T0006052

THE LURE OF
ATLANTIS

THE LURE OF ATLANTIS

Strange Tales from
the Sunken Continent

edited by
MICHAEL WHEATLEY

This edition published 2023 by
The British Library
96 Euston Road
London NW1 2DB

Selection, introduction and notes © 2023 Michael Wheatley
Volume copyright © 2023 The British Library Board

Dates attributed to each story relate to first publication.

"The Lemmings" by John Masefield © 1920, The Estate of John Masefield.
"A Voyage to Sfanomoë" © 1931 The Estate of Clark Ashton Smith.
"The Lives of Alfred Kramer" © 1932 Donald Wandrei; Reprinted
with the permission of the Estate of Donald Wandrei.
"Child of Atlantis" © 1937 The Estate of Edmond Hamilton.
"Spawn of Dagon" © 1938 by *Weird Tales*; Reprinted by permission of
Don Congdon Associates, Inc. on behalf of Carole Ann Rodriguez.

Every effort has been made to trace copyright holders and to obtain their
permission for the use of copyright material. The publisher apologises
for any errors or omissions and would be pleased to be notified of any
corrections to be incorporated in reprints or future editions.

Cataloguing in Publication Data
A catalogue record for this publication is available from the British Library

ISBN 978 0 7123 5498 1
e-ISBN 978 0 7123 6826 1

Frontispiece illustration by Sandra Gómez, with design by Mauricio
Villamayor. Illustrations on pages 6 and 288 by Henri Théophile
Hildibrand from *Twenty Thousand Leagues Under the Seas* by Jules
Verne, Sampson Low & Co, London, 1873. Shelfmark: 12516.g.21.

Cover design by Mauricio Villamayor with illustration by Sandra Gómez
Text design and typesetting by Tetragon, London
Printed in England by CPI Group (UK) Ltd, Croydon, CRO 4YY

MIX
Paper | Supporting
responsible forestry
FSC
www.fsc.org   FSC® C171272

CONTENTS

INTRODUCTION

*But afterwards there occurred violent earthquakes and floods;
and in a single day and night of misfortune all your warlike men
in a body sank into the earth, and the island of Atlantis in like
manner disappeared in the depths of the sea.*

PLATO, "CRITIAS"

The Academy. The Theory of Forms. The Apology of Socrates.
The advancements to human knowledge made by the Greek phi-
losopher, Plato (*c.* 427–347 BC), are held in universal regard. Yet,
unique among his legacy lies the ancient civilisation of Atlantis.
Detailed in two of his late dialogues, "Timaeus" and "Critias"
(*c.* 360 BC), the sunken continent has captured the imaginations
of archaeologists and authors, critics and congressmen, for the past
two thousand years.

Despite its cultural longevity, Plato remains the only ancient source
for the existence of Atlantis. And, while their specificity is substantial,
these accounts are far from historical. Dialogues, in which Plato never
inserted himself as a character, interrogate philosophical and ethical
positions. Rather than espousing answers, their participants – often
fictionalised versions of significant contemporaries – debate an issue,
while the reader is left to decide their own conclusions.

In "Timaeus", Atlantis is portrayed as a warring nation, a "vast
power, gathered into one" that aimed to "subdue at a blow ...
the whole of the region within the straits". Nine thousand years

before the dialogues, Atlantis went to war with Athens, only to be defeated. "Critias" then details the prior development of Atlantis, positioning it as the province of Poseidon. Divided between ten children he bore with Cleito, Poseidon left its rule to the eldest, Atlas.

Before they were tempted by war, Atlantis was all but utopian. Its people were "obedient to the laws", possessing "true and in every way great spirits". Their civilisation was one of moral, artistic and technological splendour, set against the lush and fertile lands which they had been gifted. Yet, as they turned from the divine, their paradise eventually fell. Becoming "unseemly" and "visibly debased", their punishment was wrought by the Gods.

For many, this is a foil, a morality tale – though, perhaps woven from elements of actual history. In "Timaeus", the hubris of Atlantis, and its eventual defeat, may have been Plato's critique of Athenian involvement in the Peloponnesian War (431–404 BC). In "Critias", the moral malaise which the people of Atlantis succumb to may have cautioned against a similar fall from the ideals of kindness, virtuosity and shirking material excess.

For others, the search for the sunken continent continues. Whether in the National Geographic documentaries *Finding Atlantis* (2011) and *Atlantis Rising* (2017), or in books such as Charles R. Pellegrino's *Unearthing Atlantis* (1991) and Frank Joseph's *The Destruction of Atlantis* (2002), expeditions still seek to pinpoint the truth of Plato's tale. Included among the possible contenders are the Doñana National Park in Southern Spain and the Greek island of Santorini.

This is not the book that finds Atlantis. Rather, it provides a snapshot of Atlantean fascination within the strange expanse of the Weird tale. In the chosen works, the various themes of Plato's Atlantis are plucked out and progressed, whether their warring spirit in the Sword and Sorcery of Robert E. Howard; their technological advancement in "Child of Atlantis"; or the awe of their architecture in "A Submerged Continent".

Indeed, since Plato's original proposal, interest in Atlantis has routinely resurrected. First published posthumously in 1627, Sir Francis Bacon's unfinished novel, *New Atlantis*, drew on the image of a once-utopian state to petition his hopes for the future. The island of "Bensalem" is described as a scientific haven, one of decency, enlightenment and religious tolerance, separated from the wider world since the days of the Great Flood.

In 1882, the U.S. politician Ignatius L. Donnelly published *Atlantis: The Antediluvian World*. Perhaps the most influential work on Atlantis since Plato's invention, Donnelly took the dialogues as truth, and proposed Atlantis to be a precursor civilisation to the Americas and beyond. In 1888, Helena Petrovna Blavatsky further developed these ideas in *The Secret Doctrine*, claiming the Atlanteans to be the fourth "root race", succeeded by the Aryans.

To represent the range of interpretations, this collection is split into four sections. "Atlantis Rediscovered" features three classic stories of deep sea exploration, formative to those which followed. "A Submerged Continent" is the sole work published outside of pulps, inescapable in its impact; "The Lure of Atlantis" was the first Atlantean narrative within the pages of *Weird Tales*, lauded among its letters; and "The Temple" marked the official inclusion of Atlantis into Lovecraft's Cthulhu Mythos.

The second section, "Atlantis Revisited", concerns tales of racial memory, in which the protagonists revisit their Atlantean ancestors through the powers of pseudo-science. In "Under the N-Ray" and "The Lives of Alfred Kramer", the narratives employ contemporary scientific theories to revisit the fall of Atlantis. Not included is Nictzin

Dyalhis' "Heart of Atlantan" (1923), which adopts a decidedly more occult approach.

"Atlantis Resurrected" features stories which subvert the sunken continent, shifting Atlantis into a concealed island ("Child of Atlantis") or a millennial miracle ("Once in a Thousand Years"). Further works on this theme include Edmond Hamilton's "The City from the Sea", within which Atlantis violently emerges from the ocean floor, and Joel Martin Nichols Jr.'s "The City of Glass", which finds the Atlantean population hidden in a desert dome.

Finally, "Atlantis Reimagined" concludes the collection with increased inflections of fantasy and spacefaring science fiction. "The Mirrors of Tuzun Thune" introduces Robert E. Howard's Kull of Atlantis, pitting him against the sorceries of a wily wizard; "A Voyage to Sfanomoë" sees the sole Atlantean survivors set a course for the stars; and, finally, "Spawn of Dagon" returns us to the eldritch horrors of Lovecraft's approach.

Explorers who wish to continue the expedition might consider longer works, such as Arthur Conan Doyle's *The Maracot Deep* (1929) or Dennis Wheatley's *They Found Atlantis* (1936). Isaac Asimov's own anthology, *Atlantis* (1988), features further journeys including Karen Anderson's "Treaty in Tartessos" (1963), Henry S. Whitehead's "Scar-Tissue" (1946) and Ursula K. Le Guin's "The New Atlantis" (1975).

Beyond the web of the Weird, TV chef Fanny Cradock penned her own Atlantis novel, *Gateway to Remembrance* (1949), to warn against moral looseness; in October 2009, Alexander McQueen's final runway adopted the theme of *Plato's Atlantis*, bringing the deep sea to surface; and Drexciya, the Black Atlantis inhabited by the descendants of pregnant slave women drowned at sea, provides a welcome counter to the monstrous ethics Atlantean narratives often take.

·Atlantis may be a myth. Yet, the sunken continent is fast becoming the precursor it has since been thought to be. As sea levels rise, as coastal communities are threatened with collapse, and as poorer countries are left to suffer the inordinate effects of climate crisis, Atlantis would seem as stark a warning as ever. Rather than the woes of warfare, however, it is the drowned reality of a nation sinking beneath the waves.

A NOTE FROM THE PUBLISHER

The original short stories reprinted in the British Library Tales of the Weird series were written and published in a period ranging across the nineteenth and twentieth centuries. There are many elements of these stories which continue to entertain modern readers; however, in some cases there are also uses of language, instances of stereotyping and some attitudes expressed by narrators or characters which may not be endorsed by the publishing standards of today. We acknowledge therefore that some elements in the stories selected for reprinting may continue to make uncomfortable reading for some of our audience. With this series British Library Publishing aims to offer a new readership a chance to read some of the rare material of the British Library's collections in an affordable paperback format, to enjoy their merits and to look back into the worlds of the past two centuries as portrayed by their writers. It is not possible to separate these stories from the history of their writing and as such the following stories are presented as they were originally published with six edits to the text and with minor edits made for consistency of style and sense. We welcome feedback from our readers, which can be sent to the following address:

British Library Publishing
The British Library
96 Euston Road
London, NW1 2DB
United Kingdom

Lost Atlantis

The blind snake crawls along the walls
Of tower and turret ages buried;
The ground swell laps within the gaps
Of the long rampart rough and serried.

There clings white brine upon the shrine
Within the temple's wave-worn glory,
And white things creep in slime, and sleep
Upon the tablet's graven story.

Soft silence reigns in those domains
Where once the trumpet rang so loudly;
And pallid gleams of phosphor beams
Glow where the sun once glittered proudly.

Oh! love, they lie beneath no sky,
Who fell by field and hill and river—
The wild seas roll from pole to pole,
And surfs above them boom forever.

Christine Siebeneck Swayne
from THE VISIONARY AND OTHER POEMS, *1905*

ATLANTIS
REDISCOVERED

A SUBMERGED CONTINENT

from TWENTY THOUSAND
LEAGUES UNDER THE SEAS

Jules Verne

Whether for his cousin, Caroline, or to satisfy his own seafaring spirit, at age eleven, Jules Verne boarded the *Coralie* and attempted to stowaway to the Indies. Caught before the ship could depart, the young Jules promised that "from now on I will travel only in my imagination". Thirty years later, in a letter to his father, Jules reflected that "anything one man can imagine, other men can make real". Such stories, widely cited, are likely to be untrue. The latter, especially, may be the apocryphal invention of another French writer, Félix Duquesnel. Yet, regardless of their fidelity, that both tales turn on imagination speaks to the near-mythical breadth of Verne's ideas. During his lifetime, he published over one-hundred novels, short stories, plays, poems and essays, and is now regarded as one of the foremost progenitors of the genre of science fiction.

Jules Verne (1828–1905) was born in Île Feydeau, an artificial island within Nantes, Brittany. With the expectation that he should follow into the family profession, Verne's father sent him to study Law in Paris at the age of eighteen. Choosing instead to pursue his passion for writing, Jules befriended the son of Alexandre Dumas, who helped him to revise and produce his theatrical debut, *The Broken Straws* (1850). His first novel, *Five Weeks in a Balloon*, was published in 1863, after which he signed a contract with the publisher Pierre-Jules Hetzel to produce two more novels a year, for the next twenty years. What followed were the *Voyages extraordinaires*, an astonishing series of fifty-four works (and eight posthumous additions) which included *Journey to the Centre of the Earth* (1864), *The Purchase of the North Pole* (1889) and *Around the World in Eighty Days* (1893).

"A Submerged Continent" is taken from another extraordinary voyage, *Twenty Thousand Leagues Under the Seas* (1869–1870). In this standalone chapter, Captain Nemo and the narrator, Professor Pierre Arronax, survey the seabed of the Atlantic Ocean. Together, they discover the "Meropis of Theopompus, the Atlantis of Plato, that continent whose existence was denied". Contrasting the modern marvel of the *Nautilus*, a submarine which would return in Verne's *The Mysterious Island* (1874), with the ruins of Atlantis, "A Submerged Continent" juxtaposes the advancing future with the ancient past. In 1978, *Journey Through the Impossible*, Verne's 1882 stage production which united elements of his various *Voyages*, was similarly rediscovered.

The next morning (19th February) Ned Land entered my room. I rather expected him. He wore a very disappointed look.

"Well, Monsieur," he said.

"Well, Ned, fate was adverse yesterday."

"Yes, because that damned captain stopped exactly at the hour we were about to get into the boat."

"Yes, Ned; he had some business to transact with his banker."

"His banker!"

"Or rather, I should say his banking-house. I mean by that this ocean, in which his treasures are more safe than in the coffers of a state."

I then narrated the occurrences of the previous evening, in the secret hope to bring him back to the idea not to abandon the captain, but my recital had no other result than to cause him to regret, in the most energetic manner of which he was capable (which was something), of not having been able to make a little excursion on his own account into the "battle-field" of Vigo.

"However," he said, "all is not lost yet. It is only a 'cast' lost. We will recoup ourselves another time, and this evening—"

"How is the ship's head?" I asked.

"I do not know," he replied.

"Well, tomorrow at noon we shall see the observations."

The Canadian returned to Conseil. So soon as I was dressed I entered the saloon. The compass did not give us any hope, the course was S.S.E. We were turning our backs on Europe.

I waited with some impatience till the bearings were taken. About half-past eleven the reservoirs were emptied, and we mounted to the surface of the ocean.

I hastened up to the platform, Ned Land had anticipated me.

Land was no longer in view. Nothing was to be seen but the expanse of ocean. There were a few sails on the horizon seeking at Cape St. Roque favorable winds to double the cape. The weather was overcast, a storm was brewing.

Ned, in rage, attempted to pierce the misty horizon. He was in hopes still that behind all this cloud there might be some land for which he was so anxious.

At mid-day the sun showed himself for an instant. The mate profited by this burst to take the elevation. Then the sea got up again, we descended accordingly, and the panels were closed.

An hour afterwards, when I was looking at the chart, I saw that the position of the *Nautilus* was 16° 17′ long. and 33° 22′ lat., about 150 leagues from the nearest shore. There was no chance even to think of escape, and I may fairly leave you to guess the feelings of Ned Land when he fully recognized the situation of things.

I did not worry myself particularly. I felt in a manner relieved from a weight that had oppressed me, and I was able to return to my usual occupations with some degree of calmness.

About 11 P.M. I received a very unexpected visit from Captain Nemo. He inquired very politely whether I felt fatigued by my exertions of the preceding evening. I replied in the negative.

"Then, Monsieur, I will suggest a very interesting excursion."

"By all means, captain," I said.

"Hitherto you have only visited the ocean depths by day and with the light of the sun. Should you like to see them on a dark night?"

"Very much, indeed."

"I warn you the excursion will be tiring. We shall have to walk for a long distance and scale a mountain. The roads are not very well marked."

"What you say only redoubles my curiosity. I am quite ready to accompany you."

"Come along, then," replied the captain, "let us put on our diving-dresses."

As we reached the room in which the dresses were kept, I perceived that none of the crew, nor had either of my companions, been selected to follow us on this excursion. Captain Nemo had not proposed my taking either Conseil or Ned.

We were ready in a few minutes. We shouldered a reservoir of air each, but the electric lamps were not prepared; I called the captain's attention to this.

"They would be of no use," he said.

I fancied I was mistaken, but I could not repeat the suggestion, for the captain had already put on his helmet. I managed to equip myself, and I felt somebody put an iron-pointed stick into my hand, and some moments later we touched the bottom of the Atlantic, at a depth of three hundred yards.

Midnight was at hand. The water was very dark, but Captain Nemo pointed to a reddish gleam in the distance, a sort of extended light, which burned at about two miles distant from the *Nautilus*. What this fire was, how it was fed, why and how it burned amid the waters, I could not hazard a conjecture. In any case it gave us light, vaguely 'tis true, but I soon became accustomed to the peculiar obscurity, and I understood the inutility of the Rumhkorff apparatus under the circumstances.

We advanced side by side directly towards the fire. The flat ground mounted gradually. We made very long strides, assisted by our sticks, but still our progress was not rapid, for our feet often sank into a sort of ooze.

But, still advancing, I heard a sort of pattering noise overhead. This sometimes increased until it sounded like a hailstorm. I soon understood the cause; it was the raindrops falling upon the surface of the waves. Instinctively I had an idea that I should get very wet. Wetted by rainwater in the middle of the sea! I could not refrain from a quiet chuckle inside my helmet at the idea; but, as a fact, in the thick diver's dress one does not feel the water, and can fancy oneself in an atmosphere only a little more dense than the terrestrial atmosphere, that's all.

After half-an-hour's walking the ground became stony. Medusæ, small crustacea, &c., lit up with their light phosphorescent gleams. I caught glimpses of piles of rocks covered with millions of zoophytes and algæ. My foot often slipped upon the viscous carpet of varech, and had it not been for my *bâton* I should have fallen more than once. When I turned round I could see the white lamp of the *Nautilus*, though paling a little, in the distance.

These stony heaps of which I have spoken were disposed at the bottom of the ocean with a degree of regularity which I could not explain. I saw gigantic furrows which lost themselves in the obscurity, and whose length exceeded all computation. Other curious experiences presented themselves. It appeared to me that my heavy leaden soles crushed a litter of bony fragments which cracked with a loud noise. What was this vast plain which I was treading? I should have liked to ask the captain, but his language of signs, which permitted communication with his companions when they accompanied him in his submarine excursions, was utterly incomprehensible to me.

Meanwhile, the flame which guided us increased, and lighted up the horizon. The existence of this fire beneath the ocean puzzled me considerably. Was it electric? Was I about to become acquainted with a natural phenomenon hitherto unknown? Or had the power of man aught to do with this? Were men fanning this flame? Was I about to meet in these depths friends and companions of Captain Nemo, living like him this strange life, and whom he was about to visit? Should we find here below a colony of exiles, who, tired of earth and its troubles, had sought and found independence in the lowest depths of the ocean? These foolish and utterly absurd ideas pressed upon me, and in my condition of mind, over-excited by the wonders I beheld at every step, I should not have been very much astonished to enter, at the bottom of this ocean, one of those submarine towns of which Captain Nemo dreamed.

Our route got more and more illuminated. The white gleam radiated from a mountain about 800 feet in height. But what I could see was only a reflection thrown up by the crystal of the sea depths. The fire, the original cause of this extraordinary illumination, lay at the opposite slope of the hill.

Captain Nemo advanced amid the rocky masses without the least hesitation. He evidently was acquainted with this dark road. He had doubtless frequently traversed it, and would not lose his way. I followed him in full confidence. He seemed to me like one of those genii of the sea, and as he walked in front, I admired his lofty stature, which was thrown out in strong relief against the luminous horizon.

It was 1 A.M. We reached the first slopes of the mountain, but to cross them we were obliged to attempt a difficult path in a vast thicket. Yes, a thicket of dead trees, trees mineralized by the action of the water, with here and there a gigantic pine dominating them. It was like a standing coal-pit, whose ramifications, like cuttings upon black paper, stood out clearly against the watery ceiling. It was like a submerged forest of the Hartz, clinging to the mountain sides. The paths were encumbered with algæ and fucus, amongst which crawled a whole colony of crustacea. I went on jumping over the rocks, striding over the tree trunks, breaking away the bind-weed that extended from branch to branch, and frightening the fish. Carried onward, I felt no weariness. I followed my guide, who knew no fatigue.

And what a sight it was! How can I reproduce it? How can I depict the aspect of those trees and rocks in this liquid medium, the black foundations, while red-tinged tops glowed in the light, which was doubled by the reflecting powers of the water? We clambered up rocks which gave way as we passed, and fell with the roar of an avalanche. Right and left there were long dark galleries. In other places were vast clear spaces, apparently man's handiwork, and I wondered whether some inhabitant of these submarine districts would not suddenly appear!

Captain Nemo still kept ascending, and I could not stay. I followed him boldly. My *bâton* was of great assistance; a false step would have been dangerous on those narrow places, but I walked carefully, and without feeling giddy. Sometimes I was obliged to jump a crevasse, the depth of which would have repelled me on land; sometimes I ventured across the unsteady trunk of a tree, thrown over an abyss; and without looking to my feet, for my eyes were fully occupied in admiring the wild scenery. Monumental-like rocks, perched upon irregular bases, here seemed to defy all laws of equilibrium. Between their stony embraces trees sprang up, like a jet under the influence of great pressure, and sustained those which sustained them in turn. Then natural towers and escarpments which inclined at an angle that gravitation would never have permitted on land.

I, myself, felt the influence of the great density of the water, for, notwithstanding my heavy clothing, I was able to scale these stiff ascents with the lightness and ease of a chamois.

In thus narrating my expedition under water, I am aware that it may appear incredible. I am merely the historian of things apparently impossible, but none the less real and incontestable. I did not dream all these things; I saw, and came in contact with them.

Two hours after leaving the *Nautilus*, we had cleared the line of trees; and the mountain, a hundred feet above us, threw a long shadow upon the opposite slope. Some petrified trees appeared to move in fantastic zigzags. Fishes rose in masses under our feet, like frightened birds in the long grass. The massive rocks were seamed with immense fissures; deep grottos, unfathomable holes, in which formidable creatures were moving about. The blood went back to my heart when I perceived an enormous antenna blocking up the way, or a frightful claw shutting with a loud noise in the depths of the caverns. Thousands of luminous points glittered in the darkness. These were the eyes of enormous crustacea; giant lobsters, holding themselves upright like so many halberdiers, and moving their claws with a clanking sound; titanic crabs, and fearful octopi, waving their arms like a nest full of serpents. What was the extraordinary world which hitherto I had never known? To what order did these articulates belong, for whom the rocks formed a second carapace? Where had nature discovered the secret of their vegetative life, and how long—how many centuries—had they lived thus in the lowest depths of the ocean?

But I was unable to halt. Captain Nemo, evidently familiar with these terrible creatures, paid no heed to them; so we reached the first platform, where there were other surprises in store for me. There were scattered ruins which betrayed the hand of man, not of the Creator. Amongst the piles of stones, rose the vague forms of chateaux and temples, clothed with zoophytes in full flower; and over which, like ivy, the algæ and fucus threw a thick vegetable mantle.

I would have fain asked Captain Nemo for an explanation of all this, but, not being able to do so, I stopped and seized his arm; but he shook his head and, pointing to the last peak of the mountain, motioned me onward. I followed, and in a few minutes we gained the top, which, in a circle of ten yards, commanded the whole of the rocky expanse beneath.

I looked down the ascent we had just climbed. The mountain was only about 700 feet high from that plain we had left, but on the other side it looked down twice the height to the depths of the Atlantic. My gaze roamed over a vast space, lighted up by a violent conflagration. The mountain was, in fact, a volcano. Fifty feet below the summit a large crater was vomiting torrents of lava in the midst of a rain of stones and scoriæ; the volcano lit up the plain below like an immense torch, even to the limits of the horizon.

I have said that the volcano cast up lava but no flames. To have flame oxygen of the air is necessary, and flame cannot be developed under water, but lava possesses in itself the principle of incandescence, and reaches a white heat, and, in contact with the liquid element, gains the upper hand and vaporizes it. Rapid currents, carrying all the gases in diffusion, and the lava torrents, flowed to the base of the mountain, like the eruptions of Vesuvius upon another *Torre del Greci*.

In fact, beneath my eyes, ruined and destroyed, appeared the remains of a town, its roofs open, its temples fallen, its architecture gone, and, in the columns still remaining, the Tuscan style could be recognized.

Further on were the traces of a gigantic aqueduct, and again the base of an Acropolis, with the dim outlines of a Parthenon. Here were vestiges of a quay, as if an ancient harbor had been existent, and had sunk, with its merchantmen and ships of war, to the bottom. At a greater distance still were long lines of sunken walls and streets—a Pompeii engulfed in the ocean.

Where was I? I was determined to know at any hazard. I wished to speak, and would have taken off my helmet had not Captain Nemo stopped me by a gesture. He then picked up a piece of chalky stone, and, advancing towards a black rock, he wrote the single word—

ATLANTIS.

A sudden light flashed through my mind. Atlantis! The ancient Meropis of Theopompus! The Atlantis of Plato! The continent whose existence was denied by Origen, Porphyrus, Jambilicus, D'Anville, Malte-Brun, and Humboldt, who ranked its disappearance amongst the old legends. Admitted by Passidonius, Pliny, Tertullian, Engel, Sherer, Tournefort, Buffon, d'Avezac, there it was now before my eyes, bearing witness to the catastrophe. The region thus engulfed lay astride Europe, Asia, and Africa; beyond the Pillars of Hercules, in which lived a people—the powerful Atlantides—against whom was waged the first battles of ancient Greece.

Plato, himself, is the historian who has recounted the events of the heroic times.

"One day Solon was conversing with some aged sages of Saïs, a town then 800 years old, as its graven annals bear witness. One of the old men was narrating the history of another town more ancient still. This first Athenian city, 800 years old, had been attacked and partly destroyed by the Atlantides. These people occupied an immense continent, greater than Africa and Asia put together, which covered a surface between the 12° to 14° N. lat. Their domination extended even to Egypt, and they wished to conquer Greece also, but were repulsed by the indomitable resistance they met with. Centuries rolled on. A cataclysm occurred—inundations and earthquakes. A night and a day sufficed for the destruction of the Atlantis; the highest summits—Madeira, the Azores, the Canaries, and the Cape Verd Islands—only remaining above water."

Such were the historical souvenirs which Captain Nemo's inscription called up in my mind. Thus, led by the strangest destiny, I was standing upon one of the mountains of that continent; I was touching these ruins, a thousand centuries old, and of the geological epoch; I was walking in the places where the contemporaries of the first man had walked; I was crushing under foot the skeletons of animals of a fabulous age, which the trees, now mineralized, once covered with their shade.

Ah! If time had not failed me, I should have descended those steep hills and explored the whole continent—which, no doubt, unites Africa to America—and visited the grand antediluvian cities. Here lived those gigantic races of old, who were able to move those blocks which still resisted the action of the water. Some day, perhaps, a convulsion of nature will heave these ruins up again. Many submarine volcanoes have been reported in this portion of the ocean; and many ships have felt extraordinary shocks in passing over these disturbed depths. The whole of the soil, to the equator, is still rent by these Platonian forces; and who knows but that at some distant day the summits of these volcanic mountains will appear once more above the surface of the Atlantic!

As I was musing thus, and endeavoring to fix the details on my memory, Captain Nemo remained immovable, and as if petrified. Was he thinking of those former generations, and endeavoring to elucidate the secret of human destiny. Was it to this place he came to revel in historical memories, and to revive the ancient life—he to whom a modern one was distasteful. What would I not have given to have known his thoughts, to share them, to understand them!

We remained in the same place for a whole hour, contemplating the vast plain by the gleam of the lava, which at times glowed with intense brilliancy. Loud noises were clearly transmitted by the water, and were echoed with majestic fulness of sound.

The moon now appeared across the waters, and threw her pale rays over the engulfed continent. It was but a gleam, but it had a wonderful effect. The captain rose, threw a last look at the immense plain, and then signalled to me to return.

We rapidly descended the mountain. The mineral forest once passed, we could perceive the lantern of the *Nautilus* shining in the distance like a star. The captain made directly for it, and we got on board just as the first rays of dawn were brightening the surface of the ocean.

THE LURE OF ATLANTIS

Joel Martin Nichols Jr.

Joel Martin Nichols Jr. (1895–1991) was an American author and journalist born in Manchester, Connecticut. After graduating from the Brown University School of Journalism in 1921, Nichols then progressed between papers before joining the Federal Advertising Agency in 1931. During his early adulthood, while exploring Europe, Nichols met the American painter, Ruth Graves. Agreeing to sit for a portrait, the resultant work was showcased at the 1926 annual exhibition of the prestigious *Société Nationale des Beaux-Arts*. Writing throughout his life, Nichols contributed frequently to pulp magazines, including "Lost Doubloons" (1925) in *Action Stories* and "The Man Who Died Twice" (1938), a wartime mystery of chemical weaponry, in *Bull's-Eye Detective*. Between 1925 and 1929, he published five works with *Weird Tales*: "The Lure of Atlantis" (1925), "The Hooded Death" (1926), "The Devil Ray" (1926), "The City of Glass" (1927) and "The Isle of Lost Souls" (1928–1929).

First published in the April 1925 issue of *Weird Tales*, "The Lure of Atlantis" concerns Professors Amos Tyrrel and Charles Randolph. Tracing the ruins of Atlantis to the Sargasso Sea—its own site of *fin-de-siècle* fascination—their exploration reveals the same wondrous architecture, "the most delicate and intricate of mosaics", alongside a temple which houses Wynona, Princess of Atlantis. Entranced by her everlasting beauty, Tyrrel and Randolph soon succumb to homosocial rivalry, all while a strange underwater vegetation begins to entangle their vessel. Whereas Verne opens this collection with an abandoned image of Atlantis, Nichols develops Plato's imagined civilization, presaging the increasingly populated works which follow. Two years later, Nichols would return to the sunken continent with "The City of Glass", a fascinating companion piece which shifts Atlantis out of the Atlantic Ocean and into the Sahara Desert.

There have been so many queer yarns in the newspapers about the sinking of the *Nautilus* that I, being skipper of the four-masted schooner *Brant*, which picked up Professor Charles Randolph, her only survivor, had better set down what really did happen down there in the Sargasso Sea.

The *Nautilus* was a steam yacht owned by Professor Amos Tyrrel, a wealthy English naturalist who had built a laboratory on the Cornish coast for the study of fish and seaweed. He and Randolph, who had been his assistant for twenty years, sailed in the *Nautilus* on the fifth of last February to do some research work in the Sargasso.

About this time the *Brant* was rounding the Horn out of Santiago, Chile, with a load of nitrates bound for Charleston, South Carolina. We struck a blow off the River Platte, and my old hooker lost her rudder. When things cleared up a bit we found ourselves pretty well out in the South Atlantic, but we rigged a jury rudder and headed northwest, figuring on dropping into some Cuban port to refit.

We struck the Sargasso about fifteen days later, and one fine morning we picked up this Professor Randolph, who was bobbing about in the open sea without the sign of a stick to keep him up. He was delirious when we brought him aboard, but after he came to his right senses he told me the queerest yarn I ever heard in my life—and I've heard some rather good ones in the forty years I've been following the sea. At first I put him down as crazy, but we'd no sooner got him aboard than hell began a-popping all around us right there on the *Brant*. When she finally got through, with two of her sticks missing and some of those hard-boiled birds in the fo'c'sl a-praying to the Almighty to save 'em from the devils of the deep, I made up my mind that maybe he wasn't so crazy after all. Then I had Randolph write down his story in his own words. I turned the original over to the authorities, and I suppose the British Admiralty has it now, but I copied the whole thing, word for word, in the *Brant*'s log. The professor headed his story in big letters: STATEMENT OF DR. CHARLES WILLIAMS RANDOLPH CONCERNING THE SINKING OP THE NAUTILUS. And this is how it read:

Captain Andrew Waters of the schooner *Brant* has asked me to write down the story of the cruise of the *Nautilus* and of what befell her unfortunate crew and my colleague, Dr. Amos Tyrrel; and since it seems certain now that the *Brant* is not to suffer the fate of the *Nautilus* I have agreed to comply with his request.

It is perhaps unnecessary for me to delineate the relationship between Dr. Tyrrel and myself, since we were students of natural science together at the University of Edinburgh, twenty years ago. His accomplishments in the field of natural history, his studies and deductions from his exhaustive researches in the seven seas, his magnificent laboratory at Bournewell—all have given him an international fame which needs no emphasizing here from me. Suffice it to say that I may designate myself merely as an unworthy assistant in his great work, a humble satellite reflecting but a dim gleam from the splendor of his genius.

The world, when it has read this statement, will realize that these are strange words coming now from me, in view of the discord (mild term!) between Dr. Tyrrel and myself, which ended in the horrifying fate of the *Nautilus*. It was a discord which really had its inception

34

five years ago, when Dr. Tyrrel exhibited the first signs of a divided interest in his life-work—an interest which led him away from his studies of undersea life and eventually found him devoting a large share of his time to archeological research.

He began this course by taking extended trips to Egypt and Central America, where he indulged in a comparative study of prehistoric architectures found on the two continents, professing to find between them a most amazing and wholly unaccountable similarity. Being engrossed with our original labors, I paid little attention to his assertions, until one day he came to me with the astounding announcement that he had evolved a tenable theory for the existence of the lost continent of Atlantis. In support of it he produced a vast number of photographs and other data, which purported to show that the pyramids found in the jungles of the Yucatan Peninsula were in reality small copies of the mighty piles found in Egypt, and that in other ways he had established an unanswerable argument for there being, in prehistoric times, a bridge of land between the African and American continents. It was his further contention that this land connection was the lost Atlantis, sunk beneath the waves of the south Atlantic ocean by some stupendous cataclysm. Egypt, in the heyday of its power, he asserted, had been naught but a poor outpost of Atlantis, reflecting only a dim glimmer of the splendors of that lost continent.

I must confess that I was bitterly disappointed in my colleague's new activities, for I had always held that the existence of Atlantis was a matter for metaphysical speculation and not one to engage the serious attention of men engrossed in the more objective sciences. I was gravely considering the necessity of voicing this conviction in the form of a gentle reproof to Dr. Tyrrel when he came to me one day in great excitement, brandishing before my eyes a piece of twisted metal.

"I have it, Randolph!" he fairly shouted at me. "This proves my theory. We've found Atlantis!"

Dr. Tyrrel was not given to practical joking, so I accepted the proffered metal, although with a preconceived skepticism. It was, I should say, a bit of framework done in bronze, very like the lintel of a door. There are many similar pieces in the temples of ancient Egypt. Carved on its surface, however, were some peculiar hieroglyphics which on closer observation I recognized as a type of cuneiform writing.

"Is this one of your Egyptian finds?" I queried, somewhat testily. He waved me down in derision.

"This," he said, excitedly, "was pulled out of the south Atlantic Ocean on the flukes of an anchor dropped overboard by the tramp steamer *Pole Star*."

"Ah, yes," said I. "A bit of submerged driftwood—"

"Nonsense!" he shouted. "Let me tell you about it. This vessel was caught in a storm somewhere down there—I've got the exact bearings—and her anchor was carried overboard by a large sea. It ran out almost the whole length of the cable before they could arrest it. When they finally had opportunity to attend to it they found that they were anchored. Think of it, Randolph—anchored out there in the Sargasso Sea where the Admiralty charts set the depth at nearly a mile! And when they got the anchor up they found this bit of bronze twisted about one of the flukes."

"A hoax!" I exclaimed. "They fooled you for a good price."

"I paid them nothing," he retorted. "They believe there was some subterranean upheaval throwing up a submerged island which by chance caught their anchor. But this bit of bronze never came from any submerged wreck as they believe. It came from one of the hilltop temples of the lost Atlantis. I have been able to translate this inscription. Do you know what it means?"

I admitted, caustically, that I did not.

"It means," he continued, "'Wynona, Fair Princess of Atlantis.' There is something more but it is unintelligible. Wynona was the daughter of the last king of Atlantis."

"Small good it will do you," I put in. "You can never prove it."

"Indeed?" he retorted. "Then you may be interested to know that I've ordered the *Nautilus* to be ready for sea in eight days. I'm going down there with our diving equipment, and if it isn't too deep I'm going to explore this watery kingdom. You may come if you wish."

To make a long story short, I must say here that I was in reality more interested than I cared to admit, and it took no great urging to get me to go along. As Dr. Tyrrel had pointed out, we were already well equipped for the contemplated cruise. The *Nautilus*, Dr. Tyrrel's yacht, was virtually a floating laboratory in which we had spent many happy months in our explorations of the seven seas. On board was every apparatus imaginable to aid in deep sea work. Many of the devices had been invented or perfected by my colleague. Chief among these were two of the latest type diving suits—glass, steel and rubber affairs capable of withstanding excessive undersea pressures. Air was furnished to the wearer from tanks at the shoulders, and thus the danger of entangling life lines and air-hose was eliminated. Now, as I write, it seems to me almost a catastrophe that these invaluable accessories have been lost forever to the world.

We steamed out of our harbor at Bournewell on the fifth of February. Our voyage was uneventful, and three weeks later we were over the spot indicated in the nautical bearings furnished us by the captain of the *Pole Star*.

How well I remember that morning of our first sounding! How well I remember my own excitement, raised to the zenith by the enthusiasm of Dr. Tyrrel! And how well I remember the look on his face and the leap in my own heart when our sounding lead showed bottom at 280 feet, even as the captain of the *Pole Star* had said! We had indeed found a submerged island. Whether it was Atlantis, I was still skeptical.

On the following morning, after having made the necessary preparations, we donned our diving suits and dropped over the side of the *Nautilus* into the sea. The spot, as I have already indicated, was approximately in the middle of the Sargasso Sea, but fortunately the surface of the ocean about us for the space of almost a square mile was free of the encumbering marine growth so peculiar to these waters. Thus, throughout the middle part of the day we expected to have the full value of the sun, thereby rendering unnecessary our electric searchlights, which were at best rather cumbersome and unsatisfactory for deep sea work.

Once in the sea, with our arms locked together we sank down—down—down. The water proved to be even clearer than we had hoped,—indeed it was almost abnormally transparent—and the shafts of the sun bade fair to penetrate quite as far as we desired to go.

We must have been descending slowly for nearly five minutes when suddenly Dr. Tyrrel loosed his arm and pointed with his gloved finger into the distance at my back. Turning my head within my helmet I saw, with a tremendous leap of my heart, that we were floating slowly down beside a beautiful, tapering pinnacle cut in a stone which appeared to be marble. Almost immediately, other and lesser pinnacles arose gradually about us, all of them glowing with varicolored tints under the penetrating rays of the sun. Peering at some of the nearer ones, I saw that they were not some mere basaltic upheaval. They had been built by human hands.

We had found Atlantis!

*

The luminous glow from above had grown only slightly dimmer when we came gently to rest on what appeared to be the roof of some gigantic building—a roof which on closer observation I saw was of a thick but lucid crystal. All about us, on a kind of ridgepole of this temple (if such it was) I saw bits of curiously carved statuary, some of them apparently broken off by the undulating action of the deep sea currents. I would have paused over them in wonderment had it not been for Dr. Tyrrel, who, without hesitation, walked deliberately to the edge of the roof, where we again dropped off into the open water. A moment later we filtered gently to rest on a wide landing in a magnificent set of marble stairs. Glancing up with thumping heart I realized that we were standing at the very threshold of a splendid marble temple!

I would that I had the time or the talent for describing the magnificence, the awe-inspiring beauty of that scene. The walls towering up before us were of purest marble, slightly tinted a bluish green by the intervening water. Above our heads the shafts of the sun, only slightly dimmed by the lesser depth, played on those lofty spires with all the colors of the rainbow—tints shading away in all degrees of green, yellow, red, purple and blue. All about us on the stairs, standing for the most part on pedestals of what appeared to be pure gold, was some of the most exquisite statuary I have ever seen. Save for a few pieces carved in the form of some hideous beast, the like of which I have never seen on earth, the majority of the effects were extremely pleasing to the eye, and were evidently from the hands of the sublimest masters, who had far surpassed the best of Phidias or Praxiteles or the unknown author of the Venus of Melos. And yet the effect in totality was marred, as I have indicated, by the weird shapes of some of the beasts.

Then, too, there was a peculiar type of fungus growing over them, a kind of seaweed unknown to me, which writhed and moved about the statuary like a thing alive. Some of it seemed actually to be coiling and uncoiling about the throat of a beautiful maiden, exquisitely carved in a pinkish marble, standing near us on the stairs. While I was charmed with the statuary, I must admit from the outset that this strange marine growth made me shudder. It was too uncannily alive. Even as we walked up the steps it recoiled from our footsteps to make way for us, but on looking back I noted that it returned again to its original resting place and seemed, in fact, to be following us up to the top!

At the head of the flight we found a pair of magnificent bronze doors, fortunately wide open. Oddly enough, both were heavily embossed with the figure of a winged animal not unlike the Egyptian Sphinx, part woman, part beast, and part bird. Although the doors were open, there was a tangle of that disgusting marine growth across the threshold, and Dr. Tyrrel with a gesture of impatience drew his knife to hack a way into the place; but even as he reached out to seize the stuff it recoiled and parted of its own accord, thereby giving us ready access.

Behind the bronze doors was a magnificent hall or foyer—I do not know how else to describe it. Half way down on our right was an open doorway leading into another and more spacious hall. Light from the ocean surface filtered into the place through the crystal roofs, but its intensity had been so greatly dimmed by the depth that we could not see clearly for more than twenty feet ahead of us.

Keeping well to the right so that we should not lose our way, we suddenly came face to face with the wall of the temple, noting with a gasp of admiration that its surface was covered with beautiful murals, apparently done in gold leaf with backgrounds of silver and a substance which might be ivory. Following the murals to the very foot of the walls, I noted that the floor on which we were walking had been done in the most delicate and intricate of mosaics.

We feasted our eyes on these beauties for several minutes, and then began following the wall at our right. I was in the act of commenting, mentally, on the absence of any furnishings or statuary in the hall proper, when suddenly there loomed before us in the greenish gloom a sizable marble cubicle. Coming nearer we saw that this was only the first of a series, mortised to the walls and standing about as high as our waists. A farther approach showed us that they were in reality a row of marble bins (to use a prosaic term). But what bins they were! What beauty, what contents! Pounds and pounds of jewels in every hue of the rainbow!

In one cubicle I buried my arms up to the elbow in the finest of rubies. From another I saw Dr. Tyrrel hold up a double handful of glittering emeralds. And diamonds!—a king's ransom in those alone.

My natural cupidity had seized hold of me, and I was for taking some of the gems with us, but I noted that Dr. Tyrrel—always the scholar—had tossed his jewels back into place; and then I shamefacedly followed his example. As we wandered farther down the hall, he informed me in the sign language we had developed for undersea work that he had concluded this was a mortuary chapel built on one of the Atlantean hilltops. If such it proved to be, he pointed out, we should soon come upon human remains, as the Atlanteans were credited by ancient chroniclers with having developed an amazing method of preserving their dead.

He was walking to one side and a little ahead of me as he imparted this information, and he had scarcely finished when I saw him suddenly pause, peer ahead into the gloom, and then hurry forward, signing me to follow. In the greenish half-light I saw that we were approaching the end of the hall and that up against the wall was what appeared to be a huge marble altar.

And then I saw Wynona, Princess of Atlantis.

She was laid out there in her crystal tomb. Her eyes, with their glorious blue, were open and smiling; the roses were still in her cheeks; the very pink was in her fingernails! I suppose I was a bit wrought up, for I could have sworn that she moved and smiled up at us. Dr. Tyrrel had dropped on one knee, his hands clasping the sides of her bier; and now he crouched there, peering through the glass of his helmet at this lovely handiwork of God. I do not know whether he cried out with the marvel of it, but I know that I did, for the sound echoed and re-echoed within the confines of my glass-and-rubber prison.

Never before had I seen so beautiful a creature. Her tomb, or casket, all of clear crystal, was tipped upward so that she appeared to be reclining there, gazing out upon the hall below her. I could see every outline of her figure, every lineament of her features. I recognized immediately the Egyptian strain in the firm, straight nose, the perfect curve of the somewhat full lips, and the exquisitely modeled chin, tender yet imperiously firm, but withal—shall I say it?—slightly cruel. Her figure, slightly swathed in a filmy lace of gold, was perfection—possibly a trifle fuller at the hips than we are wont to approve nowadays, but perfect nevertheless.

I have spoken of her contours as purely Egyptian; but here the comparison ceases, for your ancient Egyptian was of a swarthy race, but this woman of Atlantis was of the fairest, with wide-opened eyes as blue as the cornflowers in our native England, and high-piled hair as yellow as the golden fillets with which it was bound.

I can see my reader shudder at the thought of thus gazing upon the dead, but I can tell him the sight of the lovely Wynona thus affected neither Dr. Tyrrel nor myself. I do not know how long we stood there, gazing at this exquisite creature, but it must have been a very long while, for my heart began to labor and my head began to throb in a way which told me that the oxygen in the tanks at our backs must be getting low.

Almost at that identical moment I felt an uncanny tightening and drawing sensation about my legs and ankles. Glancing quickly downward, I saw something that left me cold with horror. That loathsome seaweed, unnoticed by us, had crept into the chapel and was now seemingly growing in all directions over the floor. Some of it had entwined about my ankles, producing upon them a peculiar drawing and tugging sensation similar to that felt by a person walking in the undertow on a wave-washed beach. A swift glance over to my colleague produced in me a second and greater wave of horror. I saw him there lost in contemplation of the sleeping beauty and utterly unmindful that this hideous creeping thing had gone farther on him than it had on me. Indeed, it bade fair to cover his whole body.

During the course of my twenty years' exploration of the world under the sea, I have had many occasions to be terrified by the activities of plant and animal life there, but never have I been so submerged in horror as when I beheld that slimy weed squirming and twisting over our bodies. I must have cried out with the shock of it, for my head began to ring within my helmet, and I clutched frantically for the knife at my belt, with the intention of hacking away the stuff at my ankles. My panic was short-lived, however, for no sooner had I reached for the weed than it uncoiled itself of its own free will, seeming actually to recoil at the dull gleam of my weapon.

Then, in two strides, I was at Dr. Tyrrel's side, intending to shake him back to a realization of our danger. Twice I grasped his shoulder before he paid the slightest attention to me, absorbed as he was in his contemplation of the smiling beauty in her crystal tomb. Finally, on my last somewhat rough importunity, he turned suddenly about and struck at me angrily with his hand. Almost immediately he must have regretted this act, for he signed to me that he was sorry, that he had forgotten himself for the moment.

I told him our oxygen was getting low, and pointed to the seaweed on his body, expecting him to be as horror-stricken as I had been. Oddly enough, however, he did not seem to mind it, for he got to his feet and then, to my profound astonishment, the weed slowly unfolded and left him free.

With a last glance at our recumbent beauty we started from the hall, the seaweed drawing apart before our steps until a wide lane extended before us to the door. Outside on the terrace we prepared to loose our weights for our journey to the surface, but here a new and greater horror struck me.

Glancing down from our high point of vantage before the temple doors I saw in the mass of seaweed to the right and left of the staircase the ribs, the broken stumps, the twisted stern-plates, the battered superstructures, of many sunken ships. There must have been at least a hundred of them piled together helter-skelter, and heaven knows how many more lay farther down in the valley, where the rays of the sun did not penetrate!

I do not know how long we would have paused there gazing upon this scene of desolation had it not been that the increased difficulty of breathing warned us we could tarry no longer. Accordingly we slipped our weights and arose slowly to the surface, the rose-and-nile green of the Atlantean spires dropping slowly behind us. Only once did I look down in our journey, and not until then did I realize that the seaweed from the Atlantean temple had followed us—was in fact dogging our very heels! The stuff hovered there on the surface for a minute after we had climbed aboard the *Nautilus*, and then, as if pulled by some unseen hand from below, it slowly sank from sight.

I come now to a point in my story where I am loath to continue, for it must reveal in me an atavistic strain, the existence of which, until this last accursed cruise of the *Nautilus*, I had never suspected. As may be guessed from the preceding narrative, neither Dr. Tyrrel nor myself had ever married, our labors and researches having provided us with a diversity of experience which rendered unnecessary a venture into other fields of existence. Up until the time of the last cruise of the *Nautilus*, I can say with certainty that no woman, nor even any thought of woman, has ever disturbed the quiet tenor of my emotional life. For my colleague I think I can say the same. Hence it was somewhat a shock to me when I awoke during that night to find the lovely, sensual face of the exquisite Wynona haunting me, there in the darkness of my cabin.

For a time the sensation was a pleasant one: I felt a warm invigoration of my being, a sensuous flow of hot blood in my body which, although slightly tempestuous, was not without a certain indefinable charm. I remember that I reached back to the headboard of my bed, seized there the enamel rail and stretched myself in the warm luxury of the tropic night. I felt remade—a new thing. I felt that in some indefinable way nature had poured into me renewed health, renewed youth. I wanted to arise, to pace about my cabin; I wanted to go to the decks of the *Nautilus*, to race up and down, cloaked only in the star-spangled robe of the equatorial night. I felt that I had the power to reach out and embrace the whole world.

For a time I lay there enjoying to the full this entirely new reaction and speculating on the psychological aspect of my new inspiration. In a little while, however, I began to grow too warm; the hot blood pounding through my veins became in a very few minutes a source of complete and profound and wholly inexplicable irritation. In vain I attempted to throw off the mood. In vain I attempted all the known tricks of wooing sleep; in vain I tossed and tumbled about with the gentle rolls of the *Nautilus*. Eventually I arose, drew on my dressing gown (for I had thrown aside my pajamas when the mood first came upon me), and thus attired strode out upon the decks.

Forward I saw a tiny ruby glow, which I took to be the lighted cigarette of the watch. Above, almost outshone by the brilliance of the Southern Cross, were the riding lights of the *Nautilus*. All was peace, excepting in my own brain.

I strode forward, my irritable mood pricking me onward, and reprimanded the watch for smoking on duty, although I knew such mild breaches of discipline had been winked at by both captain and mate on these long voyages. I remember how in surprize he flipped it overboard, the glowing end describing a perfect half-circle as it dropped into the sea. Somehow even that bothered me.

Presently I walked back toward the stern, and, rounding the corner of the after deckhouse, I came suddenly upon Dr. Tyrrel. He was standing there, half draped over the rail, and peering intently down into the sea. For some reason unknown to me I paused there watching him. He did not move; he might have been a statue of stone gazing over the rail. Again I felt a wave of unreasonable irritation, a veritable sweep of anger. Why should he be standing there peering so intently down into the sea? Why was he not in his cabin, where he belonged at this hour, gaining rest for the labors of tomorrow? Somehow I did not realize then that I was blaming him for the very thing which I myself was doing.

As I stood there watching him, he slowly straightened up and lifted his eyes to the stars. His lips were moving, and I thought that he sighed. It was then that I noted, seemingly for the first time in all our relationship, what a handsome figure of a man he was, with his clear-cut, aquiline profile, his full molded chin, his crisp, curly hair only slightly tinged with gray at the temples, and that magnificent figure with its tremendous shoulders, flat hips and gently sloping flanks. Somehow it made me feel small and puny and hopeless. All my new-found vigor drained from me in that moment, and I felt a strange, hot resentment against the man. Suddenly I had come to be old and worn and gnarled and terribly weary. Thinking thus, and without disturbing my colleague, I went back to my cabin and a sleepless vigil into the dawn.

That morning, while we were taking breakfast, Dr. Tyrrel told me quietly that there would be no need for my going down that day.

"Why?" I asked, somewhat testily, though never before had I questioned his decisions.

"It is exhausting work," he replied, "and we do not know how long we can stay here before there may be a storm, in which case we may have to up anchor and run before it. I think we can work best by going down in turn, I today, you tomorrow."

His reasoning seemed wholly specious, but I assented sullenly.

Throughout the four hours of his trip below I lived in torture. I thought of him down there walking through those magnificent halls, enjoying the wonders of Atlantis, the attractions of the ancient chapel, the charm of that smiling beauty there in her crystal tomb. Vaguely I wondered what he would bring up with him, and you may guess that I was somewhat startled when he came up, as he had gone down, with nothing at all.

That night, for the first time in our long friendship, we had harsh words in his cabin. I upbraided him for bringing up none of the jewels, pointing out that even if he himself had no need for further wealth, some of the rest of us were poor men and could put them to good use. My remark seemed to anger him greatly, and he lost himself in a mighty gust of wrath.

"They are not ours," he thundered, towering over me. "Not one jot nor tittle of them shall we take! They are hers. They belong to Wynona. You shall not have them."

"You are mad!" I raged. "You are inhumanly selfish! You at least owe it to these poor men aboard, who could be made independent for life. It is not within your right to deny them."

All my raging was of no avail, and the next morning I was only partly surprized, though greatly angered, when he told me curtly that only he would go beneath the waters. And for another four hours I sat there on the decks of the *Nautilus*, suffering the tortures of the damned. And again he came up empty-handed.

That night we went at it again over the teacups. I raged, I tore, I stamped about the room; but he answered me with gentle words, or, more often, not at all. For the most part he was peculiarly silent, almost uncannily pleasant. When I had finished my tirade he got up, but paused on the threshold of his cabin.

"Fear not," he said with a peculiarly quiet smile, "they shall have everything. Every foot of Atlantis shall be theirs. They shall climb its hills, wander through its halls, sun themselves on its terraces. They shall know its every beauty, all its wealth. But for you, my friend, I can promise nothing. You are not wanted down below."

His cryptic remark startled me, and I began to wonder if he were not a little mad.

That night I lay awake through all the long hours until dawn, thinking not of the jewels, of the wealth in Atlantis, but only of Wynona. At dawn I slept a little, and she came in all her gorgeous beauty and mocked me there in my cabin. That day, I vowed, it should be I who would go below.

In that I was vastly mistaken, however. We quarreled at the rail just before he went over, but he brushed me back and plunged into the sea. I saw his face, laughing up in derision through the glass of his helmet, as he slowly sank from sight.

For perhaps an hour I sat there by the rail, until the strain became no longer endurable. Then it was that the bonds of my respect to Dr. Tyrrel's judgment were broken and I realized, of a sudden, that there was nothing to keep me from going down even against his wishes. Thinking thus I got myself into my diving dress and slipped over the side.

I landed, by good luck, about half-way up the stairs to the temple. There again before me I saw that accursed seaweed, but I spurned it quickly aside and climbed the stairs. At the entrance the wretched stuff attempted to bar my way, but I drew my knife and slashed at it until it drew back. Then I walked into the foyer and from thence into the chapel.

Somehow I knew I should find him there, and I was not disappointed. As the details at the farther end of the hall were revealed to me through the dimness, I saw him kneeling before that altar with his head down across her crystal tomb, his face, behind the glass in his helmet, pressed close to hers. And then I knew that I hated him—hated him because he loved her, and because I loved her, and because in some way I knew he was the favored one. For the first time I realized that I, too, had cared nothing for the jewels; that I, too, would have scorned to rifle her chapel. Always it had been Wynona. and now he had taken her from me! I hated him with every spark of my soul, every fiber of my being.

"Dastard!" I shrieked. "Thus you have beguiled your time; thus you have hoodwinked us all!"

I had forgotten that the sound could not penetrate beyond the confines of my helmet, and now it echoed and re-echoed in my steel-and-rubber prison, ringing and screeching in my ears until the very blood seemed to well up into my eyes and the sea before me was as scarlet.

Without thought of what I was about to do I pushed forward, knife in hand. I would kill him there; I would cut him down with as little compunction as I had the seaweed before the portals. But I must be crafty! I had no intention of giving him a chance in fair fight! I would walk up behind him and strike with my knife through the rubber joints at his throat, rip the blade downward to his breast, and leave him there either to drown or bleed to death. How I would laugh as he died there at the feet of his beauty! What an outcome for his secret tryst!

And then a very strange thing happened. There was no way under heaven that he could have known of my approach, for he was kneeling with his back toward me. There was nothing to warn him, no sound from me that could have penetrated that watery space to the ears within his helmet. Yet, while I was still twenty feet away, I saw him get slowly to his feet and turn about, his hand going to the knife at his belt even before he could have realized my purpose.

Thus confronted, I brandished my weapon and bade him in our sign language to be prepared, since I intended to kill him or die in the attempt. Scarcely had I finished, when to my utter astonishment he slowly replaced the knife in its sheath and quietly awaited my coming.

Taken back though I was, I had no intention of losing my purpose. His very sureness enraged me the more. I strode forward, bending all my weight against the intervening water, holding my blade in readiness.

Now I stood before him, and saw his white, sneering face behind the glass. Shrieking aloud with a strange exultation, I raised my weapon to strike. But I never made that stroke. Even as my arm descended in its murderous errand, I felt myself suddenly and helplessly snatched away.

It was that accursed seaweed! The damnable stuff had twined about my body as I strode across the hall; and now, as I drew near enough to plunge my weapon home, it had snatched me away. In vain I foamed and fought it, slashing to the right and to the left. In vain I ripped and tore and cut, using my gloved hands where the blade seemed too slow. Where I slashed off yards of the stuff, new tendrils seemed to grow, enveloping my body.

Frothing and screaming, kicking and squirming, I was dragged across the hall and out on the steps before the temple. There, despite my weights, the weed seemed to gather under me, forcing me upward. In but a few minutes the slowly receding spires of Atlantis told me that I was on my way to the surface.

I lay on the bosom of the sea, kicking and screaming, but that diabolical stuff was determined that I should not sink again. Finally, as all strength seemed to be leaving me, I felt myself hauled slowly out of the water. They on board the *Nautilus*, seeing me struggling there in the water, had slipped a boathook under the ring at my belt and were pulling me to her decks.

But I was crafty. Once on board I revealed nothing of what had happened, merely pretending that I had been taken with cramps on coming to the surface. Then, very carefully, I laid my plans to kill Dr. Tyrrel as soon as he should return. Secretly I got out my pistol and a knife, and watched for the ascending bubbles that would tell of his coming.

But he never came. I waited there until dusk—waited until the captain came to me in alarm and begged me to go below in search of his missing employer. I should have been glad to go—for another purpose than he thought—but I knew that devilish seaweed would stop me at the outset. Looking over the side I could see it lurking there, waiting. Once I was in its clutches it could hold me there powerless while my quarry came aboard in safety and my last chance was lost. But I could not tell them this, so I cut a rent in my diving dress, telling them it would be impossible for me to venture below.

With the coming of darkness, all thought of my leaving the ship was abandoned, and Dr. Tyrrel's life was despaired of. For myself, I knew that he was still down there keeping his tryst with Wynona, and the thought of it made me fairly boil with rage. As the night wore on, I became exhausted with the play of conflicting emotions, and, pretending an illness, I went to my cabin.

I must have slept longer than I had intended, for I had many long dreams in which I saw my colleague in the arms of Wynona. The two of them stood there on one of the pillars of Atlantis, mocking me as I struggled with the weeds of the Sargasso. Each dream brought the stuff nearer my throat, while it shook and crushed me as if I were a rodent in the grip of a python. It had clutched my shoulders and was shaking me again, when I awoke and saw that I was not at the bottom of the sea but safe in my cabin, with the captain of the *Nautilus* grasping me frantically by the shoulder.

"What is the matter?" I demanded, bounding out of my bed and wondering if Dr. Tyrrel had slipped back during the watches of the night.

"The ship is sinking, sir," he said, his voice all a-tremble in the darkness. "You'd best come on deck. There's something wrong. I don't understand it."

The man's teeth were actually chattering, and the tones of his voice struck me into a panic. As I stood there, peering at his white face in the gloom, I noticed for the first time that the floor of my cabin had assumed a noticeable angle. The ship appeared to be no longer responding to the roll of the seas, but wobbled and tugged in an uncannily impotent way.

Hastily donning an overgarment, I hurried out on deck. The night was starlit, the ocean smooth, save for the gentle undulating billows from which it is never free. And yet the *Nautilus* was going down by the head! Already the angle of her decks had assumed a higher pitch while I had tarried there in my cabin. At that moment she assumed a slight list to port, the wobble becoming more accentuated with each billow. In the forward part of the vessel there arose a wail of voices, from the throats of terror-stricken, helpless men.

I turned angrily to the captain and demanded why he had not set the crew to the pumps.

"I've tried that, sir," he answered, "and I found there isn't a drop of water in her hold!"

"It's her anchor, then," I said; "it's probably caught on the bottom and the rising tide is pulling her under." (I am not a nautical man, and this seemed an adequate explanation.)

"I had the anchor up an hour ago, sir," he answered. "I tried to pull out of here—actually tried to get her under way; but her propellers won't budge her. My God, sir! it seems that we're being pulled down! We actually can't move!"

At that moment there came a ripping and creaking sound from her hold, followed by another drunken wobble to port. And that, I think, gave me my first inkling of what was really happening to the *Nautilus*. Running up into the forward part of the ship, I peered over the side. What I saw there pulled a strange cry of exultation from my throat.

Under her bowsprit and, I dare say, all along the whole length of her keel, were little, suckerlike tendrils protruding from the water, worming and squirming their way upward over her smooth white sides.

The *Nautilus* was in the grip of the Sargasso seaweed! She was being pulled under—pulled under to Atlantis! Now I understood that gruesome pile of wreckage so far below.

I realize that when the world reads this it will call me mad, and I think for the next few hours perhaps I was. I sprang into the air; I jumped and leaped about the deck. I shouted for very joy. I was going to fool Dr. Tyrrel after all! He had said Atlantis would not take me, but it was taking the *Nautilus*, and if it took the *Nautilus* it must take me!

The crew must have gathered from my yells and exclamations of triumph what had happened, for they left off their wails and went to work with hatchets, knives and axes. The weed, by this time, had crept up almost to the rails, and now, as if realizing it had been discovered, it actually began swarming over the side, on to the decks, and eventually into the masts and rigging. They, poor fellows, chopped and hacked and fought it through most of the night. It was a losing fight. Inch by inch her bow tilted downward. Inch by inch her rounded stern arose toward the heavens. Once they tried to lower her boats, but no sooner had these touched the water than the seaweed fastened its clutches upon them.

When the angle of her decks became impossible for further footing, I climbed to her stern rail, where I perched and howled and shrieked in glee.

Ah, fool, fool that I was! I had forgotten that Atlantis did not want me. Had I been more clever, had I had more of the cunning of the day before, I should have hidden myself away somewhere in the bowels of her and gone down with her to the very depths.

She went down at dawn with a dull creaking of strained timbers and a hoarse, despairing gurgle and whistle from the air expelled from her holds. And I—fool!—perched there on her stern rail, shrieked and shouted for the very joy of it. One by one I saw their bobbing heads go under; one by one I saw the last bits of wreckage enveloped by that slimy creeping thing and engulfed forever.

At noon, at night, I was still floating on.

Again and again I dived, seeking to entangle myself; again and again I felt myself thrust backward to the surface. The sun, a blistering ball of copper in the sky, sank lower and lower, and with the coming of the night I believe I must have slept there on the bosom of the Sargasso Sea.

There were other days and other nights, when I screamed and writhed in raging impotence, for I had come to realize that the sea was only playing with me, waiting there idly for me to die, when I should be carried far from Atlantis and Wynona by some swift current. But on the dawn of the third day a great ship hovered over me and even against my will I was saved.

I come now to the end of my story. I know that the world will judge me mad in the writing of it, but for the world and its judgment I care nothing, for I know whereof I have spoken. I have yet another and longer story to bring to a close and as I set this down I plan to write my finis to it out there on the decks of the *Brant*. Of this Captain Waters knows nothing, for I have his promise that he will not read this until tomorrow.

Therefore on this third day of March I hereby set my signature to this, my story.

CHARLES WILLIAMS RANDOLPH.

Well, Randolph's story as he told it to me when we first pulled him aboard the *Brant* was about the same as his statement, except maybe it wasn't so connected. But, as I said before, we'd no sooner got him aboard than the capful of wind we'd been relying on dropped off and left us in a dead calm, and then things commenced to happen.

It was about midnight that night, I guess, when we first noticed the old hooker had stopped rolling and was beginning to wobble in a queer sort of way. I didn't pay much attention to it, but turned in, leaving the deck to the mate. He woke me up about an hour later. She was down by the head and already in a bad way. I remembered Randolph's yarn about the seaweed then, and so I ran for'ard to the chains and looked over the side.

Well, sir, I could see it there on her cutwater and all around her forefoot. Then there came a creaking and a groaning from her holds, which meant that her bottom must be covered. I had the whole crew piped and we went to it with axes and knives and everything we could lay our hands on. As heaven is my judge, you could see it a-growing over her sides—it was alive! In no time at all it was on her decks and into her rigging. While we were fighting it out of the main shrouds it would get into the jigger, and when we'd get at the jigger it would get up into the mizzen, and so on. Finally we began to list pretty badly to port, and so I ordered the mate to cut away the fore and jigger, they being the ones that seemed the worst. This helped a little but not much.

And that man, Randolph! He was a fiend! He came out on deck and danced there like a maniac, yelling and singing. He didn't try to interfere with the crew, so we didn't pay any attention to him. After a while I saw him going below, and I didn't find him until afterward.

We were pretty well loaded up with Chilean nitrates—valuable stuff—and so I held on to her cargo as long as I could, hoping we might get her clear; but after a while I saw it was no go. With the cargo out of her, I knew she'd be harder to pull under; but on the other hand, when she was empty it would be easier for that stuff to pull her over on her beam ends. But it was nip and tuck for our lives then, and to hell with the cargo. So I gave the order for half the crew to open her hatches and get the stuff out.

It was in powdered form and packed in sacks, three hundred pounds to the sack. We began getting it up as best we could, and no easy job it was, with the list on her and the wobble and all that slimy stuff a-squirming over her both alow and aloft.

We'd dropped about twenty or maybe thirty bags over the side when one of them broke and spilled into the water. That was what saved us—that bag breaking over the side. I was standing by the rail helping the men, when I saw it spill into the water; and then I noticed there was a hissing and a boiling all about her where the stuff had gone in. And that weed—it just melted away all around her waterline for the distance of ten feet—curled up and dropped off! That gave me my idea. There was some chemical reaction in that nitrate which was death to that seaweed.

I grabbed the next bag and knifed it open, and we dumped it in. Then I was sure—the nitrates would do the trick.

Well, sir, we just quit fighting that stuff with knives and axes and went at it with those nitrates. We sprinkled it all over the ship fore and aft, and then we put the whaleboat over the side and sprinkled the stuff against her sides and as far down as we could get below her waterline. Pretty soon the weed in the rigging began to dry up and wither away, and then she began to roll a bit instead of wobbling. Another six hours of it, with most of the cargo overboard, and we were clear. We still had some canvas on her and a little breeze came along and pushed her out of there.

I thought maybe Randolph had thrown himself overboard and had not been noticed during the excitement, but the next day we found him hiding in the after hold. He said he was waiting for the ship to go down and that nobody would fool him this time. When I told him she was clear he began to cry like a child. Then I got him up to my cabin and set him about writing his statement.

But I'd forgotten he had a mania for making away with himself—I suppose I'm to blame for that. He went out on the deck afterward. I didn't see what happened, but the mate said he climbed up into the mizzen shrouds and then threw himself down—not into the water but upon the deck. When we picked him up he was conscious, but dying.

I felt sorry for him, poor devil! He called to me as he lay there dying, and made me promise that I'd bury him as soon as he'd gone.

"I can walk back by myself," said he. "I know the way. I'll find her."

Well, what could I do? I promised. He went, about half an hour later, smiling a good-bye. We sewed him in one of those sacks, put some scrap iron at his feet, and let him go. I suppose he's down there now, and I hope he found her, whoever she may be.

THE TEMPLE

H. P. Lovecraft

As problematic as he was prolific, H. P. Lovecraft (1890–1937) remains the most ubiquitous name within Weird Fiction. His foundational treatise on the mode, *Supernatural Horror in Literature* (1927), continues to introduce scholars into the study of the Weird, while his influence can be traced across mediums to the extra-dimensional insight of *Bloodborne* (2015) or the tentacular monstrosities of *Stranger Things* (2016–). Born in Providence, Rhode Island, Lovecraft was largely unsuccessful during his lifetime. Yet, through the preservation efforts of his close friends and disciples, August Derleth and Donald Wandrei, Lovecraft's fictions and letters have achieved incomparable longevity. Tales such as "The Call of Cthulhu" (1928), "The Dunwich Horror" (1929) and *At the Mountains of Madness* (1936) are now considered classics of horror fiction, while modern adaptations including Stuart Gordon's *Re-Animator* (1985) and Richard Stanley's *Color Out of Space* (2019) uphold Lovecraft's position as a pioneer of contemporary Weird writing.

"The Temple" was first published in the September 1925 issue of *Weird Tales*. A manuscript, allegedly composed during World War I, details the sinking of the British freighter, *Victory*, by the Imperial German Navy. A subsequent explosion in the engine room strands the German submarine on the floor of the Atlantic Ocean, where the surviving crew discover the remains of Atlantis. Here, the vivid descriptions of previous tales are filtered through Lovecraft's eldritch evils. Subsuming the myth of Atlantis into his own Cthulhu Mythos, the sunken continent would be further referenced in works such as "The Haunter of the Dark" (1936) and "Medusa's Coil" (1939), which Lovecraft co-wrote with Zealia Bishop. However, the Weirdest element of the tale may be the choice of narrator. Lieutenant-Commander, Karl Heinrich, Graf von Altberg-Ehrenstein is evoked through characteristically nuanced descriptions of his "iron German will" against the "English pig-dogs".

On August 20, 1917, I, Karl Heinrich, Graf von Altberg-Ehrenstein, Lieutenant-Commander in the Imperial German Navy and in charge of the submarine U-29, deposit this bottle and record in the Atlantic Ocean at a point to me unknown but probably about N. Latitude 20 degrees, W. Longitude 35 degrees, where my ship lies disabled on the ocean floor. I do so because of my desire to set certain unusual facts before the public; a thing I shall not in all probability survive to accomplish in person, since the circumstances surrounding me are as menacing as they are extraordinary, and involve not only the hopeless crippling of the U-29, but the impairment of my iron German will in a manner most disastrous.

On the afternoon of June 18, as reported by wireless to the U-61, bound for Kiel, we torpedoed the British freighter *Victory*, New York to Liverpool, in N. Latitude 45 degrees 16 minutes, W. Longitude 28 degrees 34 minutes; permitting the crew to leave in boats in order to obtain a good cinema view for the admiralty records. The ship sank quite picturesquely, bow first, the stern rising high out of the water whilst the hull shot down perpendicularly to the bottom of the sea. Our camera missed nothing, and I regret that so fine a reel of film should never reach Berlin. After that we sank the lifeboats with our guns and submerged.

When we rose to the surface about sunset a seaman's body was found on the deck, hands gripping the railing in curious fashion. The poor fellow was young, rather dark, and very handsome; probably an Italian or Greek, and undoubtedly of the *Victory*'s crew. He had evidently sought refuge on the very ship which had been forced to destroy his own—one more victim of the unjust war of aggression which the English pig-dogs are waging upon the Fatherland. Our men searched him for souvenirs, and found in his coat pocket a very odd bit of ivory carved to represent a youth's head crowned with laurel. My fellow-officer, Lieutenant Klenze, believed that the thing was of great age and artistic value, so took it from the men for himself. How it had ever come into the possession of a common sailor neither he nor I could imagine.

As the dead man was thrown overboard there occurred two incidents which created much disturbance amongst the crew. The fellow's eyes had been closed; but in the dragging of his body to the rail they were jarred open, and many seemed to entertain a queer delusion that they gazed steadily and mockingly at Schmidt and Zimmer, who were bent over the corpse. Then Boatswain Müller, an elderly man who would have known better had he not been a superstitious Alsatian swine, became so excited by this impression that he watched the body in the water; and swore that after it sank a little it drew its limbs into a swimming position and sped away to the south under the waves. Klenze and I did not like these displays of peasant ignorance, and severely reprimanded the men, particularly Müller.

The next day a very troublesome situation was created by the indisposition of some of the crew. They were evidently suffering from the nervous strain of our long voyage, and had had bad dreams. Several seemed quite dazed and stupid; and after satisfying myself that they were not feigning their weakness, I excused them from their duties. The sea was rather rough, so we descended to a depth where the waves were less troublesome. Here we were comparatively calm, despite a somewhat puzzling southward current which we could not identify from our oceanographic charts. The moans of the sick men were decidedly annoying; but since they did not appear to demoralize the rest of the crew, we did not resort to extreme measures. It was our plan to remain where we were and intercept the liner *Dacia*, mentioned in information from agents in New York.

In the early evening we rose to the surface, and found the sea less heavy. The smoke of a battleship was on the northern horizon, but our distance and ability to submerge made us safe. What worried us more was the talk of Boatswain Müller, which grew wilder as night came on. He was in a detestably childish state, and babbled of some illusion of dead bodies drifting past the undersea portholes; bodies which looked at him intensely, and which he recognized in spite of bloating as having seen dying during some of our victorious German exploits. And he said that the young man we had found and tossed overboard was their leader. This was very gruesome and abnormal, so we confined Müller in irons and had him soundly whipped. The men were not pleased at his punishment, but discipline was necessary. We also denied the request of a delegation headed by Seaman Zimmer, that the curious carved ivory head be cast into the sea.

On June 20, Seamen Bohm and Schmidt, who had been ill the day before, became violently insane. I regretted that no physician was included in our complement of officers, since German lives are precious; but the constant ravings of the two concerning a terrible curse were most subversive of discipline, so drastic steps were taken. The crew accepted the event in a sullen fashion, but it seemed to quiet Müller; who thereafter gave us no trouble. In the evening we released him, and he went about his duties silently.

*

In the week that followed we were all very nervous, watching for the *Dacia*. The tension was aggravated by the disappearance of Müller and Zimmer, who undoubtedly committed suicide as a result of the fears which had seemed to harass them, though they were not observed in the act of jumping overboard. I was rather glad to be rid of Müller, for even his silence had unfavorably affected the crew. Everyone seemed inclined to be silent now, as though holding a secret fear. Many were ill, but none made a disturbance. Lieutenant Klenze chafed under the strain, and was annoyed by the merest trifles—such as the school of dolphins which gathered about the U-29 in increasing numbers, and the growing intensity of that southward current which was not on our chart.

It at length became apparent that we had missed the *Dacia* altogether. Such failures are not uncommon, and we were more pleased than disappointed; since our return to Wilhelmshaven was now in order. At noon June 28 we turned northeastward, and despite some rather comical entanglements with the unusual masses of dolphins were soon under way.

The explosion in the engine room at 2 P.M. was wholly a surprize. No defect in the machinery or carelessness in the men had been noticed, yet without warning the ship was racked from end to end with a colossal shock. Lieutenant Klenze hurried to the engine room, finding the fuel-tank and most of the mechanism shattered, and Engineers Raabe and Schneider instantly killed. Our situation had suddenly become grave indeed; for though the chemical air regenerators were intact, and though we could use the devices for raising and submerging the ship and opening the hatches as long as compressed air and storage batteries might hold out, we were powerless to propel or guide the submarine. To seek rescue in the lifeboats would be to deliver ourselves into the hands of enemies unreasonably embittered against our great German nation, and our wireless had failed ever since the *Victory* affair to put us in touch with a fellow U-boat of the Imperial Navy.

From the hour of the accident till July 2 we drifted constantly to the south, almost without plans and encountering no vessel. Dolphins still encircled the U-29, a somewhat remarkable circumstance considering the distance we had covered. On the morning of July 2 we sighted a warship flying American colors, and the men became very restless in their desire to surrender. Finally Lieutenant Klenze had to shoot a seaman named Traube, who urged this un-German act with especial violence. This quieted the crew for the time, and we submerged unseen.

The next afternoon a dense flock of sea-birds appeared from the south, and the ocean began to heave ominously. Closing our hatches, we awaited developments until we realized that we must either submerge or be swamped in the mounting waves. Our air pressure and electricity were diminishing, and we wished to avoid all unnecessary use of our slender mechanical resources; but in this case there was no choice. We did not descend far, and when after several hours the sea was calmer, we decided to return to the surface. Here, however, a new trouble developed; for the ship failed to respond to our direction in spite of all that the mechanics could do. As the men grew more frightened at this undersea imprisonment, some of them began to mutter again about Lieutenant Klenze's ivory image, but the sight of an automatic pistol calmed them. We kept the poor devils as busy as we could, tinkering at the machinery even when we knew it was useless.

Klenze and I usually slept at different times; and it was during my sleep, about 5 A.M., July 4, that the general mutiny broke loose.

The six remaining pigs of seamen, suspecting that we were lost, had suddenly burst into a mad fury at our refusal to surrender to the Yankee battleship two days before; and were in a delirium of cursing and destruction. They roared like the animals they were, and broke instruments and furniture indiscriminately; screaming about such nonsense as the curse of the ivory image and the dark dead youth who looked at them and swam away. Lieutenant Klenze seemed paralyzed and inefficient, as one might expect of a soft, womanish Rhinelander. I shot all six men, for it was necessary, and made sure that none remained alive.

We expelled the bodies through the double hatches and were alone in the U-29. Klenze seemed very nervous, and drank heavily. It was decided that we remain alive as long as possible, using the large stock of provisions and chemical supply of oxygen, none of which had suffered from the crazy antics of those swine-hound seamen. Our compasses, depth gauges, and other delicate instruments were ruined; so that henceforth our only reckoning would be guess-work, based on our watches, the calendar, and our apparent drift as judged by any objects we might spy through the portholes or from the conning tower. Fortunately we had storage batteries still capable of long use, both for interior lighting and for the searchlight. We often cast a beam around the ship, but saw only dolphins, swimming parallel to our own drifting course. I was scientifically interested in those dolphins; for though the ordinary *Delphinus delphis* is a cetacean mammal, unable to subsist without air, I watched one of the swimmers closely for two hours, and did not see him alter his submerged condition.

With the passage of time Klenze and I decided that we were still drifting south, meanwhile sinking deeper and deeper. We noted the marine fauna and flora, and read much on the subject in the books I had carried with me for spare moments. I could not help observing, however, the inferior scientific knowledge of my companion. His mind was not Prussian, but given to imaginings and speculations which have no value. The fact of our coming death affected him curiously, and he would frequently pray in remorse over the men, women, and children we had sent to the bottom; forgetting that all things are noble which serve the German state. After a time he became noticeably unbalanced, gazing for hours at his ivory image and weaving fanciful stories of the lost and forgotten things under the sea. Sometimes, as a psychological experiment, I would lead him on in these wanderings, and listen to his endless poetical quotations and tales of sunken ships. I was very sorry for him, for I dislike to see a German suffer; but he was not a good man to die with. For myself I was proud, knowing how the Fatherland would revere my memory and how my sons would be taught to be men like me.

On August 9, we espied the ocean floor, and sent a powerful beam from the searchlight over it. It was a vast undulating plain, mostly covered with seaweed, and strown with the shells of small mollusks. Here and there were slimy objects of puzzling contour, draped with weeds and encrusted with barnacles, which Klenze declared must be ancient ships lying in their graves. He was puzzled by one thing, a peak of solid matter, protruding above the ocean bed nearly four feet at its apex; about two feet thick, with flat sides and smooth upper surfaces which met at a very obtuse angle. I called the peak a bit of outcropping rock, but Klenze thought he saw carvings on it. After a while he began to shudder, and turned away from the scene as if frightened; yet could give no explanation save that he was overcome with the vastness, darkness, remoteness, antiquity, and mystery of the oceanic abysses. His mind was tired, but I am always a German, and was quick to notice two things: that the U-29 was standing the deep-sea pressure splendidly, and that the peculiar dolphins were still about us, even at a depth where the existence of high organisms is considered impossible by most naturalists. That I had previously overestimated our depth, I was sure; but none the less we must still be deep enough to make these phenomena remarkable. Our southward speed, as gauged by the ocean floor, was about as I had estimated from the organisms passed at higher levels.

It was at 3:15 p.m., August 12, that poor Klenze went wholly mad. He had been in the conning tower using the searchlight when I saw him bound into the library compartment where I sat reading, and his face at once betrayed him. I will repeat here what he said, underlining the words he emphasized: "*He* is calling! *He* is calling! I hear him! We must go!" As he spoke he took his ivory image from the table, pocketed it, and seized my arm in an effort to drag me up the companionway to the deck. In a moment I understood that he meant to open the hatch and plunge with me into the water outside, a vagary of suicidal and homicidal mania for which I was scarcely prepared. As I hung back and attempted to soothe him he grew more violent, saying: "Come now—do not wait until later; it is better to repent and be forgiven than to defy and be condemned." Then I tried the opposite of the soothing plan, and told him he was mad—pitifully demented. But he was unmoved, and cried: "If I am mad, it is mercy! May the gods pity the man who in his callousness can remain sane to the hideous end! Come and be mad whilst *he* still calls with mercy!"

This outburst seemed to relieve a pressure in his brain; for as he finished he grew much milder, asking me to let him depart alone if I would not accompany him. My course at once became clear. He was a German, but only a Rhinelander and a commoner; and he was now a potentially dangerous madman. By complying with his suicidal request I could immediately free myself from one who was no longer a companion but a menace. I asked him to give me the ivory image before he went, but this request brought from him such uncanny laughter that I did not repeat it. Then I asked him if he wished to leave any keepsake or lock of hair for his family in Germany in case I should be rescued, but again he gave me that strange laugh. So as he climbed the ladder I went to the levers and allowing proper time-intervals operated the machinery which sent him to his death. After I saw that he was no longer in the boat I threw the searchlight around the water in an effort to obtain a last glimpse of him; since I wished to ascertain whether the water-pressure would flatten him as it theoretically should, or whether the body would be unaffected, like those extraordinary dolphins. I did not, however, succeed in finding my late companion, for the dolphins were massed thickly and obscuringly about the conning tower.

That evening I regretted that I had not taken the ivory image surreptitiously from poor Klenze's pocket as he left, for the memory of it fascinated me. I could not forget the youthful, beautiful head with its leafy crown, though I am not by nature an artist. I was also sorry that I had no one with whom to converse. Klenze, though not my mental equal, was much better than no one. I did not sleep well that night, and wondered exactly when the end would come. Surely, I had little enough chance of rescue.

The next day I ascended to the conning tower and commenced the customary searchlight explorations. Northward the view was much the same as it had been all the four days since we had sighted the bottom, but I perceived that the drifting of the U-29 was less rapid. As I swung the beam around to the south, I noticed that the ocean floor ahead fell away in a marked declivity, and bore curiously regular blocks of stone in certain places, disposed as if in accordance with definite patterns. The boat did not at once descend to match the greater ocean depth, so I was soon forced to adjust the searchlight to cast a sharply downward beam. Owing to the abruptness of the change a wire was disconnected, which necessitated a delay of many minutes for repairs; but at length the light streamed on again, flooding the marine valley below me.

I am not given to emotion of any kind, but my amazement was very great when I saw what lay revealed in that electrical glow. And yet as one reared in the best *kultur* of Prussia I should not have been amazed, for geology and tradition alike tell us of great transpositions in oceanic and continental areas. What I saw was an extended and elaborate array of ruined edifices; all of magnificent though unclassified architecture, and in various stages of preservation. Most appeared to be of marble, gleaming whitely in the rays of the searchlight, and the general plan was of a large city at the bottom of a narrow valley, with numerous isolated temples and villas on the steep slopes above. Roofs were fallen and columns were broken, but there still remained an air of immemorially ancient splendor which nothing could efface.

Confronted at last with the Atlantis I had formerly deemed largely a myth, I was the most eager of explorers. At the bottom of that valley a river once had flowed; for as I examined the scene more closely I beheld the remains of stone and marble bridges and sea-walls, and terraces and embankments once verdant and beautiful. In my enthusiasm I became nearly as idiotic and sentimental as poor Klenze, and was very tardy in noticing that the southward current had ceased at last, allowing the U-29 to settle slowly down upon the sunken city as an airplane settles upon a town of the upper earth. I was slow, too, in realizing that the school of unusual dolphins had vanished.

In about two hours the boat rested in a paved plaza close to the rocky wall of the valley. On one side I could view the entire city as it sloped from the plaza down to the old river-bank; on the other side, in startling proximity, I was confronted by the richly ornate and perfectly preserved façade of a great building, evidently a temple, hollowed from the solid rock. Of the original workmanship of this titanic thing I can only make conjectures. The façade, of immense magnitude, apparently covers a continuous hollow recess; for its windows are many and widely distributed. In the center yawns a great open door, reached by an impressive flight of steps, and surrounded by exquisite carvings like the figures of Bacchanals in relief. Foremost of all are the great columns and frieze, both decorated with sculptures of inexpressible beauty; obviously portraying idealized pastoral scenes and processions of priests and priestesses bearing strange ceremonial devices in adoration of a radiant god. The art is of the most phenomenal perfection, largely Hellenic in idea, yet strangely individual. It imparts an impression of terrible antiquity, as though it were the remotest rather than the immediate ancestor of Greek art. Nor can I doubt that every detail of this massive product was fashioned from the virgin hillside rock of our planet. It is palpably a part of the valley wall, though how the vast interior was ever excavated I cannot imagine. Perhaps a cavern or series of caverns furnished the nucleus. Neither age nor submersion has corroded the pristine grandeur of this awful fane—for fane indeed it must be—and today after thousands of years it rests untarnished and inviolate in the endless night and silence of an ocean chasm.

I cannot reckon the number of hours I spent in gazing at the sunken city with its buildings, arches, statues, and bridges, and the colossal temple with its beauty and mystery. Though I knew that death was near, my curiosity was consuming; and I threw the searchlight's beam about in eager quest. The shaft of light permitted me to learn many details, but refused to show anything within the gaping door of the rock-hewn temple; and after a time I turned off the current, conscious of the need of conserving power. The rays were now perceptibly dimmer than they had been during the weeks of drifting. And as if sharpened by the coming deprivation of light, my desire to explore the watery secrets grew. I, a German, should be the first to tread those eon-forgotten ways!

I produced and examined a deep-sea diving suit of jointed metal, and experimented with the portable light and air regenerator. Though I should have trouble in managing the double hatches alone, I believed I could overcome all obstacles with my scientific skill and actually walk about the dead city in person.

On August 16 I effected an exit from the U-29, and laboriously made my way through the ruined and mud-choked streets to the ancient river. I found no skeletons or other human remains, but gleaned a wealth of archeological lore from sculptures and coins. Of this I cannot now speak save to utter my awe at a culture in the full noon of glory when cave-dwellers roamed Europe and the Nile flowed unwatched to the sea. Others, guided by this manuscript if it shall ever be found, must unfold the mysteries at which I can only hint. I returned to the boat as my electric batteries grew feeble, resolved to explore the rock temple on the following day.

On the 17th, as my impulse to search out the mystery of the temple waxed still more insistent, a great disappointment befell me; for I found that the materials needed to replenish the portable light had perished in the mutiny of those pigs in July. My rage was unbounded, yet my German sense forbade me to venture unprepared into an utterly black interior which might prove the lair of some indescribable marine monster or a labyrinth of passages from whose windings I could never extricate myself. All I could do was to turn on the waning searchlight of the U-29, and with its aid walk up the temple steps and study the exterior carvings. The shaft of light entered the door at an upward angle, and I peered in to see if I could glimpse anything, but all in vain. Not even the roof was visible; and though I took a step or two inside after testing the floor with a staff, I dared not go farther. Moreover, for the first time in my life I experienced the emotion of dread. I began to realize how some of poor Klenze's moods had arisen, for as the temple drew me more and more, I feared its aqueous abysses with a blind and mounting terror. Returning to the submarine, I turned off the lights and sat thinking in the dark. Electricity must now be saved for emergencies.

Saturday the 18th I spent in total darkness, tormented by thoughts and memories that threatened to overcome my German will. Klenze had gone mad and perished before reaching this sinister remnant of a past unwholesomely remote, and had advised me to go with him. Was, indeed, Fate preserving my reason only to draw me irresistibly to an end more horrible and unthinkable than any man has dreamed of? Clearly, my nerves were sorely taxed, and I must cast off these impressions of weaker men.

I could not sleep Saturday night, and turned on the lights regardless of the future. It was annoying that the electricity should not last out the air and provisions. I revived my thoughts of euthanasia, and examined my automatic pistol. Toward morning I must have dropped asleep with the lights on, for I awoke in darkness yesterday afternoon to find the batteries dead. I struck several matches in succession, and desperately regretted the improvidence which had caused us long ago to use up the few candles we carried.

After the fading of the last match I dared to waste, I sat very quietly without a light. As I considered the inevitable end my mind ran over preceding events, and developed a hitherto dormant impression which would have caused a weaker and more superstitious man to shudder. *The head of the radiant god in the sculptures on the rock temple is the same as that carven bit of ivory which the dead sailor brought from the sea and which poor Klenze carried back into the sea.*

I was a little dazed by this coincidence, but did not become terrified. It is only the inferior thinker who hastens to explain the singular and the complex by the primitive short cut of supernaturalism. The coincidence was strange, but I was too sound a reasoner to connect circumstances which admit of no logical connection, or to associate in any uncanny fashion the disastrous events which had led from the *Victory* affair to my present plight. Feeling the need of more rest, I took a sedative and secured some more sleep. My nervous condition was reflected in my dreams, for I seemed to hear the cries of drowning persons, and to see dead faces pressing against the portholes of the boat. And among the dead faces was the living, mocking face of the youth with the ivory image.

I must be careful how I record my awakening today, for I am unstrung, and much hallucination is necessarily mixed with fact. Psychologically my case is most interesting, and I regret that it cannot be observed scientifically by a competent German authority. Upon opening my eyes my first sensation was an overmastering desire to visit the rock temple; a desire which grew every instant, yet which I automatically sought to resist through some emotion of fear which operated in the reverse direction. Next there came to me the impression of *light* amidst the darkness of dead batteries, and I seemed to see a sort of phosphorescent glow in the water through the porthole which opened toward the temple. This aroused my curiosity, for I knew of no deep-sea organism capable of emitting such luminosity. But before I could investigate there came a third impression which because of its irrationality caused me to doubt the objectivity of anything my senses might record. It was an aural delusion; a sensation of rhythmic, melodic sound as of some wild yet beautiful chant or choral hymn, coming from the outside through the absolutely sound-proof hull of the U-29. Convinced of my psychological and nervous abnormality, I lighted some matches and poured a stiff dose of sodium bromide solution, which seemed to calm me to the extent of dispelling the illusion of sound. But the phosphorescence remained, and I had difficulty in repressing a childish impulse to go to the porthole and seek its source. It was horribly realistic, and I could soon distinguish by its aid the familiar objects around me, as well as the empty sodium bromide glass of which I had had no former visual impression in its present location. This last circumstance made me ponder, and I crossed the room and touched the glass. It was indeed in the place where I had seemed to see it. Now I knew that the light was either real or part of an hallucination so fixed and consistent that I could not hope to dispel it, so abandoning all resistance I ascended to the conning tower to look for the luminous agency. Might it not actually be another U-boat, offering possibilities of rescue?

It is well that the reader accept nothing which follows as objective truth, for since the events transcend natural law, they are necessarily the subjective and unreal creations of my overtaxed mind. When I attained the conning tower I found the sea in general far less luminous than I had expected. There was no animal or vegetable phosphorescence about, and the city that sloped down to the river was invisible in blackness. What I did see was not spectacular, not grotesque or terrifying, yet it removed my last vestige of trust in my consciousness. *For the door and windows of the undersea temple hewn from the rocky hill were vividly aglow with a flickering radiance, as from a mighty altar-flame far within.*

75

Later incidents are chaotic. As I stared at the uncannily lighted door and windows, I became subject to the most extravagant visions—visions so extravagant that I cannot even relate them. I fancied that I discerned objects in the temple; objects both stationary and moving; and seemed to hear again the unreal chant that had floated to me when first I awaked. And over all rose thoughts and fears which centered in the youth from the sea and the ivory image whose carving was duplicated on the frieze and columns of the temple before me. I thought of poor Klenze, and wondered where his body rested with the image he had carried back into the sea. He had warned me of something, and I had not heeded—but he was a soft-headed Rhinelander who went mad at troubles a Prussian could bear with ease.

The rest is very simple. My impulse to visit and enter the temple has now become an inexplicable and imperious command which ultimately cannot be denied. My own German will no longer controls my acts, and volition is henceforward possible only in minor matters. Such madness it was which drove Klenze to his death, bareheaded and unprotected in the ocean; but I am a Prussian and man of sense, and will use to the last what little will I have. When first I saw that I must go, I prepared my diving suit, helmet, and air regenerator for instant donning; and immediately commenced to write this hurried chronicle in the hope that it may some day reach the world. I shall seal the manuscript in a bottle and entrust it to the sea as I leave the U-29 for ever.

I have no fear, not even from the prophecies of the madman Klenze. What I have seen cannot be true, and I know that this madness of my own will at most lead only to suffocation when my air is gone. The light in the temple is a sheer delusion, and I shall die calmly, like a German, in the black and forgotten depths. This demoniac laughter which I hear as I write comes only from my own weakening brain. So I will carefully don my diving suit and walk boldly up the steps into that primal shrine; that silent secret of unfathomed waters and uncounted years.

ATLANTIS
REVISITED

UNDER THE N-RAY

Will Smith & R. J. Robbins

While there is unfortunately little biographical information available, the pulp careers of Will Smith and R. J. Robbins can still be traced through their works. Together, they wrote one short story and two novelettes: "Under the N-Ray" (1925) and "Swamp Horror" (1926) in *Weird Tales*, and "The Soul Master" (1930) in *Astounding Stories of Super-Science*. Individually, Smith also penned "The Escape of Saemundr" (1924) in *The New Statesman*, "Wanderlust by Proxy" (1925) and "Other Earths" (1927) in *Weird Tales*, and "A Dubious Hero" (1939) in *Railroad Magazine*. Outside of a letter of 1942 to *Famous Fantastic Mysteries*, Robbins appears to have written only in collaboration.

"Under the N-Ray" was the cover story of the May 1925 issue of *Weird Tales*, and commences a couplet of tales bound by the theme of "Atlantis Revisited". In such works, the history of Atlantis is buried in racial memory, the suppressed experiences of past ancestors, able to resurface through pseudoscientific forms of regression. Madam Losieva, a medium, and Professor Ember, a pioneer of the "N-Ray", are able to project these lives onto a screen. As their subject, Jack Hodge, revisits his lineage, each ends with a death by water. Evoking the thought projection of Arthur Conan Doyle's later Atlantis novel, *The Maracot Deep* (1927), and the "N-Rays" supposedly discovered by the French physicist, Prosper-René Blondlot in 1903, "Under the N-Ray" transforms past into present, visualizing the fall of Atlantis. As the conclusion reveals, the tale can also be read as representative of evolutionary anxieties, in which humanity might revert to atavistic animals.

I

"I can't say the little party sounds alluring, or even interesting," said Hodge, with some obvious attempt to sidetrack the invitation. "I have attended these affairs before and invariably found them to be but repetitions of the time-honored table-walking and spirit-rapping that seem to be the medium's stock in trade. Can't you have a heart, Doc, and tell Madam What's-her-name that I have an important assignment slated for tonight and can't possibly make it?"

"I could do that very thing, Hodge; but I'm not going to. I made Madam Losieva a very definite promise that you would be present, and that settles it. Furthermore, I can assure you that her demonstration of the psychic forces will be vastly different from what you expect. It should provide you with some wonderful 'copy' for your paper—if you can obtain her permission to publish the details."

I was smiling, but insistent. Hodge made an impatient gesture, following it up with a characteristic shrug of resignation.

"Well, I suppose I'm elected to accompany you, though the Lord in heaven knows I'm fed up on such truck. Anyone else going along?"

The young reporter for the *Clarion* asked the question listlessly. I almost relented when I sensed his point of view. He so clearly expected a dry, uninteresting evening. Had I known the fearful termination it was to have I would have done all in my power to keep him away.

Poor Hodge! For twelve long years he was my crony, and I find it difficult to speak of him without emotion. In a way, I feel responsible for what came about, even though I did not set in motion directly the forces which wrecked his mind and transformed him into a beast.

Just how two men of such differing temperaments and tastes could get along so well together has always been a mystery to me. It is a solemn fact, however, that I have dragged him, time after time, into my library and talked Einstein, psychoanalysis or some other abstruse subject into him by the hour; and only rarely would he make a break of some kind to indicate his complete ignorance of the subject on which I was expatiating. My turn generally came swiftly enough, though. He was ever liable to tire of my line and ask me abruptly my opinion as to the probable outcome of the Haley-Brennan bout, or if the Giants had a chance for the pennant this season. Or it might be that the conversation would turn to cars. We both had them—he a speedster, while I made use of a more dignified vehicle befitting my calling as a physician.

"Unless I am greatly mistaken, you will find yourself in rather select company," I had answered his query. "Let's see. Besides ourselves Madam Losieva has invited Professor Johnson, the psychologist; Olean Davies, the radio expert; Dr. Wilbur Holmes; Amos Cronkhite, the astronomer, and his young assistant, Larry Dinsmore; Homer Day, editor of the *Argus*; and thirty or forty others whose names I can't recall. I think those I have mentioned will make it obvious enough that this is no ordinary spiritualistic performance. I understand there will be a few ladies present, and needless to say you are to be on your best behavior. I am well acquainted with your propensities where the fair sex is concerned."

"You said a real mouthful then, Doc," approved the irrepressible reporter, grinning. Unblushingly he helped himself to one of my private cigars.

"I forgot to tell you," I said, "that our friend Roger Norton is going to attend—at the insistence of his daughter, Emily—so you will have someone to talk to while the program is on."

"Aha!"

"Madam Losieva is carrying out this experiment in collaboration with a Professor Ember, who is unknown locally. Just what the nature of the work is to be she refuses to divulge, but from the hints of my colleagues it will be a sensation. Be here promptly at 8:15. I shall be waiting for you, and Madam Losieva is apt to be annoyed if we are not punctual."

"I'll be on the dot, Doc. That is, if—well, you know."

Yes; I knew. He would be prompt unless—it rained. When that happened, no promise was binding on Jack Hodge. All the galoshes in Christendom could not tempt the man to step out into the mildest drizzle. If his house were on fire I honestly believe he would burn to death rather than go out into a shower—unless firemen should play the hose near him. In that case—well, he would seek the location most remotely removed from water.

Hodge never drank water; he never bathed in water without first coloring it enough to make it look like something else; he would not cross a bridge over water without keeping his eyes tightly shut; the sight of a boat made him feel faint.

The *Clarion* people used at first to chaff him about his weakness; then they threatened. Hodge used to try honestly to conquer it, but his attempts always ended in nervous nausea followed by a fit of patently genuine illness. He gave up trying long ago. Being normal in every other way and a crackerjack news getter withal, the reporter held his job. The newspaper people at last recognized Hodge's morbid dread of water for the uncontrollable thing it was. As Hodge's physician, I called it congenital hydrophobia.

2

I shall not soon forget the peculiar sensation that came over me as I took my seat well to the front of the steadily growing assemblage in the séance chamber. Whether it was the atmosphere of strained expectancy that hung over all, or whether it was the weird aspect of the place, I cannot tell. The atmosphere was somber in the extreme, reminding me of that of certain radio broadcasting stations I had visited. The walls were hung on all sides with heavy draperies of black cloth, which effectually excluded all sight and sound of the world outside. The only illumination was furnished by a single bulb in the center of the black ceiling. The rays from this, filtering through a glass dome of a beautiful pearl tint, cast a pale glow over the assemblage. Involuntarily my mind took in the stage management of the experiment, and I found myself admiring its simplicity.

Directly in front of the audience was a small, slightly raised platform, obviously of temporary construction, on which was nothing more than two ordinary-looking chairs. On the wall beyond this stage was a large white screen somewhat similar to those to be found in moving picture theaters.

I had not long to wonder at my surroundings, for I was shortly aroused by a commotion at the rear.

Madam Losieva had entered. She was accompanied by a slight, wiry man of rather more than the medium height, quietly but expensively dressed, and plainly of a nervous mien. I had never set eyes on this man before, and I surveyed his features with an eager curiosity. Though I never saw him again after that tragic night, I still remember vividly the wide-set eyes reduced to minute dots by the immense, deeply concave spectacles he wore; the quick, darting glances he bent here and there as he scanned the faces of those present, and the impressive appearance created by a small, well-kept goatee which from time to time he stroked in abstraction.

And what of Madam Losieva herself? Just how can I give an adequate description of this colossus of mentality, this woman who has amazed the scientists of two continents with her exploits in the occult? To begin with, I may say her whole figure and personality belied the impression one had gained from reading of her accomplishments and methods. Where I expected a tall, stately woman, I beheld the exact antithesis.

The psychic was rather small in stature and well formed, and might reasonably have been of any age from twenty-eight to thirty-five. Her hair was the jet black so common in women of her race, and was done up in the simplest manner, parted exactly in the middle and combed out perfectly straight. The strands had been gathered up in two large knots, worn pendent over either ear. The features were quite strongly Russian, although a strange line of the eyes—was it the slightest bit of a slant?—hinted at a strain of the Mongolian. And what eyes they were!

As she passed down the aisle she swept the gathering with a single all-embracing glance; and as her eyes met mine for the briefest fraction of a second I involuntarily shivered. It was as if I had recognized a will mightier than my own; or was it a flashing premonition of what was to come? At any rate she exercised somewhat the same effect on all those present. Of a sudden the sounds of whispered conversation died out. The silence of the place became absolute.

At the rear Professor Ember—for it was he who had entered with Losieva—was busying himself with a complicated piece of apparatus completely covering a large, specially constructed table. The thing combined all the more salient features of a modern radio receiving set with those of a moving picture machine. Some features even brought to mind the apparatus used in taking X-ray pictures. Just how that conglomeration of wires, switches, bulbs and dials functioned to produce the extraordinary results I am about to chronicle, a good many of the scientists there present would give much to know. But the secret is locked in the bosom of Professor Ember; and that gentleman, though doubtless alive, is keeping well out of sight.

The hush that had come over the assemblage remained unbroken as the great Losieva began a few preliminary words of explanation.

"Friends, the select few to whom I have extended invitations are present tonight to witness an epoch-marking experiment—a demonstration which, if successful, will cause a complete revision of our ideas on certain subjects. For instance, what do we know of the possibility of life in the hereafter? What is the connection, if any there be, between those now living and those dead? What do we know of our previous cycles of existence? Of what transcendent heights of accomplishment is the human brain capable?

"Has any of us lived in another period? You answer, no. But are you positive that your brain cannot, under a sufficiently powerful stimulus, be made to remember strange things? With Professor Ember, who has kindly agreed to collaborate, I shall endeavor to disprove several fallacies of science which have long been regarded as indisputable facts.

"Perhaps one of the most fascinating of the dreams which sometimes come to us is that of an apparatus to bridge the gap separating us from the remote past. To the possessor of such a wonderful contrivance nothing that has ever happened could be hidden. The solutions to the world's most ancient secrets would become common knowledge.

"The mystery of life, the lost tribes of Israel, the wonder of the early ages of the earth, the secrets of the mighty empire of the

Incas—nothing could escape our eyes. The hideous monsters of the Reptilian Age would flash before our gaze, not as pictures painted by some highly imaginative artist, but rather as flesh-and-blood realities.

"Although the future may hold the solution, in the light of present-day discoveries we must brand this dream as impossible of accomplishment in its entirety. However, we have a substitute offered us even now. This is made possible through the untiring labors of Professor Ember. The secret of his invention cannot yet be made public, and I may not give details as to its operation. Suffice it to say that the apparatus has a dual identity. It consists of a manufactory for the N-ray, which stimulates the memory, and the thought projector to make the mind pictures visible to spectators.

"With the kind permission of all present we will give a demonstration which will convince the most skeptical of the absolutely authentic results obtained. Professor Ember!"

The pearl-colored dome died swiftly, and amid a chorus of subdued exclamations the room became blackness. At once a ray of unearthly light leapt into being, piercing the darkness like a great sword. The shaft was of no tint that I can name. The word "unearthly" to my mind quite accurately describes it. As it swung hither and yon, the brilliant beam played on the head of one, then another of the spectators. Finally it came to rest on an aspiring young chemist at my right, a fat fellow named Chester Tubbs.

What followed was the most curious effect I have ever seen, though phenomena perhaps similar have been noted by experimenters with radium rays. We are told by such scientists that practically all substances are radioactive in some degree. but it would have taken considerable argument to convince me that Chet Tubbs' anatomy could come under this category. Yet the bald fact remains that no sooner had the mysterious ray struck upon the fat gentleman's head than that member took on a most peculiar appearance.

Could it be that Tubbs' hair was standing stiffly on end? But hair does not grow to a length of a foot on the head of the average male American. How, then, to account for the pale streamers of light which emanated from the skull in all directions? The rising and dimming brilliance of the aura suggested the familiar aurora borealis. The young man seemed to sense something wrong, although as yet the incident meant nothing to him but the playing of strong light upon the back of his head.

The psychic again addressed the crowd.

"You have seen the peculiar effect of Professor Ember's N-ray," she began, speaking from the darkness. It was evident the thing was only beginning. "Now, if the gentleman will kindly step to the front a moment I shall ask him to be a martyr, in a way of speaking, to the thought projector. But it is only to the extent of acting as my subject for a few moments. No, Mr. Tubbs, you are not going to be mesmerized."

Somewhat doubtfully the chemist got to his feet and moved down the aisle. Guided by Professor Ember, the ray continued to play on his cranium. Many were the titters from the women, and from several of the male element came chuckles of amusement at the ludicrous pictures.

Tubbs reached the stage, and at a word from the psychic took a seat at the side of the screen.

"Mr. Tubbs, you are doubtless still under the impression I am going to mesmerize you. Please rid yourself of the idea, for all that I desire to do at this time is demonstrate the workings of Professor Ember's thought projector. I shall ask you to concentrate for a moment on that which is now uppermost in your mind. Pay no attention to me or anyone else."

As she finished a second ray of light went stabbing across the blackness toward the white screen. This became fully illuminated, and of all things I had expected to find depicted thereon—! For a brief instant there was a complete silence; then came a roar of laughter from the crowd, in which even Tubbs had to join. On the screen was a perfect picture—a close-up view of a snowy-white expanse of table cloth, a confusion of dishes and silverware, and a great, heaping platterful of corned beef and cabbage!

This was practically the only laugh during the whole program. The rest was serious enough, heaven knows.

Now the preliminary demonstration was over; and, amid considerable chaffing from his friends, the young chemist resumed his seat. The real séance was about to commence.

Right here I began to get nervous, half wishing I had remained at home myself. I began to sense impending trouble, if not a downright disaster. I cannot say just what caused this feeling—call it presentiment if you will—but remember that of a sudden I felt a wild desire to bolt the place. Turning slightly in my seat I nudged my companion. As I had expected, he was already engaged in a whispered conversation with a pulchritudinous blond—Emily Norton, whom I have mentioned previously. She was on very intimate terms with Hodge, and my existence was for the nonce a subject of total indifference. I turned away and gave myself up to the rest of the program.

"We are now in a position to continue the experiment," Madam Losieva was saying. "As I mentioned before, we have no apparatus that will enable us to plunge into the past directly; but by means of certain forces which I control in conjunction with the thought projector and through a voluntary subject, we can reproduce on this screen various incidents of the subject's past cycles of existence. These will appear almost exactly as in the ordinary moving picture, with the exception that all details will be in their natural colors. Of course no films or slides will be used. The original vibrations from which the pictures are created are supplied solely from the subconscious mind of the subject. In order to get this effect in any degree, we have found it necessary to put the energizing brain into a state of hypnosis. In such a condition and under proper manipulation there seems to be no demand to which the mind will not respond. The brain best suited to our purpose we must select by a scientific test. It is hoped that no one of those present will object to becoming the subject if called upon to do so.

"To those who have qualms in the matter let me give assurance that no harm can possibly attend your entrance into the hypnotic state. However, to make sure of no accident I shall ask Dr. Maugridge, who is known to all of you, to keep a sharp observation of the pulse and respiration throughout the duration of the experiment."

She paused expectantly as if she thought possibly some voice would be raised in protest. I thought of objecting to the part in the proceedings she had so coolly assigned to me. But I had no tangible reason. The silence continued unbroken. Losieva gave a signal to her assistant.

Again the N-ray came flashing through the gloom. This time I noticed it was rapidly dancing around the head of everyone in the room, resting momentarily on each one, but ever passing on. Again I endeavored to assign some definite color to it. All I could think of was possibly green, or an allied tint. Or was it pink? No, it wasn't that; nor was it green after all. It was not white light; assuredly it had a color. I have often thought that if I knew the color of evil I could name the color of that shaft.

The infernal radiance was swinging toward my side of the room. At times the corona effect would spring up from certain heads, but thus far the only one to produce a really noticeable aura was that of Chet Tubbs. Apparently even he had not satisfied Losieva, for still the ray searched and searched...

I thought of vaudeville shows where I had seen the spotlight thrown upon singers and other performers. Was I to be the star actor in this particular show? I had not long to ponder, for now the baleful ray swept directly toward me. It came nearer—nearer... I became conscious of an impending panic within myself. I sought to avoid coming under the all-searching glare by leaning sidewise in my seat. Too late! I felt my countenance bathed by the hateful effulgence. At once I began to experience most peculiar sensations.

The séance hall, the crowd, Hodge and all faded swiftly from my field of vision. I was for the moment in a different world. For one thing, I could have sworn that I was standing at the curb of a curiously paved street—a street totally different from any with which I was acquainted. I cannot explain where I got my impressions, as the whole experience lasted but a second. But I can state definitely that it was one in a vastly different period of time. I remember that I received a glimpse of several persons on horseback. And I will take my oath they were soldiers in *armor*!

The next moment the ray had darted to another spot, and the spectral scene vanished. What was the meaning of this strange vision? Was it a sudden lapse into a previous life, a reversion to some long forgotten ego? Who knows? Professor Ember never explained the properties of the N-ray to me for the very good reason that he never had the opportunity. And now I don't want to know.

The beam had found another victim. With a tingling along my spine I saw that it rested on the head of Jack Hodge. But with what a different result! An exclamation of utter awe burst from the whole assemblage.

As the ray touched the reporter's countenance it seemed as if a peculiar aura of green-shot purple burst into being all about his head. It reminded me of the effect sometimes obtained from high tension apparatus such as Tesla coils, or the familiar Oudin resonators. Beside the present display the aura given off by the chemist's brain shrank into insignificance. I realized as I beheld it that the psychic would look no farther for her subject.

The next instant I turned and laid restraining hands on my companion. Evidently the ray had had somewhat the same effect upon him as upon me. Almost with the instant it flashed full upon him, he gave vent to a most inhuman growl, and his face became strangely contorted. Remembering the vision that had come to me during the time the ray had played about my brain, I did not hesitate in acting. For the space of several seconds I experienced the sensation of struggling with a madman or with an ape. Perspiration broke out all over me. The reporter's strength under this unnatural stimulus was tremendous.

Now the N-ray had disappeared; Hodge relaxed limply in my hands and staggered to his chair. "Lord, Doc; I could have sworn—" Before he could finish the thought half uttered, the bulb in the ceiling flashed on, and the great medium was speaking.

"The test is ended; we believe we have located a subject who will react favorably. His brain aura under test shows great sensitivity and response to the psychological manipulations which are so necessary to a really successful demonstration. Of course any person in the audience would make a passable subject; that is, we could always get some results. But it is a lamentable fact that in most cases a subject picked at random could progress backward but one or two cycles before the pictures on the screen would become very indistinct.

"I should explain here, perhaps, that my control extends beyond the subject's physical brain to the astral double of that brain. And on that double are impressed undimmed the experiences of the ego through all its cycles of existence. But not all subjects have so close a connection between the physical brain and the astral.

"In the case of Mr. Hodge I hope to show you five or six cycles of his life periods before his mental effort weakens—or my control ceases. The balance of the program depends on his willingness to undergo a half hour or so under hypnosis."

This last was addressed more to Hodge than to the general assemblage. I looked at the unlucky reporter. Clearly he was still in somewhat of a daze, and I felt a nameless kind of pity for him. Yes, I had to admit it to myself; Hodge, the man who held a reputation as the most aggressive reporter on the *Clarion*'s staff, was giving every evidence of going into a blue funk!

I had anticipated some sort of scene from him, but the reporter remained meek and inert. Madam Losieva was talking to him in a smoothly modulated tone which was having an oddly quieting effect upon him. He was drinking in her every word with an intenseness almost ludicrous. And as she talked on, the voice took on a peculiar monotony of cadence—a singsong tone if you will—and I rather fell under its spell myself.

Of a sudden I gave a start as I gazed at Hodge. Was he getting pop-eyed? That queer glint as the light struck his eyeballs and reflected into my own! The light? It was that of the N-ray. The other light—that from the pearly dome—was all but gone.

That stare—Losieva's voice has sunk to a barely perceptible murmur. The silence is intense—it is a palpable thing—Hodge's head is still held stiffly upright, but his eyes—the psychic has directed them to the dying glow in the ceiling—they are rolling upward—.

"Sleep, sleep—you are to dream of the past;—deep, deep slumber—. Sleep with your eyes on your dreams—deep—sleep—deep—deep—sleep—" The chamber was swept by the long, soughing aspirations of the drugged.

Too easily I can recall that dread scene—the tense little throng of spectators—the slight, sinuous figure of the mystic—the weird light of the N-ray—the unconscious form of my poor friend. Dimly seen, the huddle suggested not a living thing, but a statue of pitch-black clay. The eyes gleamed out as gray-white sculptures, gazing at that which statues see.

3

"I shall require a little assistance from one or two gentlemen. I desire that Mr. Hodge be placed in a chair on the left hand end of the stage, in a sitting position."

Norton and I volunteered for the service, and shortly the subject was so placed as to be dully perceptible to the whole assemblage. Taking a position near by, I noted the pulse and respiration. Beyond a barely noticeable decrease in the rise and fall of the abdomen, I could not thus far detect any abnormal conditions. I was thoroughly alive to the possibilities of the situation, however. As I resumed my chair I resolved there should be no unnecessary risks.

Certain grating and rustling sounds coming from the rear of the chamber told me that Professor Ember was making further adjustments to his apparatus. The inevitable sound of excited whispers came from all directions. The voice of Madam Losieva could be heard softly addressing the subject. Hodge remained immovable, rigid, as the baleful effulgence continued to scintillate in minute pinpoints of ghastly radiance. The reporter's colorless countenance, bathed and aureoled by the brilliancy, gave a grotesque suggestion of the man in the moon. But no one laughed.

"You may start the projector now if you wish, Professor Ember." The medium still used the monotonous quality of voice that had overcome the reporter. Was the tone used merely to preserve the general atmosphere of the séance, or was it that Losieva feared her subject's awaking? I do not know. Certain it is that no telltale tremors of the reporter's body were transmitted to my fingers as I touched him gingerly. His was the stiffness of the dead. Better had my friend been dead in actuality.

I was aroused to a realization that things were happening, by chorused exclamations from all sides. I glanced in the direction of the screen. A hazy something was slowly but definitely taking form before us. Nebulous and indistinct, it wavered and flickered, every moment growing clearer. Finally it resolved itself into the image of a human being. It was a very lifelike reproduction of the medium herself.

For a moment I had an idea that the operator might be making use of a slide, in some final adjustment to his mechanism, but on glancing in the direction of the machine I found that the professor was nowhere near it. Evidently satisfied that the apparatus would take care of itself for the time being, he had taken a seat among the lookers-on. The movement on the screen suddenly quieted and the form of Losieva stood out sharply, limned on dazzling white. Perhaps the most curious feature of the picture was its total lack of any background.

"The picture before you," began the great psychic, "is not a stereopticon slide as some of you may think, but rather is a picture that exists in the brain of the subject. As you can perceive, he is under complete hypnosis. Although conscious in one sense of the word, he is unable to move a muscle or perform any of the ordinary functions of life without controlling suggestions. His brain is now in such a condition that it can entertain but one thought impulse at a time. At present his mind is completely given over to one image, which is necessarily uppermost—the picture of myself. This picture will remain stationary until I cause him to exert his mind in other directions. Even though the ramifications of the average human brain are almost limitless, I hope to show very shortly that Mr. Hodge's mental power is quite exceptional.

"Please do not be surprised at times if the subject talks aloud and in unknown tongues. As far as I know he is unacquainted with any language other than English, but we may hear strange things. The subject's present ego is of the American nationality, but who can tell what the previous ones have been?

"The fact that there is no background shown on the screen while the image of myself is quite clear, indicates that the mind of the subject has no conception of his present surroundings. Yet it retains a sharply defined image of the agency which caused his state of suspended animation.

"John Hodge," addressing the still form in the chair, "do you know where you are?"

"Yes," came the answer in a dead, colorless voice. I shivered.

"Where?"

"In the séance chambers of Losieva, the psychic."

As he spoke there was a slight, a very slight, tremor of the aura about his head. Simultaneously the picture on the screen dimmed slightly, and other things began to come into view—a table, a chair, and a very good likeness of myself and of one or two of the other persons present who had happened to come under the reporter's attention.

An embarrassed little exclamation escaped from the magnate's daughter and chuckles emanated from several of the older persons present as Emily Norton's picture suddenly flashed conspicuously into view. Momentarily it outshone even the previously predominant image of the medium. The latter evidently feared loss of control over her subject, for she (rather hastily it seemed to me) began to voice a series of questions. The subject answered them all in the same lifeless tone.

As he made his answers, scene after scene slithered into view before us, remained for an instant, and as swiftly faded as new ideas were continually introduced. The strain was beginning to tell on the relentless psychic. Occasionally, when a desired answer was not immediately forthcoming, her voice would break with impatience. As she continued her apparently aimless interrogations it slowly dawned on me that she was striving to call to the subject's mind events of years before.

I remember one scene reproduced very vividly, one which I noted with more than casual interest. It dealt with a boyhood quarrel in which Hodge was badly beaten by a much bigger boy. I was little stronger or older than he, but I remember of injecting my presence—and fists—into the conflict to such good effect that the enemy finally beat an inglorious retreat. I was startled to see this scene re-enacted with absolute distinctness and fidelity of detail, even to school buildings and neighborhood fences.

"You may wonder," interpolated Losieva, "why, if these are really pictures that the subject's eye has imprinted upon his brain—why those scenes do not appear as he actually saw them. You see, when Mr. Hodge was knocked down in the fight we have witnessed, he did not see himself go down. He saw, rather, the ground come up—or perhaps his eyes were really closed, and he saw nothing. But in retrospect we picture events as we believe they occurred, casting our own figure in with the other actors. In other words, these are scenes not as registered by the subject's physical eye at the time of enactment, but rather as seen by his mental eye at this moment.

"This psychological bent is most fortunate for our experiment. Without it, we should be unable to see the subject himself on the screen—our point of vantage would always be the subject's eyes. As it is, we are given the point of view of an entirely detached spectator—or of a motion picture camera."

The medium may have said more, but if so I did not hear it. My mind was elsewhere. I was being entertained, to my consternation, by a very realistic repetition of my own wedding—at which I got most gloriously drunk. This scene was greeted by a ripple of laughter. Most of the audience were personal acquaintances and could appreciate the humor of the situation—for them. I remember a feeling of intense gratification at the extreme darkness of the room.

I shall not attempt to mention all the scenes that followed. There passed several of relative unimportance, and then came the most remarkable one so far. This one gave us a passing glimpse of an infant lying in bed beside the quiet form of Hodge's mother. The child could not have been more than two days old. The woman was easily recognized. And Mrs. Hodge had but one child!

I gasped. By no other means could all this have been produced save by exercise of an abnormal stimulus over the man's own memory. If his memory could be sent back so far as this, what of the man's life before birth? Did the ego extend back beyond that? Did the subconscious brain hold memories of a former ego? If so, then—. I shuddered for the hundredth time.

Losieva's voice became audible, her words uncannily in line with my thoughts. The voice was now soft, crooning.

"You are now but the embryo of a man, without material brain or incarnation. The present cycle, the eleventh of human existence, has become as nothing to you. Back, now, to the tenth cycle. I desire to know your identity and under what circumstances you lived in that cycle. Think; think, and allow no detail to escape you in this—. Ah-h-h!"

The screen became a confused blur as seemingly thousands of indistinct, shadowy images flitted past us like gray ghosts in a fog. Some would be startlingly vivid for a brief instant, then flash away as quickly as they had appeared. At one time I seemed to perceive the reporter in all the regalia of an Indian chieftain; again he appeared in the guise of a printer in a very ancient-looking establishment; still another—no more than a flash this time—showed us a densely packed mass of struggling men, of which the subject was the center of interest. By the uniforms worn by the contending forces and by the comparatively ancient type of weapons, it was a scene which took place during the Civil War.

"Come, come, Mr. Hodge!" the medium snapped. "These scenes are too indistinct to be genuine. Your material brain is struggling with the astral. Forget the physical brain—it cannot hold memories of events before your birth. It is trumping up scenes now that have been impressed on it only yesterday—things of the history books John Hodge has read. Let the astral memory have sway. That's it!"

The visions so rapidly flitting by had suddenly crystallized into a picture of cameo distinctness. This one was far different from any of its predecessors and quite clearly indicated a period of remotest antiquity. Indeed, from evidence gleaned from later developments, I should judge it to be laid in the time of King Arthur.

The scene depicted the interior of a room, or cell. From the pronounced concavity of the walls and the rough stonework I concluded that it was the interior of a fairly large castle tower. The furniture reminded me strongly of pieces I had encountered in museums. The room, untenanted at first view, suddenly became occupied. So quickly had the new picture flashed into being that I was given no opportunity to see just how the emaciated man seated at the table had entered.

One look at this fellow was sufficient. The whole form showed the ravages of starvation; the cheeks were sunken, the arms wasted away. Tattered raiment hung on the feeble frame like the vestments of a scarecrow. But for all this I knew the man in such evil case to be Jack Hodge.

Dropping horrified eyes to the flagged floor, I noted another distressing fact. I was sure now that this was the interior of a prison cell, for shackled to the prisoner's leg was a massive iron ball which he was forced to roll in order to move about. The point of view shifting rapidly, I got fleeting glimpses of a small, square window set high in the concave wall and well protected by both vertical and horizontal bars. Clearly, escape from such a place was hopeless.

The prisoner was spending most of his time at the table, working with quill and parchment. Feverishly he worked, ever and anon casting anxious glances in the direction of a heavy oaken door, the one entrance. A parchment filled, he would move with laborious haste to the window and, having made the scroll into as tight a package as possible, throw it into the outer air. In most cases the wind would catch it and whirl it away. What his object could be I could not fathom, unless he were endeavoring to acquaint persons outside with his whereabouts.

Picture after picture came into being only to fade into obscurity. I judged the series to cover a considerable space of time. All the scenes showed the hapless captive ever toiling at his parchments. It could be seen that hope was failing him. Before our eyes he grew more and more feeble and emaciated.

There came a time when the oaken barrier slowly opened, and a file of men in armor entered, carrying huge swords and battleaxes. They removed the ball from the wretch's ankle and dragged him, struggling in feeble strength, down a winding stairway. At length the frenzy of despair subsided, and the man allowed himself to be led along unprotesting.

I watched the execution party—such I felt it to be—proceed down flight after flight of worn stone stairs. Such a multitude of flights there were, indeed, that I began to wonder. Why did they not reach the ground level? Downward and ever downward they went; I wished I had counted the flights. The prison cell must have been the topmost room in a veritable Tower of Babel, or—. Or had the party passed the ground level long ago? I believed the passage they now entered was one of a system of subterranean corridors.

There was nothing to confirm this belief except perhaps the rough masonry everywhere in evidence. That told little, however, being illuminated fitfully at best by the guards' torches. Evidently in a hurry to get the thing over with as soon as possible, the soldiers strode along at a great pace. At length they came to the end of the corridor and stepped quite without warning into broad daylight. I now saw that the passage was indeed a tunnel, ending in the side of a rocky hill. The entranceway was protected against attack by a large, heavily barred gate, on each side of which stood a sentry in armor. As the party passed through this portal, both sentries raised their right hands stiffly in salute, then slammed the gate shut.

Finding himself in the bright daylight that had so long been denied him, the captive renewed his struggles to escape, once succeeding indeed in wrenching himself free. But upon finding himself surrounded by relentless warriors he gave up sullenly and was dragged into the mouth of another tunnel close at hand.

This one proved to be shorter than the first and terminated in a small, cylindrical chamber with a domelike roof. The flare of several torches held in cressets here and there showed the set, grim faces of two men who stood silently awaiting the doomed man. They were dressed in the coarse black robes worn by the ancient monks. What sect they represented I cannot guess; but surely such evil faces could belong to no Christian priests. As I surveyed the sinister pair I shuddered. Their aspect was in complete accord with their surroundings. I hope never to witness another such spectacle as I shortly was to see.

Upon entering the death chamber, the leader of the armed men performed the customary salute and signaled to the two soldiers who held the prisoner in an iron grip. At his word they dragged the cowering wretch forward and flung him down before the two somber ones. One of these advanced a single step and rapidly administered the last rites of his religion—whatever that religion was. Meanwhile the other made certain preparations. A table of unusual length and with ponderously heavy legs he ordered dragged forward and placed in the center of the room. One at each corner of the table and fastened securely to the legs by means of heavy staples, were four iron rings. A torture table!

At a word from the leader, four men leapt upon the shrinking victim and once more bore him to the floor. I boiled at this utterly unnecessary cruelty. Surely the man's meager reserve of strength was about exhausted. Nevertheless he struggled in futile desperation until might prevailed, and he was placed, writhing and twisting, upon the horrible table.

The séance audience gave signs of a growing uneasiness. More than once the psychic had to speak sharply to insure absolute silence, explaining that it was in the interests of the subject. Indeed he was being subjected to a terrific strain, his life forces taxed to the uttermost.

*

The rest of the ghastly drama of the tenth cycle I shall record as quickly as possible. Even now, as I recall it, I feel a deadly nausea overcoming me. Let me get it over with, once and for all.

The prisoner was laid flat on his back; his limbs were drawn out and down to the four iron rings and lashed there with rawhide thongs. His face, contorted by fear and realization of the inevitable, became a thing of horror. Several soldiers withdrew, each to return bearing a bucket of water. One of the priests removed from a peg in the wall a huge metal funnel, which he examined for a moment with an evil smile. Now, being careful to keep out of the victim's limited field of vision, he crept up toward the table.

My God! How can I go on?

Before I had time to shudder, the prisoner's jaws were sprung wide apart—by a deft pressure of finger tips on certain nerve centers in the face—and the horrible funnel thrust between the teeth. The writhings of the doomed man now commenced anew; the black-robed executioner had some ado to maintain the unusual instrument of death in position. A soldier came forward and, standing close, glared into the prisoner's eyes with the gleeful hate of a maniac. Suddenly he reached down, grasped a brimming pail and thrust it high over his head. A moment he poised it there; then slowly, carefully, he lowered the forward edge. Without spilling so much as a drop, he poured the whole of the great bucketful into the trembling funnel. This man's expertness bespoke long, loving service of a similar nature, for most of the several others to pour bungled the job badly. One man spilled half a pailful in his nervousness.

As the water forced its relentless way into the victim's body, his eyes bulged wildly from their sockets, and his fettered limbs became as flails. Another pail was raised on high—the priest holding the funnel with both hands now in a deadly grip—another pail—my God!—the pictures became but a mass of throbbing, pulsing waves of shadow—or was it?—I had fainted.

4

Evidently my brief lapse had not been observed in the general gloom of the place. As I came to I heard as from a distance the voice of Madam Losieva.

"Deeper, deeper," she was saying, "into the ages. Tell me what you see in your ninth cycle. You are going back—back—. Think deeply, sleep deeper—. Now—."

The pictures were again rushing by at a tremendous rate, presenting for the most part a confused blur. But after a time they began to slow down as before, until finally they could be followed fairly well.

"Doctor Maugridge!" Losieva called out sharply.

The anxiety in her tone cleared the last of my brain fog. She pointed, and I hastened to see to the subject. He was breathing stertorously, but the heart action still appeared normal. I nodded a reluctant okeh—I had no really sensible reason to disapprove—and was about to resume my seat when I noted that Hodge's lips were moving. Wondering if he were not struggling against his mental fetters, I pointed mutely at his face to draw Losieva's attention.

"Speak, if in that way you can more readily recall the past," she suggested to the tranced form. "The effort is great, but you are equal to it and more. You are now existing in your ninth cycle, before the days of the water torture."

At this suggestion a visible tremor passed over Hodge's body.

"Ah-h—. Slower please; we cannot follow you at all. Fine!"

Almost upon the heels of the suggestion to speak enunciated by the medium, the reporter did a thing I have never been able to explain satisfactorily to myself or anybody else. He raised himself slightly on one elbow and passed his hand—which before had been rigid as so much stone—before his eyes, clearly in an effort to think.

At once he began to talk, but in an absolutely unknown jargon. The pictures simultaneously became more vivid and coherent, and it was not difficult to form a fairly good connection between them. From time to time Professor Ember at the machine made slight adjustments calculated to keep the N-ray at full intensity on its object. The weird aura continued to stream unabated from Hodge's head.

Clearly the ninth cycle had been spent in a far different clime than the tenth. In place of the English castle with its torture room and horrible black-robed priests was a picture of a tropical region. In the immediate foreground could be seen a sharply sloping river bank covered with lush vegetation. Farther back, the soil had a sandy aspect, and here and there protruded a boulder badly eroded from centuries of contact with the elements. A number of lofty palms in the distance completed the picture.

The point of view must have been located on the river itself. As the scene clarified I made out the outlines of a galley; now the lines of the deck planking became apparent. Soon about a score of people of both sexes were to be seen aboard. Some were walking along the deck, but the greater part lolled on the profusion of many-colored cushions in attitudes of indolent ease. Some of them strummed idly on peculiar stringed instruments, while others wove garlands of beautiful blossoms with which they gayly bedecked each other.

The center of attraction was a young woman who reclined languidly under a striped canopy. Like the others her skin was dark, although it was not black like that of her scantily clad Nubian slaves which were in some evidence. Rather it might have been termed a light olive. Her hair, of a jetty black, was smooth and silky, and dressed in the familiar bobbed mode of the ancient Egyptians. Her form was slight but willowy, and the contour of beautifully rounded breasts and wide hips partially revealed aroused all the artistic instinct within me.

At her side lolled a handsome youth. While most of those in the party suggested in costumes and facial expression the ancient people of the Nile, this youth was clearly of a different race. His skin was nearly pure white, and his robes suggested nothing of the Egyptian. Rather was he a Greek, or mayhap a Roman. Yes; surely that was it. Those severely plain accouterments were reminiscent of High School days when I, finding my Latin study period too long for concentrated thinking, had amused myself by looking at the colored illustrations. Well I remembered that short toga or tunic, the sandals and the shortsword.

Did I neglect to say the man's face was identical with that of Jack Hodge! I had noted the fact without surprise.

I did feel a pang at having to be a mere spectator while my crony made love to Cleopatra. I felt not the slightest doubt that the lovely creature in the center of the screen was that wicked queen. Which one of her lovers Jack had been I cannot guess. History has perpetuated the names of several of these unfortunate gentlemen, but not their likenesses; and just what this youth's full name was I never knew. Marius, the name shortly repeated by the subject, could have been only a given name.

A deeper hush had descended upon the assembled crowd. The reporter was again speaking, sometimes in the peculiar jargon before alluded to, sometimes in clean-cut Latin. The Roman was evidently endeavoring to carry on a conversation with the dark siren, and, owing to the imperfect knowledge each had of the other's tongue, was experiencing some difficulty. My knowledge of Latin being imperfect, and of ancient Egyptian nil, I will not attempt to reproduce the actual words. Suffice it to say that the conversation seemed to consist mostly of impassioned marriage proposals and smiling, cool refusals. Though of course no actual word of the fair Egyptian could be heard, in most cases her gestures and Marius' subsequent words made her part of the talk fairly clear.

At length the young fellow gave over his efforts and allowed his gaze to wander disconsolately shoreward. There was little in the dreary landscape to inspire him, however, and all attempt at conversation ceased. Once, though but for a fleeting instant, I could have sworn that a sinister expression distorted the queen's face—one in which struggled both fear and hatred. Had Marius, the Roman, perceived it, mayhap he would have been more on his guard later on.

However, the fellow's subjugation at the hands of the dusky houri had been quite complete. Plainly he had no thought of danger from the fair creature leading him on thus shamelessly. After witnessing the abrupt end of this cycle I for one can understand why history speaks so scornfully of this woman.

For several minutes the scenes shifted so rapidly that their trend could not coherently be followed. Presently a curt word from the psychic slowed down the temporary activity of the subject's mind, and Professor Ember adjusted the N-ray to a greater brilliance. Stimulation thus increased, Hodge's memory continued the orderly progress of the cycle as before, and the finale of this ancient drama was presented for the last time.

The galley had reached a good-sized cove, stalwart rowers had leapt ashore and by their combined efforts were dragging the craft through the bulrushes to a secure landing place. There was a general rush to the side, and one by one the youths and maidens leapt to the ground. All seemed imbued with the spirit of a modern picnic party, and with signs of hilarity proceeded up the bank. As they walked, the ground rose in a succession of terraces until finally they came out on a barren plateau which extended, sand-swept and dreary, to the horizon.

The Sahara! Into the sea of sand they plunged under the leadership of the queen and her companion. For what seemed to me endless miles the revelers traveled, until a final turn around a particularly high sand dune revealed a tremendous object directly ahead of them and not a hundred yards away. A pyramid it was, and truly a thing of wonder. In awe I gazed at the thousands of huge blocks of roughly dressed stone piled here solely by the physical strength of sweating slaves. My gaze darted here and there in vain search for an entrance-way, but at every hand naught save a solid front of rough stone met my eye. Evidently, I thought, the builders had some well-defined motive for concealing the method of ingress into the royal sepulchers. Though the entrances to several of the pyramids had been discovered by modern investigators, I knew this was not accomplished easily.

The queen and her companions came to a halt at the foot of the pile. For a brief space a whispered colloquy took place with Cleopatra, Marius and a huge, ebony-black Ethiopian. It became evident to me that the greater part of the company was to be left behind, the Ethiopian having doubtless been chosen to go along as a guard. This man was a gigantic fellow, with great rippling muscles and the form of a god. He was unadorned except for the loin cloth worn by most male slaves of the period. He carried no weapon except a dagger which depended from a strap at his waist, and as far as I could see he had no need of that. His terribly strong hands looked an all-sufficient protection.

Signing to the two others to follow, the queen began to skirt the pyramid. She, apparently, was the only one who knew their destination. Soon the fair guide began to climb the rough side of the pile, making easy work of the natural staircase afforded by the out-jutting blocks. The others, being made of heavier stuff, followed at a rather more laborious pace. As the trio made their way upward, the picture changed continually, eventually omitting all view of the ground. Occasionally I would get a glimpse of the desert stretching off in endless desolation until finally the dun sky seemed to blend into it. Once I got a flashing view of a cluster of palm fronds in the distance waving gently in response to the hot breath of the Sahara.

At last the climb came to an end. Cleopatra had led the two men well-nigh to the summit of the huge man-made mountain before locating her goal. How she knew the exact stone was a mystery to me. My puzzled eyes could detect nothing to distinguish the block beside which she paused from the thousands she had passed by.

Under the queen's direction the men inserted their fingers into certain tiny crevices and exerted their strength in a mighty heave. A small stone came outward a few inches, only to stop as if held by a concealed protuberance. The Ethiopian unsheathed his knife and pried about the stone here and there. Again he and the Roman heaved, and this time succeeded in dislodging the stone. Motioning the others aside, Cleopatra thrust her arm into the opening. What movement she made with her hand I can never say. All I can remember is a general gasp from my companion spectators at what she accomplished. Whether the queen had actuated the mechanism of a pneumatic or hydraulic lift, or whether it was simply a crude form of lever, is a mystery. At any rate a seeming miracle was worked.

A gigantic section of the pyramid's surface, weighing probably hundreds of tons, slid slowly, smoothly downward and disappeared into the body of the pile! Both men leapt back affrighted.

The woman waited coolly enough for the entrance to yawn fully open and then stepped in, motioning for the others to follow. The Ethiopian was plainly demoralized by fear, and his eyes rolled wildly. The young Roman, in spite of the well advertised valor of his race, seemed strangely ill at ease. There ensued a period in which the evil queen's plan threatened to fail of its sinister purpose. Both men had evidently refused to enter the Stygian tunnel before them. The Ethiopian, doubtless smarting at the remembrance of tortures undergone in the past for hesitating at the queen's orders, finally agreed to go on. Marius still hanging back, Cleopatra changed her tactics from pouting and pleading to tempestuous scorn and ridicule for his courage. This the Roman could not endure. He shrugged, and without a word turned and led the way into the tunnel. At once the screen before us became night black.

I stooped over the body of my friend. Without a reasonable doubt the blackness was but a reproduction of the inside of the tunnel, but—who could say what moment the subject might crack under the strain imposed upon him? And even though the reporter's physique could bear up under the psychic's mental flail, how could I be sure that she herself might not break down? Suppose she left him stranded in some far past epoch! At thought of this most terrifying of possibilities a cold sweat broke out all over me, and I felt what I honestly believe was a premonition.

I found the subject's heart action and respiration to be somewhat slower than normal, and I seized upon this not alarming condition as an excuse to have the unwholesome affair ended. I turned to Losieva.

"Madam, I must protest against this thing being carried farther. It is dangerous. I believe we are all satisfied with the success of your experiment. May not the séance be closed now, and our friend brought back to present-day life?"

The psychic addressed the subject.

"I wish you to return to the eleventh cycle of your ego. Back—to—the—present. Now! Answer me! Who are you?"

"John Hodge."

It was the same lifeless tone, but what a thrill of joy it sent through me. Good old Hodge brought back to life!

A relieved murmur ran through the audience. I raised my eyes to where the pearly dome should directly be glowing. I was consumed with impatience: why didn't they light the place up? And for heaven's sake, why not shut off that ghastly ray?

But there the thing still streamed, its vicious radiance even growing in intensity; there still danced about Hodge's inert head that most unholy, glaring halo.

5

"You have just finished your second glassful, Mr. Hodge. Go easy, or your friends will have to pilot you home. What, another? You are going too far with the stuff. No more—too late! For shame, sir!"

Damn the woman, what was she up to now!

Of a sudden, the hazy pictures thrown by the thought projector became slightly less blurred, and I saw. The screen was filled with a vision of distinctly pre-meddling days—a wild jumble of jugs, bottles and glasses, some of them overturned and varicolored liquids flowing out of them. I remember distinctly that one spilling bottle bore the label, "Johnny Walker". Tears came to my eyes—being caused by the eye-torturing wavering, teetering and increasing blurriness of the picture. Finally the jumble became altogether unintelligible. A smacking and gurgling came from the reporter's lips.

"Drunk, Mr. Hodge; shame on you! Don't you realize the stuff you are imbibing will have an unpleasant effect on your heart? It is pumping now like mad, and see how your respiration has speeded up! Why, if you—put down that glass, sir, and listen to me."

Losieva's voice became a dreary monody.

"You are falling into a drunken, fevered stupor—your drink-fired brain will torment you with nightmares—you will dwell in other days—back in the ninth cycle—the days of Marius—and Cleopatra—and the visit to the tomb—the tomb of Rameses the Second. Back—"

A clear-cut picture springing to the screen and a great burst of incoherent Latin from the subject told us he was indeed back. I was torn between disappointed anger and real admiration. The woman had induced an artificial drunkenness in my friend, either by recalling to him some spree in his immediate past or by suggesting a wholly ficti- tious orgy. Venomously I wondered, if the scene had been trumped up out of her own mind, where she got the material for all the lifelike stage properties.

At any rate, the trick had succeeded so far as she was concerned. My examination showed Hodge's heart action greatly stimulated, his body filled with a new vitality. Should I allow the experiment to progress? How could I prevent it, if the psychic was determined? And I repeat—I fling in the faces of those who have condemned me—I had no tangible, physical reason to do so. I—I let the morbid business go on.

The scene now vouchsafed us showed Cleopatra, the Roman and the slave in a small chamber of stone, their faces when visible presenting a weird aspect in the flare of a torch held by the queen. Marius was pale, but his face was set in a grim determination to see the thing through. The woman showed a buoyancy of spirit border- ing on the hysterical. As for the Ethiopian, he looked quite frankly near to a collapse. His eyes stuck out in a most grotesque fashion, reflecting the fitful light of the flare like two lambent, white globes.

The three were bending over a roughly rectangular object which occupied the center of the crypt. The illumination was so poor that at first I was unable to identify the thing. But presently the queen held the torch directly over it, and the flesh writhed on my bones.

They had unwrapped and were pawing over the shriveled body of a mummy!

An increasingly loud coughing and choking sound forcing itself on my consciousness, I looked to my charge. The spasms were not danger-ously violent, however, and reluctantly I kept silent. And on glancing at Hodge's counterpart on the screen I immediately perceived the cause of the trouble. Marius was racked by coughs timed exactly with those of Hodge. Cleopatra was plainly struggling for breath and wiping her eyes constantly, while tears streamed unchecked down the contorted face of the Ethiopian. Strongly spiced indeed was the dust they were profaning.

It seemed the Ethiopian shortly got his fill of it. He suddenly jumped up, gasping and clutching at his throat, and staggered out of the circle of light. Cleopatra curled her lip and motioned Marius to continue to help her in her grisly labors. What the object of those labors was I understood when, the queen having brought to light a sizable excavation in the mummy's abdomen, they began to remove therefrom double handfuls of precious stones.

At a time when the couple were most engrossed, this pleasant occupation was interrupted. They had whirled about as one, to fix startled eyes on their gigantic guard. The fellow was backing slowly toward them, swinging his dagger wildly as if defending himself from a score of assailants. Eyes rolling and white teeth flashing in weird grimaces, he had evidently gone stark mad with fright. Neither I nor the noble couple on the screen could perceive a single enemy in the vault. Was the crazed Ethiopian seeing some hideous guardians of the dead man's outraged spirit? The Roman grasped his shortsword in an instinctive movement to go to the slave's assistance. But at this moment the guard, as though pursued by a relentless fate, dashed wildly from the place and disappeared into the depths of the pyramid.

The others followed, Marius, sword in hand, far in the lead. Cleopatra, however, seemed in no great hurry, and soon the Roman had to stop to let her bring up the torch. She stepped calmly ahead, holding the light behind her to guide her companion. Certain it was that she was not afraid, yet it was patent that she had no interest in finding her recreant servant.

She walked onward with a sureness of step that bespoke long familiarity with these dim galleries and chambers of the dead. In spite of the torch, however, Marius stumbled constantly. The brave determination on his face gave way to an expression of grim dread as he glanced down dark branching corridors. The pair proceeded what must have been a good mile, and I decided there was no end to the honeycomb of passages and shadowy tombs. Several times they had encountered stairways, and in every instance they had gone *downward*. Could it be that they were already far below the surface of the desert? Had we long since entered the base of another pyramid? Was the work of the Pharaohs so much more extensive than any living man had dreamed? And why was my friend being urged into such an ill-omened place?

At last came the dreadful, sickening dénouement. To this day I do not know whether the fate of poor Hodge—or Marius—should be laid at the door of Cleopatra, or whether it was but an accident. If mischance it was, it is certainly strange. Cleopatra, with her familiarity with the ground, must have known what lay at the end of that particular tunnel. Otherwise, why did she—? But I cannot conceive of it. It seems impossible that any woman, however wicked, could deliberately plan such a thing. To take her lover ostensibly on a pleasure trip only to employ him as a guard while she replenished her perennially wasted coffers—and then thank him by murdering him!

Cleopatra, several paces ahead of the Roman now, had suddenly stepped into a side passage. The screen went black, and a wild screech rent the séance chamber. I got a last flashing view of an expanse of inky, noisome water, a speck of a torch far above in the hand of that evil woman, and a dim, sprawled body hurtling down—down—down—...

6

Physically the subject was unharmed by the strain of recalling the end of the ninth cycle. His auto-suggested jag was lasting well, for all his functions were obviously still operating under a strong stimulant.

"Backward, Marius; back to when time was young," Losieva was urging the silent thing in the chair. I call the subject "thing" because somehow it is impossible for me to think of the unconscious form as my old friend. Indeed it is a question whether he was really anybody in particular, suspended as he was between identities.

A new ego shortly became his, and upon glancing at the subject's face I gave a violent start. In place of the rather decent features of Jack Hodge were those of another man—a most unkempt, uncouth, and withal fierce kind of man. This time my friend's immersion in another self must have been an extremely potent thing, strong enough to wrench his features until they matched those of the man of the eighth cycle, the man who lived before the age of Cleopatra.

The first intelligible scene was a fleeting glimpse of the ocean. It was an immense expanse, on which were riding several curious craft. At first no land was in sight, the fleet of queer ships steadily sailing toward the setting sun. The action continued considerably faster than had been the case in other cycles, for in a matter of minutes a long coast-line appeared directly ahead. On the deck of one of the boats, and staring shoreward, was a tall man whom I seemed to recognize. Yet I knew for a certainty that I had never seen him before. For some minutes I pondered these contradictory facts, and then the solution came over me. That fierce countenance was none other than that I had seen reflected on the features of Hodge at the opening of the cycle.

Evidently the control was bad, for the action alternately slowed and rushed, and the scene continually shifted. Indeed, throughout the epoch these conditions obtained, making it difficult at times to follow the thread of the story. However, there was a certain advantage in this, because it made possible the unfolding in a few hours of the events of several days.

I remember distinctly my disappointment at not seeing the ships make port, the scene having suddenly moved to land. Here the tall man was still visible, this time striding rapidly along an avenue of beautiful tropical trees. On each side could be seen most handsome, albeit fantastic, structures. Some of them I conceived might be dwellings, others shops, and one or two had every appearance of being temples. Here and there were strolling groups of people, and only rarely a person walking with any definite destination in view. For the most part I was impressed by the lack of any apparent employment. It seemed to be a city of affluent idleness.

I noticed that the loiterers in the fierce-looking man's path made way quickly enough, and in a servile sort of manner. But as soon as he had passed, invariably they made a point of turning and bending in his direction the blackest of looks. It occurred to me that the man, judging by his unpopularity, must have a great deal of power. Possibly he was a naval commander, or some high government official. I never learned.

Again the scene had undergone a complete metamorphosis. It was night. Illumined in an unearthly kind of glow, I could see a small city square, packed with thousands of struggling people. Where was their languid ease? What had stirred them to this mad activity? As if to answer my question a huge mass of fire came winging from nowhere, curved downward and dropped straight into the center of the milling multitude.

A horrible debacle took place before my eyes.

In seemingly no time the nearest of the houses had caught fire. Another enormous, flaming ball dashed itself to earth; another, and another. Everywhere there were flames and fighting, surging throngs. And in the crazed thousands, not one person stood a chance of safety; not one—. But yes, here was a man whose brute strength might yet save him.

It was our tall man of the sea. Ruthlessly he slashed through the press, tossing and trampling those who would delay him. At last he put them all behind him, and dashed toward the red-spangled sea. On the beach our man stumbled upon a comparatively light craft obscured in a multitude of heavier ones drawn up on the sand. Two sailors were vainly heaving and tugging in an effort to launch the thing before all was lost. Grasping each by a shoulder, he bundled them into the vessel. Next he had lifted the dragging prow clear of the sand, run splashing into the sea with it and then leapt nimbly aboard.

Behind him in the flame-swept street an enormous red-hot crack yawned suddenly open, to engulf a score of burning houses and a hundred writhing bodies. Tongues of flame shot hungrily skyward while the crack gaped wider. A deluge of fiery meteors fed it for a space, and then there rolled in a monstrous wave. Great billows of red steam burst from the rift, and the crumpled remains of houses and men were belched skyward.

The crack is glowing again with a dry, hot incandescence—another great wave—it has closed tight—it has *sunk*. The city—where *is* the city? There is naught here but madly lashing seas and floating things unspeakable.

Meanwhile, what of that cockle in which the three seafaring men pushed off and wildly poled away? That dancing mote in the red eye of the rising sun! Can that be our bark? Impossible, yet—*it is!*

Everywhere was a desolation of dark water. The surface was never calm, being rent and tortured by what must have been the remnant of those volcanic and subterranean forces that had destroyed the land. What a contrast was this churning sea with the picture of that proud, serene fleet sailing so majestically homeward. Instead of the clean sunshine of that time, the light now was a bloody glow from a smoky sun. Extending for leagues in every direction hung a dense pall that was ever blotting out the sun completely, turning scarlet day into pitch-black night.

On the ship all was numb despair. From time to time the leader could be heard, evidently giving listless orders. The tongue, as reproduced by the subject, was one to defy analysis by the most accomplished linguist of our time. In all the words spoken by the man of the eighth cycle, only one to us had any meaning. This was uttered several times during the cycle, each time in a voice of tenderness surprizing in one so stern—the word *Atalanti*.

What joy those four syllables must have engendered in the little group of savants present! Here was solid support of an ancient legend that was familiar even to me. Could the fair city we had just seen be that fabled metropolis said to have flourished eons before the Egyptians conceived their pyramids? On a lovely isle risen from the ocean bed that city had been built. There great kings were born, reigned and died. Mighty navies had there a home port. A civilization famed to this day for its beauty and richness had developed—and then the whole marvelous perfection was undone in a night. Volcanoes had spat, the waters had reared; and the island had been enfolded into the bosom of the broad Atlantic that had given it birth.

That the name of the city had undergone some slight change in being handed down from survivors of the holocaust seems probable enough. The sibilant on the end of our modern name may have been accidentally left off by Hodge in the word he repeated, but anyone present at the séance would doubt this. The name we are familiar with is "Atlantis".

Again the erratic memory of the reporter raced the action ahead. The little ship was still before us; but now it was night, and tortured clouds streamed across a cold moon. All sail bravely spread, the tiny craft scudded through the foam at a terrific rate. The three men could be seen huddled at the helm. All were looking backward to the horizon where still hung a shredded, smoky smear.

What agony must have been their thoughts! Had they been compelled to leave behind the incinerated bodies of loved ones—of wives, and little children? Had one, perchance, been the possessor of great wealth, only to witness its total destruction before his eyes? One of the men surely gave an impression of the bereaved husband. Could any mere material loss cause such an expression of utter unhearting? Even as I speculated, the man darted to the side, and only by force was he restrained from jumping overboard.

Another shift of scene disclosed the tips of two masts protruding from a smiling, sunny sea. A short distance away and playfully caressed by little lapping waves lay a sun-heated knob of rock. The knob was only as large as this table, and its rounded apex was perhaps two feet above the tranquil sea level. Nevertheless it afforded refuge for a pair of castaways. I wondered if the tide were at its height...

Other questions followed in quick succession. Who were these two, and how long had they been here? Were they the survivors of Atlantis? If so, why were there only two? Their forms were emaciated to the point of scarecrow thinness: that would suggest they had been here for days. Then the tide had spared them; but had there been no stormy waves? A man lying prone on his stomach lifted his face for an instant in some mute appeal to the heavens, and in the simple act I perceived the answer to some of my questions.

The terrible face was that of our Atlantis naval man; the features, puffed and blotched so that recognition had come slowly, had been mutilated by days of contact with hot, unclouded sun and hotter rock. One question remained to be answered: what had become of the third fugitive, who I saw must be the one whose disheartened state I have mentioned?

I remembered his suicidal tendencies. Had he succeeded in plunging overboard before the vessel was wrecked? Or had he lived through the crash and landed here with the others? In that case, supposing he should resume his attempts at suicide after a day or two here, how hard would his starving companions strive to restrain him? There was something gleaming just beneath the surface on a jagged slope of the rock. The shimmering water made the thing hard to identify—is there a species of clean, white coral?

This picture, the last of the Atlantis era, was mercifully short. For a few minutes I watched the tide creep up and up until the men were forced painfully to stand up. Then a peril I had overlooked entirely made itself manifest. Here and there little darting arcs began to describe themselves on the smooth surface. More and more joined them until there was a complete, ever changing circle. Now and then a section of the strange circumference would detach itself and launch inward toward its human center a fearsomely few feet away. The flirting lines were drawn by little triangles projecting above the water, the fins of sharks.

Many times the men must have been subjected to these same attacks and I asked myself what had held the brutes away. I remembered the shape of the rock as I had first seen it, and therein lay the explanation. The beasts could come to within four or five feet of the castaways, but nearer than that the shallowness of the water fooled them.

Ah, but here was something that could not be fooled!

The drooping men saw the thing at the same time I did, and at once were galvanized into frenzied action. A snakelike arm studded with deadly, cuplike suckers writhed from the water six feet away and rippled tentatively toward them. Our tall man hacked frantically at it with his knife, while his crazed companion clawed with palsied, futile talons of hands. Others of the slimy tubes wormed along the surface to lay the victims by the nethers. A monstrous, shapeless head, with two hideous red glaring eyes and a wicked beak, emerged from the churning water. It was joined by another and another, and the delirious denizens of a bygone deep closed in.

The picture became a confused mass of flailing tentacles—of wildly distorted human limbs—of great, horrid eyes—of gaping, pulsating craws—a scream—

High pitched, piercing, a new scream from behind me shocked me back to the present. A girl—Emily Norton—had fainted.

7

It was dawn. Over the slowly waving tops of somber pines flew a raven. Shortly followed two more, and still another. In an ever changing geometric pattern, they described weird curves and angles as they took flight across the desolate wastes. From the tangled thickets and swamps rose more birds, until a mighty escadrille had formed and streamed across the sky.

Now from a dim forest aisle stepped a youth. He wore a short tunic of a color closely resembling that of the surrounding foliage. Crude weapons he carried—a short javelin in the right hand and a long bow and quiver of arrows swinging from the shoulder. His features suggested rude material from which might be chiseled the well-shaped lineaments of Jack Hodge.

I was hard put to it to place the period of time represented in this picture. Something told me the era was not many centuries advanced from the Stone Age. Prehistoric I at once classified it. What caused this conviction I cannot say, unless it was that the whole atmosphere of the picture seemed newer and the sunshine brighter, cleaner, than any I have ever seen. Surely this was a younger sun than ours.

The hunter came to a stand at the head of a steep declivity. Some hundreds of feet below lay a little green valley, through which wound the silver thread of a river. Nearer at hand I could glimpse through the tops of giant conifers the deep blue of a mountain lake. Toward this the huntsman for a moment directed his gaze. Having apparently located something on the lake shore too far distant for me to recognize, he uttered a grunt of satisfaction and turned away.

Unslinging his quiver, he selected an immense, red-tipped arrow. This he bore to the base of a pine tree, where he plunged it repeatedly into a great lump of oozing pitch. After smearing the end well with the sticky substance he brought the shaft to the edge of the cliff and laid it down. Next he busied himself at rubbing two splinters together until they had produced a smoking spark and, with many great distendings of rough cheeks, blowing the spark into a tiny flame. With this he ignited the pitch-smeared end of the arrow. Fitting the arrow to the rawhide string, he drew it back—back until it seemed the mighty bow must break. Now he looked once more at the spot on the lake shore, raised the bow a little and released the fiery shaft.

Up and up it sped, leaving as a wake an immense arc of brown smoke. Up, and still higher, until reaching its limit it began to drop. It fell slowly at first; but by the time it had dipped from view behind the farthest treetop its speed was that of a meteor. One moment the youth stood with folded arms, watching the course of the flight. Then, apparently satisfied that the arrow would hit its mark, he suddenly wheeled and darted into the forest.

There came a view of a group of rude, thatched huts on a beach by a lake. On the right side of the screen was a sharp upslope surmounted by a little bluff easily recognizable as that from which the hunter had loosed his quarrel. Swarms of rough warriors could be seen toiling up the slope, while in the village nothing was left but a few women who stood with shaded eyes watching the progress of their protectors. An arrow stood still burning and untouched where it had plunged into the ground at the center of the compound.

To the screen sprang a close-up of a hut I had seen standing a little apart from the rest. In the doorway stood a broad woman holding a wooden platter in her hand. On her face was an expression of helpless fright. Following her line of vision to a near-by thicket, I beheld our archer of the cliff. Apparently realizing he had been seen, the youth now bounded from cover and pursued the woman into the hut. He made short work of binding her wrists and ankles with thongs of hide, and then turned to the slight figure of a girl cringing in a dark corner. With one motion he spun her about and tossed her roughly on to his shoulder. Now he ran from the hut and headed for the beach, where was drawn up a little dugout. Urgently placing the girl on a seat, the fellow pushed off, sprang in, grasped the lone paddle, and with great thrusts began rapidly to put distance between him and the cabin.

I studied the not unbeautiful face of the captive, and in spite of myself was amused at her expression. Where were the loathing glances one might expect? There were none; the girl showed rather a shy admiration for her captor. His bronzed face bore little expression at all, unless perhaps a trace of triumph.

And who could blame him? To start the village men off on a wild goose chase as he had done and carry off doubtless the prize specimen of their women! I glanced up at the hillside. So bold a plan deserved to succeed.

But it could not. Already the men had realized they had been fooled. Brandishing their weapons and uttering perfectly visible yells of rage, the whole party was swarming down toward the lake. Already they were within fair bowshot of the canoe, and one after another dropped to the knee to release a winged missile. In all too short a space they were at the shore. Some few hastily launched canoes, but the greater number set off on foot around the shore to head the elopers off.

The young man in the boat plied the paddle with renewed vigor. The girl sat quietly in the bottom of the dugout now, and kept her eyes glued upon the shore they had left. As she watched every movement of the pursuing party, the first glint of anger came to her eyes.

Far ahead where the lake dwindled to form the source of a mountain stream I saw a single dwelling. The straining youth fixed his eyes on this and redoubled his efforts. But all was useless now; the flight had been discovered. The hutch was too flimsy to withstand any half-determined siege. And furthermore—the running men had reached it first. Now they had set fire to it. The last vestige of hope left the youth's face. With a look of grim determination he ceased paddling and faced the girl.

Her face went white, but she answered the question in his eyes with a nod. The man resumed his paddling, but now his eyes were fixed on the stream banks. He sent the dugout straight on beyond the burning hut.

Those on shore seemed now to divine his purpose. Gesticulating wildly, they ran to the stream. The girl in the dugout raised her chin defiantly and pointed straight ahead. A huge fellow drew back a bowstring, but instantly the girl threw herself into her companion's arms. Torn between two fears, another man, whom I judged to be the girl's father, restrained the archer, then covered his eyes with a hairy paw.

The dugout went on with an ever increasing current. The banks of the rivulet drew nearer together and rose towering over the little craft. Faster and faster it flew, while the young warrior tightened his grip on the girl who had elected to die with him rather than leave him to his fate at the hands of her people. The stream became a mill race—the little boat was as a javelin cast by some battling merman—or had the rock walls on either side so rank with slime and ooze taken on a backward movement of their own?—faster—a million disordered shapes leered from out the swirling mist clouds—the maiden hid her face in the youth's tunic—the dugout dipped, righted, swung completely around. Now the craft hung suspended in space—a swift vision of a long slant of green water—jagged snags—the bottom had dropped out of the universe—down—...

From the mesmerized form of Jack Hodge came a choking whimper; the tortured body fell writhing to the floor.

8

I shall never forget the terrible countenance that met my gaze when I bent over the supine figure of the reporter. The eyes were open and staring glassily. The lips were drawn back so tightly they had cracked open and were bleeding. The teeth and gums were exposed in a manner horrible... That protruding tongue!... I drew back. Bestial! I dared not touch the man.

I watched the hands which before had been so white and nerveless. They were slowly turning a deep red, as if the man were being filled with a new, bursting life. The backs flattened and broadened; the fingers lengthened before my eyes, curved upward from the backs and downward to form ugly claws. Any moment, I expected the fellow to spring to his feet and run amuck. For I knew as well as Losieva what had happened.

She had lost control of her subject! At the end of the seventh cycle—that of the prehistoric lovers—the mind had failed to assume the usual state of coma. Instead, and contrary to the suggestions of the psychic, the ego had leapt backward another cycle. And judging from the distance separating the other cycles from each other, this one must be back before the time of man!

I whirled to confront Losieva. Just what idea I had in mind I cannot remember. I was beside myself. I remember only one transcending thought—to break up this wicked séance! Madly I rushed at the woman...

I seem to remember hearing the softly modulated voice of the psychic addressing me; of a strange something enveloping me, a twilight—no, not twilight; that thrice-damned N-ray! Now I began to fight, but it was too late. My muscles refused to respond to the urgings of my brain. I remember particularly that I wanted to strangle that fiendish professor and smash his miscreated machines. No use; I could do nothing except at the mystic's command. The ghastly light had me nearly blinded, and within a few seconds I was suffering inexpressible torture. When the pain in my eye-sockets reached an intensity unbearable I must have passed out entirely. I have a confused sensation of falling—falling—recurring flashes of dazzling light—a monstrous whirling vortex into which I was being drawn—one pitying thought for Jack Hodge—oblivion...

The rest of the story I pieced out next day with the help of Roger Norton and the heavily scare-headed *Clarion*.

Roger tells me that my subjugation had taken but a moment—that it was over before anyone in the audience had decided on definite action. It had consisted only of a few purring phrases from Losieva and a momentary stab of the N-ray in my direction. Next the mystic was making slow passes over me which had—heaven be praised!—sent me into a normal, exhausted slumber. The ray had again lighted on the head of the creature on the platform; and after that things had happened too fast to permit any thought of me.

What had been Hodge had arisen heavily from the floor, to stand glaring at the audience and weaving slowly from side to side. Norton swore the thing's chest had swelled to enormous proportions and that as it stood half bent forward the hands hung on a level with the knees. While the crowd cowered in horror, the being stood gibbering and grimacing for a moment and suddenly plunged down among them.

There had been pandemonium, during which had been made frantic efforts to locate Losieva and Ember. But these two had deserted, leaving their victim despoiled of humanity. Worse still, the professor had left his rays going full blast and casting pictures unspeakable to the screen. Roger learned that at the moment the monster set upon his daughter the screen was lurid with a picture of a hulking, manlike brute overtaking and subduing a big she-ape. Of course he never saw the picture—mercifully no doubt—as he and four or five other men had their hands full with the ogre and Emily. It seems they tore the screeching girl away and got the beast pinioned to the floor finally, but only after the girl had sustained ugly tooth-marks on her throat.

Just then, as if to make a fitting climax, the place had caught fire. Norton thinks some of Ember's contraptions got overturned and caused the blaze. At any rate the whole room had become a roaring furnace in a twinkling—I remembered those flimsy cloth draperies—and the crowd had barely time to get outside. Good old Roger passed lightly by any mention of who rescued me, but I can easily guess why it was that at the moment I was seized and rushed out, the Frankenstein made its escape.

I agreed with Norton in the belief that the creature had perished in the flames, until in the afternoon I read the *Clarion*. That sheet held a hectic account of the séance, called upon all the powers of heaven and earth to search out and punish "those black mountebanks," contained a glowing eulogy of "our beloved associate," and went on to recount his death:

> The man who was supposed to have been burned to death was seen this morning by a party of school children. They described him as a monkey dressed in men's clothes but without shoes. He was first sighted when he darted out of the shrubbery on the Hallet estate near the East Fairbrook bridge. The children

declare the animal "swarmed" over the wall (Mr. Hallet's wall is 15 feet high at this point) and made for the bridge.

Here, instead of crossing as a man would do, he swung himself under the planking and, monkeylike, attempted to cross on the iron string pieces. Half-way across, where the current is swiftest, he somehow lost his foot-grip and fell fifty feet to the water. The body was recovered this noon at Douglass Mills.

I read the piece over again from end to end. Norton and the others had missed it, but could it be that the newspaper was blind, too! Yes; evidently it was I alone who had noted the most salient fact of the whole affair.

In all phases of his ego, Jack Hodge had met death through water!

THE LIVES OF ALFRED KRAMER

Donald Wandrei

Donald Wandrei (1908–1987) was an American author and editor born in Saint Paul, Minnesota. In 1928, he graduated with a BA in English from the University of Minnesota, where he also edited the student newspaper, *The Minnesota Daily*. The year previous, in late 1927, Wandrei had hitchhiked over one thousand miles to Rhode Island to visit his friend and mentor, H. P. Lovecraft. Lovecraft subsequently led him on an antiquarian tour of his home, and together they would further explore Salem, Boston, Marblehead and Warren. Most prolific between the 1920s and the 1940s, Wandrei published myriad short stories, poems—including his series of "Sonnets of the Midnight Hours" (1928–29)—and the novel, *The Web of Easter Island* (1948). A member of the "Lovecraft Circle", a collection of authors which extends throughout this anthology, his tales frequently expanded upon the myths and themes of Lovecraft's own fiction. Alongside his original works, Wandrei also co-founded Arkham House in 1939, a publishing venture which endeavoured to preserve Lovecraft's writings.

"The Lives of Alfred Kramer" was first published in the December 1932 issue of *Weird Tales*, and later collected in *The Eye and the Finger* (1944) and *Don't Dream* (1997). As in "Under the N-Ray", the eponymous Alfred Kramer has discovered a powerful new form of radiation. "Kappa Radiation", he explains, allows an individual to revisit the suppressed memories of past lives housed within their cells. Yet, as Kramer tells his narrative, tracing his ancestry to Atlantis and beyond, regression starts to take its toll. Where Smith and Robbins drew on the ideas of Blondlot, Wandrei employs those of the English biologist, Thomas Henry Huxley. Ending the tale as a "writhing mass of protoplasmic slime", "The Lives of Alfred Kramer" grotesquely conceptualizes *Bathybius haeckelii*, Huxley's debunked discovery of a primordial ooze on the ocean floor from which all organic life evolved.

Though my train did not pull out till eleven p.m., I had boarded it at ten. While the berths were being made up I strolled around. There were few passengers this early in the week. Indeed, when I walked back and took a seat in the smoking-car, I noticed but one other occupant. To my casual glance, he appeared singularly repulsive. His grayish face, an immobile setness of expression, burning black eyes in which no pupil was visible, his gloved hands folded stiffly in his lap, all combined to give me an immediate dislike.

I paid no further attention to him during the quarter of an hour or so that I sat smoking. Several times, however, I had an impression that he was intently watching me.

When I arose and began to walk toward my berth, I had an equally vivid impression that he addressed some remark to me in a low and extraordinarily husky voice just as I was passing him. So inaudible was his voice and so marked my aversion that I pretended I had not heard and continued on my way.

Dismissing the incident from mind, I prepared for slumber. A variety of noises kept me awake. I heard brakemen call, the train pull out, its wheels clack rhythmically.

An hour later I was still tossing restlessly.

At about twelve-thirty I gave up my futile effort to sleep, climbed from my berth, and slipped on a dressing-gown. Cigar in hand, I again made my way back to the smoking-car. Its lone occupant had evidently not moved, for he was still sitting where I last saw him. I did not notice his lips move, but plainly this time I heard his abominable husky voice.

"Won't you join me for a few miles?" it said. "I am an invalid, you see."

Perhaps his appeal for sympathy touched me, or perhaps his obvious loneliness. At any rate, I suppressed my unpleasant reaction to his physical appearance and dropped into the chair opposite him.

I made some reference to my unconventional garb, and idly remarked, "I thought I'd have another smoke. Sleep was impossible."

"Yes," he responded, "there are times when one would like to sleep but can not. It is worse," he added cryptically, "when one would prefer to remain awake, but can not."

A bit puzzled, I waited for him to continue.

"I have not slept for three nights," he volunteered.

"Indeed? I am sorry if your illness prevents you from sleeping," I said politely.

"No, it is not that. My indisposition is of such a nature that slumber is dangerous. I have kept myself awake by stimulants. And the long night hours are monotonous when one is alone."

Casual though our conversation was thus far, and despite my friendly resolve, I had been becoming more uneasy. There was a kind of psychic chill in the air which early autumn could not entirely account for. My companion's repellent aspect was hardly modified by the soft lights around us. For all the expression on his grayish face, an automaton or ventriloquist might have been speaking. No muscular change had yet livened his countenance, his lips had made no perceptible movement. His unrelaxing gloved hands, the unnatural shine of his black eyes, and his rigid carriage were as disquieting at close range as they had been at a distance. Nor could I accustom myself to the throaty degeneracy of his speech. About his person there was in addition an odor that bothered me. It was quite indefinable, but had an element of the beast in it, and of corruption, and stagnant sea-water, and mildew.

I now noticed what had hitherto escaped me, that a pile of books lay beside him. The topmost was Strindmann's monograph, *Racial Memory in Dreams*. Other books underneath it dealt with abnormal psychology.

"Are you a student of psychology?" I asked.

"To some extent, yes, but I am more interested in dreams. You see, I have been troubled by nightmares for some time. I am on my way to Vienna to place myself under Strindmann's care.

"Allow me to introduce myself: I am Alfred Kramer."

"And I am Wallace Forbes. Your dreams must be rather upsetting to necessitate a trip half-way around the world."

I, who never dream, had always been fascinated by that phenomenon in other people. Kramer himself must have desired sympathetic ears to receive his story, because, hesitantly at first, then more directly and swiftly, he began to tell his narrative.

"From early childhood," he commenced, "I was inquisitive into the world around me. I seem to have been born with a scientific and inventive bent. At the same time I was a dreamy child. My nights were vivid with a constant stream of images. Sometimes these were pleasant, often they were terrifying. I saw scenes and had strange experiences that I could not explain on the basis of anything I had read, or witnessed, or heard.

"Because of these visions I acquired a profound interest in brain processes as I grew older. My studies dealt with dream psychology, racial memory, and mental inheritances.

*

"A certain dream kept recurring over a period of years: I stood in the midst of a somber glade. All around rose the vast and evil boles of monstrous trees. Long shadows lay athwart the sere grass of autumn at my feet. There were indistinct figures at a little distance which harmonized curiously with the colossal trees. They were watching me intently. In my hand I held a wicked sacrificial knife. Before me was a great stone altar, stained with the blood of countless victims. It stood by the hugest of the trees, and it had a slanting trough so that the spilled blood would water those gnarled roots. A naked young girl of goddess-like beauty lay upon this altar. Her gray eyes regarded me with a baffling mixture of religious ecstasy, terror, and love, as I slowly raised the knife to plunge it into her breast.

"Time after time that vision came to me as clearly as an episode from life. But I never dreamed of what preceded the scene, nor did I know what followed.

"Out of my wish to know the full episode, and from my belief that many dreams were memories of past events, I conceived a hypothesis. The unbroken stream of life had descended from parents to children throughout the ages. Why might not major experiences have been so deeply impressed upon the brain that they too were inherited? Perhaps they were latent, awaiting only a magic touch to awaken them into reconstructed pictures. If this were true, possibly it would account for hitherto unexplained dreams. My own persistent nightmare was like an inherited image, surviving in me, of some impressive episode in the life of a long-dead ancestor.

"Under proper conditions, why shouldn't it be possible to release these ancestral adventures?

"Fascinated by the thought, I plunged into years of labor. Mental therapy, psychiatry, brain surgery became my special studies. I exhausted all sources of information on every phase of the brain, in health and disease, infancy and maturity, life and death. I made elaborate investigations into physiology, the nervous system, motor stimuli, 'why the wheels go round,' in other words. I began a thorough and detailed research into the structure, nature, function, purpose, and action of brain cells.

"Behind my wild idea and its resulting intense activity was a coldly logical plan. If past events could be retained in memory by descendants, they would be recorded somewhere in the brain itself. And among its component parts the source most likely to offer fruitful results was the cells. Of these there are several millions, a vast majority of which seem never to be used. In fact, the average human being requires the services of only a few thousand cells during his lifetime. The remaining cells apparently are capable of storing up facts but simply are not called on except by individuals who pursue knowledge inexhaustibly. It was my belief that this enormous number of unused cells retained, but ever so slightly, impressions of the dominant incidents which had affected the lives of all one's forebears.

"I next supposed that when a cell was required to store away a fact or event in one's life, its latent memory of ancestral experience was obliterated. But if it were not used, the latent memory continued to exist, sometimes never to be realized, sometimes, however, to flash forth vividly in sleep or subconscious dreams.

"For a long time I pursued a wrong path. I thought that the memory-impressions made a physical change in the cells, just as a particle of metal changes in shape when you strike it violently: and that all I needed to do was to invent some sort of sensitive electric device which would tap these cells by means of their specific differences.

"Vain delusion! I wasted two precious years pursuing a ghost, as it were.

"And like many another person who deals with complexities, I found simplicity the keynote to my riddle. It was in 1931, not long after the cosmic ray was discovered and the electrogenetic theory of life propounded, that a brilliant idea occurred to me. You are acquainted with this theory? Its assertion that the human system is somewhat like a battery, and that what we call life lasts while a positive-negative interaction of electricity continues, while death is the complete cessation of that activity? Well, the thought came to me that by increasing this electrical energy of the body, and more particularly by heightening this activity in the brain, each cell might release its individual retained fact or ancestral memory. Recent impressions, being nearer and therefore stronger, would be unloosed first; but by gradually building up activity, older and yet older events ought to permit of resurrection.

"I worked with new energy. Light, wave-lengths, rays occupied my attention. Weird and intricate machinery accumulated in my laboratory.

"And now at last I began to feel success approaching with my isolation of the Kappa-ray. I found it in minute quantities in the bright sunshine that poured down, found too that it directly supplied human beings with much of that electrical energy which gave them life.

"I toiled feverishly until I succeeded in crossing my last barrier. I constructed a sort of Kappa-battery that would isolate from sunshine and store up in concentrated form the Kappa-ray! Day after day, as my black metal box stood in the open glare of the sun, charging itself with precious invisible stuff, I watched it, fondly, jealously. I would have killed any one who chanced to come upon it.

"Then came that evening when its capacity was reached. Carefully I closed it and carried it to my quarters as gently as if it were nitro-glycerin. Worn out and prematurely aged from my years of intense labor, tired in body yet wonderfully excited in spirit, I lay down on my bed with the black box beside me.

"With a strangely steady hand I reached out and opened its shutter and pressed a switch.

"An invisible warm radiance flowed and flooded and poured into me. My head swam with an indescribable nausea, a kind of opiate thickness combined with an increasingly rapid surge of extraordinarily lucid thoughts. My mind seemed to be working faster and clearer than it ever had before. But at the same time, that soothing warmth stole pleasantly over me. Lest there be danger, I extended my arm and closed the box.

"Almost instantaneously I slept.

"A panic-stricken mob, fleeing in terror, bore me along in its mad flight. I fought and struggled to prevent myself from being crushed to death. A confused roar deafened my ears. Cries of racing figures, groans of injured and dying men, crackle of flame and howl of wind blended into a hideous noise. Buildings appeared to speed by me as I forged ahead. I knew I must be in some large city.

"My bursting lungs gasped for clean air but only drew in acrid smoke. The sky glowed redly, flame-shot darkness swirled around me, from behind came the glare of a vast conflagration. I saw swaths of fire leap from building to building on the wings of a stiff wind. Clouds of smoke billowed up, drifted upon us, choked the lungs of refugees. Ever and again, some poor devil fell, and the sheeted flame raced inexorably over him.

"A lumbering brute crashed into me. I cursed savagely and plunged after him. He tripped. I saw him no more. A frail woman with two children, crying as the mob jostled past her, leaned helplessly against a door-stoop. I caught her in one arm and swung her along with me, the children folded to her. And all these people were dressed in the fashion of a full half-century ago!

"We struggled onward in the midst of this livid nightmare. The city's heart was an inferno, a raging furnace.

"But now we were approaching outskirts and less thickly populated districts. Gradually we forged ahead. Smoke and blistering heat still smote us, but the danger region lay farther behind.

"Then, abruptly, the scene changed.

"I was at a ship's wheel. Under full sail we scudded along at a fast clip. Stretching to every horizon, with no land visible anywhere, a white-capped sea surged under a strong trade-wind. The sun poured warmly from a sky in which only a few clouds floated high.

"With terrifying suddenness came a cry from the lookout.

"'*Derelict dead ahead!*'

"I swung the wheel mightily. The ship skewed. Crash! She quivered a moment, began to sink. I saw a waterlogged hulk, black, submerged, hover by our ripped bow. There was a pandemonium of leaping men, despairing shouts where boats fouled in their davits or capsized when badly launched, a bitter fight for positions in those that remained. One went down, overloaded. Another was drawn by suction and followed our ship as she sank.

"At the first shock I tore my clothing off and dived far overboard, swimming rapidly to escape the deadly suction. I was hauled aboard one of two boats that survived. In all there were eleven men left out of thirty-two.

"Then came tragedy in the days that ensued as thirst, starvation, and a blazing sun took their toll. We knew of no land closer than five hundred miles. Some time during our second night adrift, the two boats became separated.

"Six survivors had manned our boat to begin with. At the end of a week we were four. This number was reduced to three on our tenth day afloat when Olaf went mad from drinking salt water and leaped overboard. That left Petri, Andrews, and myself. I think Petri recklessly committed suicide rather than suffer a lingering death of torment, but I can not be sure, for I became delirious on the twelfth day.

"I returned to my senses strangely refreshed. A rain squall had evidently struck and passed. I greedily lapped up warm, fresh water from the boat's bottom and revived still more I noticed that only one of my companions was now left—and he had been dead for I know not how long. I heaved his body overboard.

"Two days later a little palm-fringed island came in sight. With what desperate anxiety I watched it grow larger, and how eagerly I stumbled ashore to drag myself feebly up its beach! I was saved! Saved! And without warning the scene vanished.

"Then followed a couple of less interesting dreams with whose details I will not bother to tell.

"When I at length awakened at dawn, I could scarcely keep calm because of the excitement that possessed me. Columbus could not have been more thrilled when he discovered a new continent. I had made a discovery that might open up unguessable stores of knowledge to mankind, or that might clarify many obscure and forgotten pages of history. Yet I had no intention of announcing it publicly until I had first explored for myself in full its potentialities. I hoped that I would sooner or later have a complete re-presentation of that persistent but fragmentary vision which I alluded to earlier. I speculated on what fascinating episodes from ancestral life might present themselves as I continued using the Kappa-ray. For insofar as I could tell, it left no ill effects. Indeed, I felt unusually energetic, my thoughts came with exceptional clarity.

"That day I spent much of my time obtaining books from libraries and dealers. These were mainly works on genealogy, history, costume, antiquities, biography, and sciences.

"I pored over these till late at night. Two items rewarded a tedious search. One brief record told how my father had escaped in his youth from the great fire of Chicago. The second excerpt, which I ran across in Cooper's *Maritime Disasters*, narrated that a whaler, the *Nancy R.*, disappeared in the South Seas, A.D. 1809; and that her fate was not learned until two years later when the clipper *Seagull*, anchoring for repairs at an atoll southwest of Keaua, found the sole survivor of that tragedy, my grandfather, who had been living there ever since.

"I was happy as a child over this verification of my theory, even though I had strained my eyes by such intensive research. More than satisfied with my achievement, I again opened the Kappa-ray battery and felt its radiant-soporific energy pour through my head just before sleep came to me.

"1638. They were ready to burn a condemned witch in England. A wizened, half-demented old woman, she was already tied to the stake. A crowd of stupid faces and stern persecutors ringed her in. I had somehow been drawn there but now looked at her with compassion in my eyes and would have turned away, sick to my heart, if I could. Any movement was difficult, wedged in tightly as I was.

"A vicious mob shout arose as the executioner advanced, torch in hand. Above that babel the old woman's voice suddenly ascended.

"'Innocent! I am innocent!' she croaked. 'Burn me, will you? May your heart turn to the stone that it is!'

"A startled expression came into the executioner's eyes. He paused in his stride, clutched his breast, plunged to earth dead before he struck.

"Supernatural fear laid an absolute quiet on the crowd. One of the witch's relentless tormenters, bolder than his associates, walked forward and picked up the fallen torch.

"'Sorceress!' he cried. 'Prepare to meet thy God and be sentenced to eternal damnation!' And he flung the torch among the faggots heaped around her. It caught, a thin flame sprang up and raced from stick to stick.

"'Fools! Fools!' the old crone cursed. 'May the vengeance of God and Satan, for this day's work, pursue every one—*except you!*' And she raised a withered hand toward me. 'Only you have pity—may you and your descendants be blessed, even unto the tenth generation. But after the tenth generation, beware! *We shall meet again, yea, three hundred years hence, and you will tell me you remember!*'

"Without willing it, I cried, 'I will remember!'—and awoke to hear my own voice, *'remember—remember,'* echo hollowly in my room and die away. I tossed fitfully, dropped into a sound sleep."

But this account is growing longer than I intended. I must omit many details, fascinating though they would be. Flying miles accompanied flying minutes while I listened spellbound to Kramer's husky voice, and looked into his fever-bright eyes, and wondered how he managed to speak with any distinctness when his lips had not yet visibly moved. His story flowed on—or shall I say continued backward?—through Henry the Eighth's court, the Spanish Inquisition, Constantinople at its fall, Paris of Villon's day, the Norman conquest, weaving its way through earlier and yet earlier centuries.

"So I finally came to my puzzling dream," Kramer went on. "I do not know exactly what year it was, but from its place in my sleep-atavism, I would guess the Fifth or Sixth Century.

"Autumn had come. Dead leaves and withered grass marked the dying year. I was a high priest among the Druids. Each year, upon the last evening of fall, we sacrificed our loveliest virgin to the forest god so that her blood would appease him and cause him to let our sacred trees grow green again when spring returned. I, as high priest, must offer the sacrifice—and she whom they had chosen was Neridh, beloved of my heart.

"I had done everything in my power to save Neridh, until they had grown suspicious. One desperate hope of success remained, but the ritual had been chanted, Neridh lay upon the altar, and a semicircle of dark faces watched me from all around this woodland glade. I dragged out my invocation and supplication. The sun sank lower, and shadows crept longer on blown leaves and brown grass.

"There could be no further delay. Sacrifices must be made before sunset. I raised my arm slowly and held the knife high, poised for its downward plunge into my beloved's heart. Anguish, terror, love, resignation struggled for expression on her face. Already the sun's rim was dropping, and—

"Somewhere afar a tree gave forth a sharp crack. Fear leaped into those eyes that watched me. I heard a heavy groan, a series of sounds from rending boughs, then a booming crash as a giant tree toppled.

"'The wood-spirit is angry!' I shouted. 'Our sacrifice displeases him! To the Great Hill, fly! and witness the evidence of his wrath!'

"Terror gripped the Druids, they melted away like ghosts. I knew what they would find—a forest monarch half chopped in two, and a slow fire that had eaten its way in. My work, my secret efforts to rescue Neridh were triumphant.

"I bent over and slashed her bonds. Swiftly but gently I set her on her feet.

"'Follow me, there is not a moment to lose!' I whispered. 'Make haste before they return!'

"Hand in hand down the endless forest aisles we raced. Neridh ran like a nymph, her graceful body flashing white among the shadows. Night drew on, and I saw her shiver with the chill of early evening.

So intent had I been on saving her that I had forgotten her lack of raiment. I unloosed my outer robe, and scarcely pausing in my stride threw it around her as we sped onward. She gave me a quick glance of pleasure and clutched the warm ceremonial garment close to her.

"And so, deeper and deeper into the vast forest, through thickening darkness, by trails that only I knew, we ran toward safety, weaving our way past immemorial oaks and gigantic boles that had stood even before the coming of our people.

"There my dream ended. I can merely surmise that we escaped into the fastnesses of that forest. There too, since I had discovered what I sought, I could have ended my experiment and ceased energizing myself with Kappa-rays. Such self-denial was beyond either my will or my desire. I was caught in a maelstrom, farther goals lured me on, I succumbed to a magnetic spell which my own imagination had woven. How much more could I learn of what my forebears had lived? I wanted to carry my experiment to its limit. Night after night I therefore utilized the Kappa-ray in pursuit of those adventures which a part of me had long ago experienced.

"A year that I do not dare to guess. I must have been a merchant, and I had gone on some annual trip to a town far from my native land. It was a rambling town, a town of crowded, connected little clay and stone houses. It lay beneath the glare of a scorching sun, and farther out the shifting desert dunes melted into bleak, red wastelands. Its men were swarthy, bearded. They wore long and flowing robes and spoke a language that I could understand but little.

"As I walked down the narrow streets, I heard a sudden hubbub above the usual street cries. When I came to a sharp curve that had interrupted my view I halted abruptly. There was a crowd of the curious, the holy, rich and poor alike, following a stranger who paced along the sunbaked street. He was simply clad. On his face was an expression of such glory, and in his eyes a light of so divine a purity, that my first instinct was to recoil in humility. He was radiant, and the very air about his head seemed luminous with a light I have never seen elsewhere. Then I felt a great serenity come upon me, and my spirit was lifted out of me, cleansed as if I had bathed in some mystical, immortal essence.

"There came a woman who flung herself at the feet of the stranger. Her left hand was hooked like a claw, and splotched with ominous patches of white. The fingers of her right hand were withered away, and her face was disfigured. The crowd shrank back, muttering 'Unclean! Unclean!' But the woman heeded them not and pleaded to the stranger with sorrowing eyes.

"He paused. I saw an expression of infinite pity and compassion shine through his eyes. I was reverent in the presence of ineffable beauty and transcendent wonder.

"The stranger stretched out his arm, and blessed the woman in a voice melodious as distant bells. I saw the claw-shaped hand become firm and rosy, the withered arm fill out to its former symmetry, the mutilated face glow with the happiness of restored health.

"The stranger continued on his way. The woman transfigured knelt in the dust...

"Day after day I kept drawing aside the veil of oblivion. Night upon night I lived again in my dreams my previous lives and ventured still farther back through vanished years. I saw Phryne pose for Praxiteles at Athens in 338 B.C. when the Aphrodite of Knidos was taking immortal form under his hands. In Egypt I witnessed the wakening of a mummy from its tomb of ten centuries, and saw the doubtful Egyptian gods arise from crypts older than civilization. I dwelt at a lamasery near Tibet when all my future was foretold to me by priests of a forgotten cult. And ever I pursued my ancestral life backward through mounting ages. There came a night whose dream no history records, the memory of an event that must have occurred more than ten thousand years B.C.

"My lives had turned away from Asia and gone westward, beyond Egypt, beyond Greece, beyond all Europe, to a vast island or little continent far out in the wastes of the Atlantic. It was a fertile country, a land of mists and sunshine, whose people were happy in the unbroken advance of their civilization. In bays by the murmuring sea, and on slopes of the central hills, golden spires rose high above cities of white and black marble. This continent was a world by itself. There were legends of lands that lay far east from which the ancestors of these inhabitants had come, and there were occasional voyages to nearer countries westward. But they were an indolent race, safe from attack, undisturbed by strife, living in plenty, and rarely venturing afar since there was no need to.

"So the fruitful years marched by, and now there came to this island kingdom the rumor of approaching disaster. In Ixenor, capital of Atlantis, Lekti, high priest of the sun-worshippers, made a prophecy of doom.

"'Our god is angry. The sun shall fail above Atlantis.'

"What did this strange forecast mean? The Atlanteans looked at their sun-god smiling high in the heavens and could not understand. They asked of Lekti that he interpret the warning, or tell them how to appease Elik-Ra, god of the sun. But Lekti had spoken, and answered that he could only receive the message of Elik-Ra and that it was not for him to explain.

"'The sun shall fail above Atlantis.' A hundred virgins were sacrificed with prayers and supplications for mercy to Elik-Ra. The foundations of a great new temple facing east were laid. Days passed and there was no sign that the prophecy would come true. Gradually the Atlanteans regained their faith, and went about their usual tasks again, and believed that their sacrifice of a hundred virgins had satisfied Elik-Ra. Even the prophecy began to fade from their minds, and no one quite remembered why another temple was being erected.

"But superstitious fear had taken root in my heart. I felt that words of warning, however obscure, should be heeded. There was a legend that fertile hot countries lay far east of Atlantis, beyond where any of us living had gone, whence our ancient fathers were supposed to have come and where the home of the sun-god himself was said to be. I reasoned that some terrible menace might be threatening Atlantis the golden, while the gods bided their time. And if Elik-Ra was really angry, I could either save myself by fleeing westward, or take an offering with me and strike out east to seek the god's home across the great sea.

"I set to work and had a large new galley built for me. When the inhabitants of Atlantis heard of my undertaking, a few thought my mission could be successful, some said I was foolhardy, but the majority mocked, saying that I was mad or presumptuous since Elik-Ra had been appeased by the sacrifice of the hundred virgins. Their scorn raised momentary doubts in my mind, but I went ahead with my plans.

"Thus there came a day when sixteen slaves took their places at the sweep-oars and we set off across dark waters to seek legendary lands of the rising sun. My galley had one mast whose sail could be used in emergency or when the crew was exhausted. There was a great store of provisions aboard, and as much wealth as I owned. Beside me in silver chains lay the sacrifice I intended to offer Elik-Ra when the time came: a young girl, lovely as the fading spires of Ixenor, and with red-gold hair that flamed like the setting sun.

"We had left Atlantis at dawn. Hardly a breeze stirred. The ocean heaved undulantly in slow, sinister swells. By noon we were entering that trackless wilderness of waters where no living man had penetrated. Far behind, my island kingdom, the only land I knew, dwindled toward the horizon, becoming dream-like and misty and unreal.

"And now as the oars pulled rhythmically a strange thing happened. The waters around us changed from heavy green to a complete and frightful black. Thousands upon thousands of dead fish floated to their surface, whales, tarpon, swordfish, octopi, sailfish, and a dozen other varieties of monsters of the deep such as had never been seen, all dead. Bubbles oozed out, vapor and wisps of steam drifted up. The sea boiled with a vast and nauseating motion. All in one instant Atlantis vanished from the horizon as the ocean reclaimed its own.

"'The sun shall fail above Atlantis.'

"To me alone was given understanding of the prophecy, unless my slaves remembered. Blind terror had come upon them, and they shouted wildly. I followed the direction of their eyes. From sunken Atlantis a colossal, a mountainous plateau of water extending across the whole horizon hurtled toward us. We saw it coming and we were helpless. We saw it tower overhead and engulf our galley as if it were a fleck of sand. Something bumped me and I grabbed it unthinkingly. An infinite roaring deafened my ears, I was sucked under and flung violently ahead, furious forces raged everywhere. I crashed into something else, hung on, half-drowned pulled myself and my burden up. A freak of the great wave had righted my galley. With two feet of water in its bottom it raced along with the sea-wall. Not one of the sixteen slaves had been saved, only myself and Teoctel, the flame-haired, who had been thrown against me when we capsized, were left of all the millions that had dwelt in Atlantis...

*

"I dreamed again, in search of my ancestral lives, and for many nights my visions became increasingly barbaric. I wandered through hills in what is now Spain, where swart people dwelt in caves. I fought a woolly rhinoceros in the Balkans, ruled a tribe of blond giants in the Rhine valley. Time and again I brought down my prey with primitive weapons, or even made my kill with only my bare hands and sharp teeth. More than once I fought, like the savage I was, to get or to keep the female of my choice.

"When the fire people discovered again the lost art of building a fire, it was I who found that meat improved by being burnt. Then the great cold and the field of ice crept down from the north, and my lives were passed in a strange warm country far to the south where my tribe had fled. And always the faces around me became more bestial, the marks of civilization fewer, until finally the only law was the law of one's strength.

"There, more than fifty thousand years ago, I halted my dreams. Did I say halted them? No, that is not quite true.

"For a week I had been feverishly writing my observations during the daytime, and poring over piles of books in order to localize in time and place the substance of my released memories. I begrudged the moments necessary for eating; it was many days since I had shaven or paid any attention to myself.

"But, as I said, my visions were becoming more savage, primitive, less varied the farther back I went. My initial excitement had begun to wear off, and on this morning, despite a certain heaviness that appeared to possess me, I felt the need of attending to my long-neglected personal appearance.

"When I bent over to draw the water for my tub, some unexpressed thought vaguely puzzled me. That thought continued to bother me while I slipped from my clothing. There is, in my bathroom, a full-length mirror; and not till I was passing it did my feeling of unease receive expression.

"For I glanced at my naked body in the mirror, and such a shock of utter horror froze me as I can never again experience on earth.

"*What I saw in the mirror was a massive, shaggy, beast-like man of fifty thousand years ago!*

"I can not relate the rest of that fateful day. I tried to convince myself that I was the victim of an optical illusion. Perhaps my dreams had become so vivid that they persisted even in my waking hours. My mind may have temporarily given way, I thought, and made me a victim of hallucination.

"But it was all in vain. The mirror did not lie. Each time that I returned to it, drawn by a morbid curiosity, the same appalling figure leered back at me, ape-like, brutish. Slowly the bitter truth forced its way in, though I tried to evade it. Some powerful element in the Kappa-ray, or some unknown organic change that it had influenced in my physical system, was causing my body to revert, to follow my brain as it went back through the ages in the trail of my ancestral lives. I had played with mysterious forces and I was paying the penalty. A physiological atavism or throwback kept pace with the transformation of my mind.

"Shuddering, sickened, I gave way to a frenzy. I raged and stormed around like a trapped animal. My hate concentrated on the Kappa-ray. That was the source of all my misfortune. But at least I could prevent this abominable devolution from going any farther. Perhaps I might even be able to regain my old self when the source of that malignant energy was destroyed. And so, hardly realizing what damage I did and caring less, I kicked the Kappa-ray box across the room, smashed it, trampled it under my feet and ground it into wreckage. Even though

I could never again become as I was, yet I would check this degradation before it went farther and before it was too late.

"I do not know how long the madness ruled me. It must have been far into the night that I finally managed to drop into the deep slumber of exhaustion.

"*And that night I dreamed again!* I re-lived a fierce, nomadic life in southern Italy, followed the first glacier as it retreated north, hunted the mammoth, and then roamed anew through the valleys of central Europe in the warm days before the glaciers came.

"When I wakened at dawn, I was beyond any paroxysms of despair. An apathy came upon me. I walked with dull and heavy tread, listlessly pondered over my fate. I realized now that the Kappa-ray had done its fatal work, and that I had saturated myself in an energy which I no longer had power to control. Whatever changes the ray had begun to make in my brain and my body were proceeding as freely as if they were a natural part of me.

"I could only hope that the effect of the ray would wear off in time. Sedatives, drugs, opiates, alexipharmics—I tried them all and without success. Nightly I lived backward through obscure dawn ages. Daily I wakened to find hideous and subtle changes metamorphosing me into a prehistoric creature. And what faint hope I had held died in my heart when I discovered that the rate of my nocturnal return to former life was accelerating with ever-increasing rapidity. At first I had spanned a few decades in a night, then it became a few centuries, now I bridged thousands and tens of thousands of years each time that I slept.

"I followed primitive man when he crept out of Asia half a million years ago. I lived in a luxuriant land that is now the desert of Gobi. Earth itself underwent great transformations. A continent sank under the waves, another one rose from the Pacific deep. Beasts that no living man has seen appeared in growing numbers, the curious vegetation of vanished eras became my habitat. There were vast saurians on land, ferocious nightmares of air, gigantic marine reptiles and monsters that battled in the warm seas.

"And always, too, there came a hotter, damper climate upon earth. Swamps and marshes became more numerous. Tropical jungles flourished everywhere, with weird, conical trees and hundred-foot ferns and evil flowers growing to incredible heights.

"So the years mounted by millions and the geologic ages were born again in my dreams and drifted on like a camera film run backward. The Carboniferous Age became an era of the future, the giant beasts of land decreased in number, steaming jungles and poisonous marshes covered what ground lay above water. The seas grew almost boiling. Terrific storms and deluges of hissing rain swept the globe. Not a single vertebrate now roamed upon land, only a few ephemeral moths winged their brief way through air, moths far larger than any we know, soft, immense, and spotted with gold, scarlet, indigo. But even these passed away; and life swarmed only in the almost universal sea.

"How long I have retrogressed in years I do not know, but it must be millions upon millions, beyond any computation. And it has been not only a dream that came to me, but a reality overshadowed by abysmal terror. My brain has tottered on the brink of madness and I am so far degenerated physically that for three nights I have been taking powerful injections to keep me awake. I fear another vision more than I fear death."

The husky choking voice trailed away in a low gurgle. Over me as the hours waned there had been creeping a nausea, a kind of revulsion against my loathsome acquaintance and his mad story. A perspiration had broken out all over me, and I was about to make a hasty departure when that disgusting voice continued but in a more uncertain and throatily tired way.

"That last dream—Ugh! I shall never forget it. It haunts all my thoughts and hovers deep within me like an evil incubus ready to descend whenever I weaken.

"Dim sunlight filtered down through water that was thick with sediment and vile with elementary life. In masses of subaqueous growths lurked nasty pulpy things. The black ooze beneath heaved with soft, wriggling forms—gastropods, univalves, protozoa, cephalopods, infusoria, animalcules, and gelatinous forms of a myriad other kinds. A shadow enveloped me—I stared up. Not far above, a giant cephalopod settled toward me, its beak open, innumerable suckers quivering on tentacles that were mushy as worms. I moved slowly aside—and found myself enveloped in the ichorous filaments of a gigantic and viscous jellyfish. I do not know what happened—I do not wish to know. Ugh! I can not convey the vertigo caused by that sticky stuff—and the clammy life-forms that originally rose in the ancient seas that once covered earth."

The voice trailed away and died, and silence descended stealthily. It seemed to me that the invalid's figure had relaxed, and I thought his head fell back. I did not wait to make sure as I stiffly stood up, for I felt uneasy, yes, and slightly afraid. I do not know why it was, but even as I recoiled physically from the stranger, so my spirit shrank as from a thing unclean or accursed. Trembling a little, I steadied myself and paced down the aisle after the briefest of muttered phrases, to which I heard no answer, if indeed my acquaintance made one.

I had about reached the vestibule when a peculiar sound impinged on my consciousness. I paid no attention to it, and tried to quicken my step. My hand was outstretched toward the door, I believe, when that primeval cry froze me in my place and brought me facing about.

It was a whispered scream that died away hideously; a sub-human, sub-animal wordless gurgle, like the death rattle in the throat of a drowning person.

Alfred Kramer may have dreamed his last dream. Psychologists tell us that the subconscious mind may work at abnormal speed when the conscious mind is at rest; and it is at least possible that a lifetime's visions paraded through the fitful slumber of Alfred Kramer during those long seconds that I required in approaching the door. I do not know. And it may be true also that I was temporarily insane. Again, I do not know. But the sight that met my eyes when I whirled about could have been merciful only to madness. One may preserve an equilibrium in a completely normal world; and a madman would find, I suppose, a certain unity in his completely abnormal world; but to face the abnormal in the midst of everyday life, to find the incredible exchanging place with the usual, that is to unite insanity with sanity and make one doubt whether normality exists at all.

For when I spun around, I saw that Alfred Kramer had somehow risen to his feet. And as I stared in his direction, a frightful change took place.

His hands dropped from his wrists and thudded to the floor. His face suddenly went awry, slipped, melted away. The clothing squirmed, bulged, ripped off.

And now I knew the meaning of those motionless lips and that pasty face. It was a mask that I had been watching.

Swaying horribly for an ageless second, what was left of Alfred Kramer shook convulsively and collapsed.

On the floor lay a writhing mass of protoplasmic slime.

ATLANTIS
RESURRECTED

The Lemmings

Once in a hundred years the Lemmings come
Westward, in search of food, over the snow;
Westward until the salt sea drowns them dumb;
Westward, till all are drowned, those Lemmings go.

Once, it is thought, there was a westward land
(Now drowned) where there was food for those starved things,
And memory of the place has burnt its brand
In the little brains of all the Lemming Kings.

Perhaps, long since, there was a land beyond
Westward from death, some city, some calm place
Where one could taste God's quiet and be fond
With the little beauty of a human face;

But now the land is drowned. Yet we still press
Westward, in search, to death, to nothingness.

John Masefield
from ENSLAVED, AND OTHER POEMS, *1920*

ONCE IN A THOUSAND YEARS

Frances Bragg Middleton

The identity of Frances Bragg Middleton proves as strange a story as any here included. Slivers of information arise, some clear, some contradictory. In *The Shudder Pulps* (1975), Richard Kenneth Jones describes her as "a facile exponent of the masculine point of view". Both Eric Leif Davin's *Partners in Wonder: Women and the Birth of Science Fiction, 1926–1965* (2006), and Frank M. Robinson and Lawrence Davidson's *Pulp Culture: The Art of Fiction Magazines* (1998), include her among their company. Charles H. Baker's *Rejections of 1927* (1928) provides the most substantial detail, claiming she lived in Texas and "witnessed the destruction of Galveston by the great hurricane of 1900". Yet, both the *Internet Science Fiction Database* and *The FictionMags Index* suggest Middleton to be a pseudonym for Frank Richardson Pierce. While no conclusion can be offered, the name, whether her own or otherwise, can be attributed to over two dozen works of short fiction in publications including *Dime Mystery Magazine*, *Red Star Mystery*, *Horror Stories* and *Terror Tales*.

"Once in a Thousand Years" was originally published in the August 1935 issue of *Weird Tales*, and was Middleton's sole contribution to the magazine. Inspired by John Masefield's poem, "The Lemmings"— which, as with Ella Wheeler Wilcox's "The Lost Land", thematises longing for that which cannot be attained—the tale concerns Shane

O'Farrell, who finds himself swept out to the Sargasso Sea. Rescued by a fleet of advancing ships, his saviours lead him to Atlantis, "a country so completely governed by science that its people can always avoid their enemies". Alongside Edmond Hamilton's "Child of Atlantis" and Joel Martin Nichols Jr.'s "The City of Glass", "Once in a Thousand Years" thus presents an image of Atlantis as a recluse, having long since retreated, rather than as ruins. Preceding the tale, find the full text of Masefield's original poem.

I t was a mad thing to do, of course. But the three of us were together, perhaps for the last time. And we were all just out of school, and none of us was twenty-two, and each of us had had one drink too many. Also, the night was one of those mad, intoxicating nights that rarely come more than once in any man's lifetime.

Glamor. The night was thick with it. A blue, blue, star-shot sky. The Gulf spread out to meet it, white under the breath-taking beauty of the great white moon. All the rippling, gurgling voices of a summer sea, all the Circe-scents of jasmine flowers, magnolias, and orange trees in bloom. We couldn't sleep. We couldn't stay inside.

I don't remember who suggested swimming out to the float. We were none of us accountable, exactly. But I remember we all agreed to it, though we all knew that the tide was out and running strong. Indeed, I never knew such another ebb as we felt that night. It swept us out with all the force of the current of a great river in flood-time. And it served to sober us. We were glad to reach the float and lie on it and rest. We knew we could never go back against a tide like that. We'd have to wait till morning.

So Nelson Todd and I made the best of it and slept. But when the hot sun waked us, Shane O'Farrell was gone.

It did not occur to us then to be uneasy. We swam in, dressed, and went down to breakfast. It was only then, when we couldn't find him, and when Todd's family and Todd's servants—it was Todd's father's house where we were staying—declared they hadn't seen or heard him, that we began to be alarmed. And by that time it was too late to do any good.

Of course, we searched everywhere, notified his uncle and the authorities. There was a terrible rush and scramble of coast guards, police, and newspaper men for a while. It actually looked at one time as if Todd and I might be accused of making away with him. But O'Farrell's old uncle wouldn't hear of that. Neither would he admit that O'Farrell was dead. Todd and I had no doubts on that score. We knew what that tremendous ebb was like. If it had got O'Farrell... but it was more than three years before we knew.

For Shane O'Farrell came back, as suddenly, as unexpectedly, as he had gone. He simply walked in on me, in the office where I was strenuously trying to learn my father's business. And when I had begun to get over the shock of his return, and to get a good look at him, I began to realize that he had changed immeasurably. He had always been tall, I remembered. Now, by some trick in the carriage of his head, in the pitch of his shoulders, he seemed inches taller. His blue eyes were clouded with something I couldn't fathom. His big, generous, Irish mouth, that had used to laugh so much, was etched in sensitive, wistful lines. And his movements were more deliberate. His old impulsiveness was gone.

Shane told me, in answer to my questions, that he had been globe-trotting a bit, that he had already seen his uncle, but hadn't been able to locate Nelson Todd.

"Todd's on an engineering job in Yucatan," I told him.

He gave me a startled look.

"That's queer," he said.

But when I asked him what was queer about that, he only shook his head absently. And it dawned on me suddenly that it was his own voice that was queer, as if it hadn't been used much lately, in talking English, that is.

I began to get a little warm under the collar. After all, we'd been brought up next door to each other, gone to school together, eaten each other's bread, fought each other's battles, spent each other's money, almost all our lives. He had dropped into the sea that night from within a yard of me. And I wasn't going to be put off by that cool, detached, new manner of his, if I could help it.

"So you mean to tell me," I accused, "that you got tired of the float, so you just dropped off into the water, were swept out to sea and were picked up, and that you've just been wandering over the face of the earth ever since, without money, without letting your friends know—"

"Oh, I was with friends," he told me casually. "That is," with the manner of one conscientiously trying to tell the exact truth, "that is, they were friends after I met up with them."

And for a while he just sat there, staring out the window of that eighteenth story office, but seeing nothing, hearing nothing, I could have sworn, of the dingy, humming streets below. And my patience broke all of a sudden, like a blown-up balloon.

"But where have you been?" I almost yelled at him. "Great Scott, man, do you think you can go out like the flame of a candle and then bob up again without a word of warning, and expect nobody to take any notice of it? Haven't the reporters got hold of you yet?"

"No," he answered mildly, still staring out toward the smoky horizon. "Uncle John and you are the only ones who know yet that I'm back. I don't want—publicity."

"Well, you'll get it," I exploded. "Dead men can't come alive without getting into the papers. Where have you been?"

"In the Sargasso Sea," he answered quietly, and smiled a little, secret smile.

I think I was never quite so angry in my life before.

"So that's what you mean to tell the papers!" I snorted witheringly. "I suppose that wouldn't get you publicity in large, handsome gobs? The Sargasso Sea that's so famous and so reeking with mystery! And you mean to tell me you got there—by swimming, was it?—with nothing but a pair of bathing-trunks to help you along?"

He burst out laughing, quite like his old self for the moment. It was the first sign of *reality* I'd seen in him since he came.

"Oh, I had a striped silk dressing gown before I got there," he explained. But then his laugh broke off in the middle and his eyes grew vague again. "Saint Brandan's Isle, you know. You've read about it—"

"Sure," I snorted. "I've read about it. About the Seven Cities of Cibola, too, and the voyages of Madoc and Maeldune, and a thousand other marvels. But I never expect to see any of them, and you don't either."

"No, I never expect to see any of them," he repeated, and his eyes grew more clouded than ever.

I banged the drawers of my desk shut and dragged him out to lunch. That night I took him to a show. But he never really waked up. He still liked me, I think—as much, that is, as it was left in him to like anyone. He dropped in every day. But he wouldn't talk. And that queer, detached manner of his bothered me.

When he did break silence, it was always to say something strange and unexpected.

"Do you believe in the impossible?" he asked one night, when we were smoking in the living-room of the two-by-four apartment which was all I could afford in town.

"It depends on what you call the impossible," I answered, puzzled. "Columbus did it in his day. Peary did it in ours. So did the Wright brothers. Everything was impossible till somebody did it."

"In other words," he said slowly, "nothing is really impossible?"

"Not after it's been done," I told him, with all the wisdom of twenty-five.

"Then if I told you—"

But he broke off there, and that absent look came into his eyes again. I admit I was worried about his sanity. His uncle was, too. I know, because he told me. But we didn't either of us know what we ought to do.

He grew more and more restless through the winter. He went to the public library almost every day and dug into a lot of what would have been called ungodly volumes not so very many years ago. Folklore. Old legends about Atlantis, Antillia, Lemuria. All he could lay his hands on about archeological research in Crete, Egypt, Mexico, Yucatan, a dozen other moldy civilizations. There was nobody to interfere with him. He had money enough, which his old uncle had carefully nursed along for him while he was gone. He didn't have to work. But it did seem a pity for him to throw his life away—as he seemed bent on doing.

And that word "impossible." It seemed to haunt him. He wanted to believe something, or to make me believe something. I got wise to that fact at last. I'd known for a long time that he must have stumbled on some discovery or other, probably remarkable, even epoch-making. He was eating his heart out about it too. He needed, desperately, to let it to the air. But it was a long time before I could get him to talk. And when he did start, it was just by bits and snatches. I had to piece them together myself. But when I did begin to get his drift I was eager enough for him to go on.

"Do you know anything about heredity?" he demanded once.

"Only that most people look more or less like their parents and inherit their debts or their property," I said.

"No, I mean—" He stopped, and it looked as if he was going off into one of those far-away silences again. But he didn't. "No, I mean the principles of heredity that make us what we are. A man doesn't always resemble his close kin. There are throwbacks sometimes. You take a case where two dissimilar breeds have been crossed, white man and Indian, say. No matter how carefully the alien blood is bred out, sooner or later a child will be born into that family who has all the marks of a full-blood Indian. Now such things do happen, not frequently, but often enough to establish a rule. How do *you* explain that?"

"I don't know that I ever tried," I told him. "But I suppose it was because the kid in question wasn't very choosy. Instead of taking his hair from granddaddy Jones and his eyes from grandmother Smith and his short temper from great-great-grandfather Whosit, the cattle rustler, he just grabbed off all the characteristics of old Chief Rain-in-the-Face and let it go at that. I dare say such things happen oftener than we think. Where there is no mixture of races it isn't noticeable, but lots of times you hear people say, 'I declare I don't know who that child takes after, nobody in the family that *I* ever saw.' But what's the point, O'Farrell?"

"Just this," and his face was very intent and sober. "Suppose someone could inherit *all* his characteristics from just *one* ancestor, with nothing at all from any of the others—what then?"

"Why, then, probably, he'd be a monkey," I grinned. "At that, they're born with tails sometimes, you know. You see it in the papers. And it probably happens sometimes, too, when it doesn't get into the papers."

"Yes, but"—O'Farrell was dead in earnest now—"but if he inherited everything from just one ancestor, all his characteristics of mind as well as body, then wouldn't he remember *all that that ancestor ever knew?*"

I was dumfounded, and uneasy. But I tried to hide my fears. I wanted to draw him out, if possible, get at the thing that was festering in his mind.

"You mean," I said slowly, feeling my way, "that you would explain in that way the queer feeling we have sometimes that we have lived before, that we can almost remember things which we know we never saw—"

"Exactly!" eagerly. "But if you had inherited *all* your brain from just one ancestor, then you'd remember clearly, wouldn't you? Don't you see that that *could* happen?"

"Oh, yes," I granted carelessly. "It might—once in a thousand years."

"Once in—" He stared at me, his face as white as paper. He looked so sick I ran and got him a drink. But he got over his agitation shortly. His color came back. "But that was only a guess you made," he finished, as if taking comfort in the thought.

"Of course, it was a guess," impatiently. "A guess just like yours."

"No, I'm in earnest," surprizingly.

But he wouldn't say anything more then. It was weeks before I *got* the rest of it And even yet I doubt if I ever did get it all.

It seems that he couldn't sleep that night, out there on the float. That luminous, glamorous moonlight, the swiftly running ebb, all the scents and sounds and witchery about him wrought him up to a tremendous pitch. He said he just lay there repeating lines about the sea that had stuck in his mind from English Lit., especially from

Swinburne and Tennyson—he'd dug in pretty deep, I remembered, that last year at the U. He quoted a lot of it. He said that night, for the first time so far as he was concerned, "The sea moaned round with many voices"—and he understood them all. That for the first time he could actually feel all "the light and sound and darkness of the sea." And at last he found himself repeating that thing of Masefield's:

> "Once in a hundred years the lemmings come
> Westward, in search of food, over the snow,
> Westward, until the salt sea drowns them dumb,
> Westward, till all are drowned, those lemmings go."

And then, he said, altogether without his own volition, he had slipped into the water, and the tide was racing with him out to sea. He wasn't drunk on liquor, I could swear to that myself. A glass too much, maybe, but not drunk. But the night had got him, the night and the ebbing tide and the moon that controlled the tide.

He said he wasn't worried at all. He exerted himself very little. The tide was carrying him. Even when he began to tire he wasn't actually alarmed. When he came in contact with some wooden thing that floated by him he pulled himself aboard without any particular feeling of eagerness or relief. The moon had paled by that time and the sun was not yet up; so he couldn't see much. He could hear a sort of drowsy chittering and squeaking, though, at the other end of the raft he was on, a noise that reminded him of mice. But he didn't investigate. He was tired. And, unbelievable as it sounds, he stretched out on the wet boards and slept.

The sun roused him to what, he assured me solemnly, was to be the most stupendous day of his life, up to that time. He found himself on a raft, all right, though he was sure it hadn't been built for that purpose. It looked more like the side of a heavily timbered house, a house that perhaps had been washed away and broken up in flood-time. It rode low in the sea, and shipped water constantly, enough to keep everything wet. O'Farrell didn't mind that especially, but his companions did.

For he wasn't alone. At the end of the raft farthest from him were clustered somewhat less than fifty little brown furred animals with small ears and short tails and tiny, white, sharp teeth. They wrinkled their noses at him and made complaining noises and seemed very damp and unhappy. He supposed they were some sort of field mice, though they were a little large for that. They reminded him of prairie-dogs, he said.

He began now to be actively concerned about his own safety. There he was, well out of sight of land, aboard a makeshift raft which the most sanguine couldn't have called seaworthy, with no food unless you counted the field mice which he wasn't hungry enough to do yet, and no clothing but his bathing-trunks. Fortunately the sea was calm. Clumsy as it was, the raft rode levelly, driving as straight ahead as if by rule and compass. And when he looked overside he understood the reason. A current as strong as that strange ebb tide of the night before was sweeping it onward—a current where by rights no current ought to be—a current of purple-blue, transparent water that was less than fifty feet wide.

O'Farrell came cautiously upright in the center of the raft. As far as he could see ahead of him, that dark-colored current cut the gray Atlantic in two. And on its flood drifted boats of many sizes, of many designs, led, or so it seemed to him, by a stately yacht, white and misty in the distance, her sails all furled.

He simply couldn't believe what he saw. He looked and looked, but the scene remained unchanged—a plain sweep of sunlighted ocean, empty but for that weird, incredible procession.

He was hungry by noon. So were the field mice. They scampered about uneasily, chattering at him, beseeching him with their little bright eyes. He was thoroughly alarmed by this time, finally decided to signal the nearest craft. It was too far away for his voice to carry, but, caught in a splinter of the raft, there was a weather-stained strip of sodden canvas; so he used that to signal with.

The boat just ahead of him put about and drew slowly toward him, fighting that powerful current every foot of the way. O'Farrell said it was the trimmest gasoline launch he ever saw, fitted up with a high-powered engine, but still almost powerless against that inexorable current. Its only occupant was a girl. She threw him a line as she came alongside, and he made it fast to a splintered timber. And then he got the biggest shock of the day.

For the girl suddenly cried out in a voice that was high with ecstasy and amazement and incredulity all at once. She leaped to the raft, ran over to those shy, furry little creatures and went to her knees and held her hands out to them.

"Oh, the dear, dear, funny, timid little things," she cried, a sob in her throat. "And you brought them! You lucky, lucky man! We didn't know we had any of them along."

O'Farrell said he just stood there, gaping at her, while the little field mice sniffed at her fingers and crept into her hands. He had felt like a man in a dream ever since he waked, and now he felt more like one than ever. Even the girl was unlike anyone he had ever seen before. She was as tall as he was, very fair, yellow-haired, blue-eyed. But that doesn't mean much. It was her features, he said, the pure Greek lines like those of the old statues, the grace and swing of her perfect body, which he found impossible to describe. Even her white middy blouse and skirt, her white shoes and hose, couldn't keep her from making him think of the Winged Victory. But her voice, her accent, were, incredibly, as truly American as his own.

"Oh, it's wonderful, after all our years of dreams, to see them coming true!" she was murmuring. "I never thought I'd actually *travel* with them. Oh!" her voice rose on a note of purest music. "All our old dreams, changing into reality!"

O'Farrell was stupefied, she was so amazing, so utterly different from anyone he had ever known. And she was plainly so rapt with ecstasy, so absorbed in her happiness, so sure of being in the presence of an understanding and sympathetic listener, that she had thrown all reserve to the winds.

"You know how it begins," her soft voice was almost crooning. "Back in your childhood, when you first begin to remember that other world—when bit by bit you understand the destiny you were born to—when you first realize why it is that you love and long for the sea, though you never saw it in this life—why you yearn for a burning moon in place of the cold, pale moon you know, for the low, yellow stars instead of the far-off points of light you live under, for a sky of gorgeous blue instead of the dull sky up above you—"

She drew a deep, long sigh. The little furry things had taken complete possession of her now. They were as friendly with her, O'Farrell said, as kittens. It was pretty to watch her with them, or would have been if he hadn't been so completely bewildered by it.

"And you come upon pictures that make you ache with homesickness—you don't know why. Pictures of the sea—and long, smooth beaches of shining sand—and ships of long ago. Pictures of Greece, Crete, Spain, Philistia. And your half-dreams taunt and mock you, till at last, just all in a sudden flash of light, you *know*."

Her voice trailed off into contented silence. O'Farrell made no effort to break it. He couldn't think of a thing to say. And when she spoke again her tone had changed.

"Why, they're hungry!" she cried. "There is no food! Why did you bring no food along? Whatever in the world—"

"I didn't know I was coming," he told her bluntly. "This whole business"—he waved his hand toward the sea, the current, the parade of boats—"is no more than a nightmare to me. Maybe you can explain it?"

She sat back on her heels, staring at him in an amazement that matched his own. Her eyes were enormous in her suddenly pale face. She caught her breath sharply in a sudden rush of emotion, the nature of which he could not have told.

"But this is beyond a miracle," she cried. "If you aren't one of us—if you didn't hear the call—how could you come?"

He told her. She listened intently, nodding her head from time to time, slowly and thoughtfully. She looked squarely at him out of eyes that were the steadiest, the most candid that he had ever seen.

"But this is terrible," she told him when he had finished. "I don't know what they'd do to you," with a sudden, apprehensive glance at the line of boats ahead. "You can't possibly escape, and if you don't even know where we are going—"

"I don't. It's the most impossible adventure any man ever dreamed about. Can you tell me? Do you know?"

"Oh, yes, I know." She smiled. "I am one of those who were born to know—by inheritance, rather than by learning. All of us," again that gesture toward the boats ahead, "are bound for the same place—to the kingdom of Atlas—the Garden of the Hesperides—the Isles of the Blest—"

She broke off, watching his face, which must, O'Farrell confessed, have seemed a mask of stupidity.

"Can't you even guess?" she cried.

But he could only shake his head.

"Do you mean," she asked him incredulously, "that you know nothing at all of that first great civilization from which all others spread—that land of tall, fair men—'for there were giants in those days'—which sent its adventurers into so many lands? Did you never hear of Cro-Magnon man, who left his drawings and his bones in the caves of France and Spain? Or the legends of the giants who lived once in the British Isles? Of the Pelasgians, the Cyclops, the Titans of Greece and Asia Minor? Of Hiawatha, who came to teach the savage Iroquois? Of Quetzalcoatl, the Fair God, who came to the Aztecs? Does the tale of the sunken land of Tristram's Lyonesse mean nothing at all to you?"

"Mighty little," O'Farrell admitted. "Either you're crazy or I am. I've read myths and folklore, of course, and as much of the *Morte d'Arthur* and its kindred 'literature' as they made me swallow. But it never occurred to me that I'd ever meet up with anybody who *believed* that stuff."

"But it isn't written—what *we* know," the girl said solemnly. "As for those legendary remnants of an ancient history that you mention—why, don't you realize that there never was a myth or a legend yet that did not have some foundation in fact?"

O'Farrell said he couldn't answer her. What with the hot sun on his head, the glare on the water, and no food for almost twenty-four hours, his head was going round and round. Perhaps the girl saw that. Anyhow she came deliberately upright, and the little animals she had been petting clustered around her, running over her feet.

"Did you ever see anyone just like me?" she demanded.

"No," O'Farrell muttered. "No."

"Yet all my people are like me. I don't mean the family I was born into. No. I mean my people"—she waved her hand—"there—in front of us." She looked at him, long and hard. "And you are not one of us. You know none of the things we know. That will be very bad for you, because you can not escape. And yet you might pass for one of us, being fair—and tall—though not quite tall enough. And you brought these"—she pointed to the little creatures at her feet.

"I don't want to see you made a sacrifice," she went on earnestly. "Maybe if I tell you—but first we must get aboard the launch. It isn't wet and sloppy like this thing, and I've plenty of food aboard."

So they made the transfer, field mice and all. The launch was fairly comfortable, well stocked with eatables, cushions, summer blankets. The girl gave O'Farrell a lounging-robe of hers and a complete man's yachting-outfit which she had worn in a college play. She had always played men's parts in the girls' plays, she said.

He went into the tiny cabin and tried them on. They fitted him—and O'Farrell was six feet tall! But she advised him to save the suit for the day of their "arrival", so he wore the lounging-robe instead.

It must have taken about a week, he reckons, to make that incredible journey. He lay on the deck most of the time, under the awning, trying to figure things out and not succeeding. He had no theory, no answer to the puzzle presented by that girl. She spent the nights in the little cabin, but all day she was outside, always in fresh, plain, white clothes, always as perfectly appointed as if she were actually chiseled of the marble she so resembled. And she was always coolly, impersonally friendly toward O'Farrell. But she showed actual tenderness toward those pets of hers.

She had told him her name the first day. Diana. That was all. It fitted her superbly, he thought.

They were evidently quite off the steamer lanes. They met no craft, sighted no land; till, early one morning, the hazy outlines of lofty hills stood blue against the sky.

"The Isle of Saint Brandan," the girl whispered softly. "Sailors used to sight it, but when they tried to reach it, it was never there."

"Is that where we are going?" O'Farrell wanted to know.

"That is where we are going. For *we* shall reach it—we and the lemmings. We were summoned, as others are summoned—once in a thousand years."

Lemmings! He understood now. Those lines of Masefield's went swimming through his head again, and he repeated them under his breath:

> "Once, it is thought, there was a westward land,
> (Now drowned) where there was food for those starved
>   things,
> And memory of the place has burnt its brand
> In the little brains of all the lemming kings."

"Yes, it was there—the Greek Isles of the Blest—Odysseus sailed west to find them—and they still are there, only the land between is lost and drowned—lost and drowned as the poor little lemmings are, those who try to go when it is not the appointed time."

"Do you remember the last lines?" O'Farrell asked. "Listen!

> "But now the land is drowned, yet still we press
> Westward, in search, to death, to nothingness.

"Is that for us?"

"No, not for us. That is—"

And she sat there for a long time, her chin on her hand, watching the cloud-like hills on the far horizon. Yet it must have been by faith alone that she was so sure that the land was there. To O'Farrell it seemed much more like a mirage, a fantasmagoria, a fata morgana. The hills changed so, now like a low continuous range, now rearing in tall spire-like peaks, now resembling glaciers, icebergs, or ruined, battlemented castles. And as they drew nearer, the land seemed actually to divide, to break up precisely as a fleet might do, even to advance and recede in strange and complicated evolutions, while over it hung always a wavering mass of rainbow-colored mist.

"Do you wonder now," the girl asked him in a hushed, enraptured voice, "that the sailors used to tell such strange tales of Saint Brandan's Isle—how they sighted its green hillsides and its clear streams, and how it vanished like a mirage whenever they came near it?"

"I can remember one legend about a Portuguese who landed there," O'Farrell answered dryly. "The natives feasted and wined him to the king's own taste. But when he awoke he was adrift alone on the ocean. And when he reached home he found his sweetheart had been dead a hundred years or so. They showed him her tomb, I remember, by her husband's, along with the tombs of her seven daughters and her seven sons. I wouldn't like that."

"That was only a myth," she objected.

"Haven't you said a hundred times that all myths have a foundation in fact?"

"Yes," reluctantly. "And it might have happened with him as it has happened with you. It is a miracle, of course. But miracles can happen—once in a thousand years."

"You mean, I suppose, that the summons—as you call it—comes just once in a thousand years?"

"Yes, that is what I mean."

"And what is to happen to us?"

For the first time, O'Farrell said, he saw trouble in her face. Her eyes, when they met his, were clouded, her fine mouth quivered.

"For myself there can be nothing but good," she answered. "But for you, who come by accident, I don't know. They will not like it. And it lingers in my mind, like some far-off recollection only half remembered, that they can be very cruel, at times."

"In the matter of human sacrifice, perhaps?"

She winced. Her breath came sharply.

"It used to be so," she admitted, unwillingly. "And I suppose they still offer sacrifices to their god of the sea—Poseidon. You know"— gently—"the Mayas of Central America did that too; only, being an inland people, they had to throw their sacrifice into an artificial pool. They had had their messenger, too, just as the Aztecs and the Iroquois had, from Atlantis."

"Atlantis!" But he realized that he wasn't really surprized.

"Atlantis, which was never completely destroyed, which still exists in the Sargasso Sea, a country so completely governed by science that its people can always avoid their enemies, so never have to fight them."

"So that tale Plato told of the Atlanteans attacking Athens is substantially true?"

"Of course. And if you want to live, you must believe as I believe, and seem to remember as I remember. For if you show doubt or ignorance, I am afraid you'll die."

And then, O'Farrell said, she talked to him a long time, carefully going over and elaborating all she had told him—all that he must, for safety's sake, be able to "remember". He had been through so much already, he said, that nothing had the power to astonish him any more. And in spite of the threat of danger in it, this unheard-of adventure began to appeal to his Irish soul. If he could ever get away and tell the world about it—

The girl's voice broke in upon his thoughts.

"You'd better dress now. I imagine our reception will be something gorgeous. Atlantis welcomes visitors from the outside world just once in a thousand years, you know."

He obeyed her, as he had got in the habit of doing. When he came out of the cabin again, he noticed for the first time long streamers of drifting seaweed. It grew thicker and thicker as they went along, swirling down the current ahead of them, behind them, beside them. But it did not interfere with them. The current took care of that.

And always the land ahead continued its changes before their eyes, resolved itself at last into a wide-horned crescent of flat white beaches and tall palaces and towers and fair, green, colorful gardens, against a background of softly folded, mist-enshrouded hills. The pure beauty of it made them gasp.

The boats were crowded closely together now. O'Farrell could see the occupants of several of them. And they were all very much alike—all tall, all fair, all yellow-haired and blue-eyed, like the girl Diana. And they, like her, were all tremendously excited. Well, O'Farrell was excited too, but not so enthusiastic as the rest.

And then, before O'Farrell's dazed, incredulous eyes, dozens of islets broke away from the tips of the crescent's horns, came swinging through the quiet sea toward the boats. Each of these tiny isles was perfect in itself, seemed to be the very embodiment of some artist's dream of an enchanted land. Many were flower gardens, ablaze with unbelievable color, alive with circling song-birds. One held a lonely palm tree, leaning a little in the southern wind, rooted in a long narrow beach where bits of white coral rolled in the swirling water. Another bore a shrine with a white altar, vine-wreathed and smoking with incense, before which a group of children decked in the goatskins and hoofs and horns of fauns were playing on flute-like pipes made of reeds.

"'Pipes o' Pan'", O'Farrell thought. "'Horns of elfland'—and all the rest of it. The thing's impossible. Thirst and the sun got me on that cursed raft and I'm delirious. Well, it's a pleasant enough way to die."

But even as he told himself that, he says he knew he lied. And,

"Remember the floating gardens of Mexico," the girl murmured, very low. "No doubt they were copied from these."

The boats were drawn into a line now, a line that curved in the middle, a crescent to match that other crescent of the shore. And the islets swept together in a circle about them, formed an atoll, leaving the boats in a still lagoon. The current which had brought them had spent itself, dissolved. Another force had swept the islets into place, was moving the boats toward the land. And, as a climax to all the rest, the mists which had hung above the hills swept downward and outward into a vast, circular curtain, completely blotting out all the world outside.

"Now, in the name of all the pagan gods at once!" muttered O'Farrell to the girl beside him. "Do these people know how to control the elements too?"

The girl Diana smiled serenely.

"Atlantis is very old and very wise," she told him quietly. "And its people have known neither war nor invasion nor famine nor pestilence for eleven thousand years. So, why shouldn't they have learned all that man can know in this world?"

The boats swept nearer and nearer toward the shore, with constantly diminishing speed. The sheer beauty and perfection of the scene, O'Farrell said, struck him dumb. The broad white beach, the steps and balconies of the tall white buildings, the terraces of the green hills—Plato's mounds, O'Farrell recognized—swarmed with tall, fair people. The men were garbed in tunics and kirtles, white in color, sandals and greaves of yellow leather, and great tall head dresses ornamented with yellow feathers set in a fanwise spread from left to right. The women were bareheaded except for jeweled fillets, and wore soft flowing robes of every imaginable tint. And in the foreground, extending all along the beach, was a chorus of young men and maidens, singing. The sound of their voices surpassed anything O'Farrell had ever heard.

But the girl Diana put out a hand and touched him on the arm. She was trembling violently, and when he turned to look at her, he saw that her face was as white as chalk.

"That song," she whispered in a shaking voice. "I can understand every word of it—and you, of course, nothing at all!"

"Not one word," he said.

"Then—then—" Her tormented eyes were pleading. "Oh, I never thought once about the language! I never dreamed that I'd understand it! I had never heard it in the world outside, so how could I know? But—don't you see?—you must be careful. You must say that the ancestor from whom you inherit left Atlantis in the earliest times. They were invaded from the mainland once—the language must have altered—"

O'Farrell shook his head slowly. He felt, he said, as the "hero" of an old Greek tragedy must have felt—like one caught in a net and dragged, compellingly, inexorably, toward some unknown and unwelcome end. His had been a passive part from the beginning.

He was utterly helpless, and knew it. He had no idea what might be coming, but whatever it was he must take it with as much fortitude as he was able.

"What is the use of lying?" he whispered back. "I'll never be able to get by with it. They'd better know in the beginning—"

"No, no, no!" She was tugging at his arm with both hands now. "Promise me you'll do as I tell you. Promise me!"

"All right," he assented, "but I'm afraid it won't help much. I know so little—Plato's writings—what I can remember of them—and what you've told me. They'll soon know I'm a fraud—"

"No!" she cried in a vehement whisper. "No! They shan't!"

The boats touched land. O'Farrell and the girl got ashore somehow. The lemmings scampered after them, were snatched up and petted by a hundred hands. And then the chorus of voices and of strings rose to an exultant, triumphant pæan of joy and praise. The crowd pressed close. The whole scene became utterly unreal and dream-like. A perfect babble of incomprehensible words assailed O'Farrell's ears. He could not have made himself heard if he had wanted to. A group of old men, dressed in long yellow robes embroidered with curious, mystical designs, and miter-like head-dresses of gold, appeared suddenly in front of him. They were, he surmised, priests of the Atlantean religion. The foremost, doubtless the high priest, waved a veritable caduceus over O'Farrell's and the girl's heads in a gesture of consecration. Then they passed on, were hidden by the crowd.

With a little cry the girl Diana broke away and ran toward one of the newcomers, who was looking at her with a wild, delighted incredulity. It was a man who wore the uniform of a colonel of English infantry, with a string of ribbons across his breast. He looked to be nearing fifty, lean and tall and weary. He walked with a limp. His left arm was stiff. And a long scar, as if from a bayonet cut, ran down his left cheek. The girl had gone straight into his arms.

The throng divided. Great swaying elephants, caparisoned in yellow silk, and bearing howdahs of white ivory, made a lane for the newcomers. An elderly man wearing priestly garments emerged from the crowd and pressed a sort of diadem set with flashing stones down upon O'Farrell's head. Metal pads fitted firmly behind O'Farrell's ears, and on the instant, though the words of the singers, the babble around him still sounded outlandish and strange, it all became intelligible to him.

"I am Otar," the old man said, smiling at O'Farrell's look of incredulity, "of the healing branch of the priesthood. And this instrument is a mechanical interpreter of tongues. We find it useful in helping newcomers to adjust themselves for the first few days. So today we are all wearing them in one shape or another." For a moment he studied O'Farrell through his shrewd, keen eyes. "And who was your honored Atlantean ancestor, my son? Do not hesitate to use your native tongue. Whatever you say, I shall be able to understand." And he touched his head-dress significantly.

O'Farrell braced himself. It was, he realized, now or never.

"My ancestor left Atlantis very young," he improvised with the facility of desperation. "Atlantis had been invaded, and he remembered little of it but the misery and oppression his people suffered at the hands of their conquerors. He had dreams of human sacrifice and games that ran with blood. He went as armor-bearer with an expedition to the mainland to make war upon a city afterward known as Athens. He was captured by these early Athenians and so never returned to Atlantis."

"Ah, that is extremely interesting!" exclaimed Otar, his blue eyes bright with interest. "And what was that armor-bearer's name?"

"His name was Gadir." O'Farrell pronounced firmly the only Atlantean name which Plato knew. After all, it was something to claim descent from the man for whom the Pillars of Herakles—the Rock of Gibraltar—had been named!

"Then you shall be called Gadir among us—Gadir, the bringer of the sacred lemmings. Your old name," with a slight gesture of his hand as if flicking from him a grain of dust, "your old name will be forgotten. Let me have your left wrist, if you please."

O'Farrell obeyed. How could he do otherwise? But he watched with some trepidation while the priest-physician drew what looked like a capsule of glass from a pocket and held it against O'Farrell's wrist. He felt but the slightest prickle. Then the old priest pocketed the glass again.

"A matter of precaution," he explained. "The outside world is, we know, a place of hideous suffering and disease. But now—you will not believe me, since your ancestor left us before our great discoveries were made—but now you will never know a moment's illness again."

And before O'Farrell had time to thank him he had bowed ceremoniously and vanished in the crowd.

Others, many others, came up and spoke to O'Farrell now, briefly or at length, making him welcome, praising him for the bringers of good fortune—the lemmings—which he had brought, asking him eager questions of the outside world, of which they had had no news for a thousand years. But now a procession was forming. O'Farrell was led to a kneeling elephant, helped into the gorgeous howdah. The girl Diana and the English colonel followed. The elephant lurched to its feet and they were off.

Before them paced at least two score of elephants. As many more were behind them. Only the newcomers and the body of priests rode. The rest of the people danced. Danced, literally, to an almost delirious music, in what seemed to be a complete abandon of joy. Escorted by the whirling figures, they turned into a wide, white-paved avenue. Towering buildings stood on either side, flush with the pavement. But there were no people at the windows or on the balconies. Everyone, plainly, was in the street.

The girl Diana leaned forward from her seat between O'Farrell and the Englishman. Her eyes were rapt, ecstatic.

"It's like the rarest sorcery," she sighed. "If one hadn't been prepared for it so long, it would be unbelievable."

"A land so self-contained," the Englishman mused, "that it has no need of the rest of the world; so versed in the arts of concealment that it need not fear the world; so wise, so happy that it does not envy the world—yes, it is, as you say, unbelievable."

The girl looked shyly at O'Farrell.

"Colonel Carter's ancestor who bequeathed him his memories was the father of the ancestor who gave me mine," she said simply. "We knew each other instantly."

"And," interposed the Englishman, before O'Farrell could speak, "since she can not remember her father, and since my daughter—an only child—was killed in an air raid over London nineteen years ago, we have agreed to be as father and daughter. It is very good of her," he added, gently.

"It's more than I can quite take in," O'Farrell ventured dazedly. His eyes were on that beautiful, gracious street, on the lumbering elephants ahead, on the beautiful, rejoicing people who whirled and danced. His ears were hypnotized by a music of voices, of pipes, of strings, of horns, such as surely the world outside had never known. "There's something in the air that—lifts you up," he added.

The Englishman laughed gently.

"Not in the air, my lad, but in that ichor in your blood-stream," he amended. "Crock that I am, it has made me feel different too. No more pain—no more disease. No death till the heart simply wears out and stops its work—or is stopped by violence. Ah, but one must wish he could tell the world about it."

"The world wouldn't believe," the girl Diana said. "Or if it did, it would want to rob us of our secrets and then, most likely, destroy us."

The Englishman sighed.

"You are probably right, my dear." He turned to O'Farrell again. "You and my new daughter are the only Americans here. I am the only Englishman. There are two Irishmen, a Welshman, and a Scandinavian. The rest, as one might expect, are from the rim of the Mediterranean—from Egypt, Spain, France, Crete, Greece, Italy, Asia Minor—where Atlanteans settled long ago. There were eleven Greeks who came together on that yacht. But then, the old Greeks were certainly direct descendants."

Again his keen blue eyes rested in what seemed a trace of puzzlement on O'Farrell's face.

"And you brought the lemmings. That was a fine thing, certainly."

"More an accident than anything else," O'Farrell told him. "I stumbled on them, on the way. It was Diana who fed and cared for them. Thank her, not me."

A faint pucker grew between the Englishman's fine brows. The girl gave O'Farrell a warning look.

"He was washed off his own—craft," she hastened to explain. "I was lucky enough to be able to pick them up. We came on together, you know."

"Yes, I know. Poor little beasts," returning to the lemmings. "To think of remembering for more than eleven thousand years! Tiny, tiny brains to nourish faith so long. Because their ancestors made annual migrations, like the wild geese and the ducks and the ill-fated passenger pigeons, they still try it 'once in a hundred years.' If only they knew that it is only once in a thousand!"

"It puts our own faith to shame," the girl said.

"And yet inherited memories are probably more common than we think. Ours are entire. But consider the broken ones. And there are so many! One man may be lucky enough to be born with the genius of a great poet of centuries ago, and 'gain much fame thereby'. Another gets enough to put him in a madhouse—dreaming that he is King Solomon or Napoleon Bonaparte. Oh, I speak feelingly on the subject! I raved of my Atlantean memories so much in that French hospital back in 1918 that they thought I was mad. If I had not been lucky in my connections, and known to be greatly interested in ancient civilizations, I should be in a straitjacket now, I dare say. As for those other poor chaps—" He made a quick gesture with his uninjured hand. "Well, we are lucky. Let us be thankful."

He fell into a brooding silence. O'Farrell had no wish to break it. Nor did he dare to ask where they were going. Doubtless he was expected to know.

They paced slowly down the street. A great arch presently confronted them. The elephants passed through into a narrow, shadowy enclosure, began the descent of an ever winding, ever darkening road. It must lead to a temple, O'Farrell surmised. All the old races had worshipped in caves, he knew, as witness the Cretan labyrinth. He hoped, with an inward shudder, that there would be no sacrifices.

They went a long way. Where the light came from he could not tell, but though they must have penetrated deeply into the earth, the darkness never became complete. Always they could see the elephant ahead of them, the howdah swaying, ghost-like, on its back, till suddenly it knelt, then lurched to its feet again, then disappeared.

Their own elephant knelt. Shadowy forms helped them to alight, lowered voices bade them follow. So they climbed a high stairway of broad, shallow steps, fairly well lighted though they could not tell from what source, to a narrow doorway. Still following their conductors, they went through.

They came out into an enormous balcony, set with tables and benches. Other balconies were above this, still others beneath, sweeping in immense circles above the huge arena below.

The central feature of this arena was a high altar smoking with incense. Its white marble sides were painted with beautifully executed designs—the swastika; the Cretan double ax; Atlas with the sky on his shoulders; a winged horse, soaring; Medusa's head; the lemmings; Poseidon riding a storm at sea; the bucranium—the head of the sacrificial bull—with fillets; the minotaur.

Above it all arched a dome of the color of a summer sky at midnight. The sweeping zodiac with its twelve signs, the twelve planets which the Atlanteans, and—later—the Aztecs had known, blazed in this artificial heaven, giving light.

The girl Diana touched his arm, drew his attention from the unparalleled grandeur of that gorgeous ceiling to his more immediate surroundings. He followed her and the Englishman to one of the tables and sat down. He saw that the balcony was filled, though not over-crowded. Filled too were such portions of the other balconies as he could see. All about him was a hushed murmur of conversation.

Boys and girls came in presently, bearing trays of food and wine which they placed upon the tables. These young people, O'Farrell decided, were neither slaves nor servants. They had all the air of hosts looking after the comfort of honored guests. Indeed, he realized suddenly that he had not yet seen anyone who seemed to be a servitor, nor any officials other than the priests. And he found the food, the drinks, though utterly unfamiliar to him, to be extraordinarily good.

Into the arena below filed the chorus which had welcomed them on the beach. Their musicians were with them—with harps of various shapes, though none too large to carry, pipes, small horns, odd-shaped lutes, a drum. A vast wave of melody rolled up to the silent people.

Dancers swept in, a medley, unearthly, beautiful yet somehow terrible, an awful unmasking of the ancient pageantry of the new-made earth. Goat-shepherd Pan with his fauns and satyrs, who hunted animals and dressed like them. A god-like, golden Prometheus, who brought down a flaming torch from the sky. The first horse-tamers, the centaurs. Nymphs and dryads decked with leaves, and with flowers in their hair. Warriors in helmets and armor. At last, the thinkers, priests of Atlantis in their yellow robes.

In turn they wove an intricate pattern of a myriad figures, fantastic yet weirdly beautiful. And suddenly O'Farrell began to understand. The music, the chanting, the dance, were all parts of a single symbolism. The age-old history of Atlantis was being enacted before him.

There was shown the slow, measured development of a primitive people, the constant outflow of the more restless to neighboring lands of the north, south, east and west; recurring earthquakes and human as well as animal sacrifices to placate the gods; invasion by an alien people and exile of many of the original race; finally the great ocean wave which broke up and almost destroyed the kingdom.

O'Farrell had sat spellbound. He had forgotten himself, his predicament, his danger. It was as if the panorama of thirty thousand years had been unrolled before him.

But now the scene changed. Dancers, chorus and music-makers drew aside, became a background for the procession which now entered the arena. These were the older priests in their lavishly embroidered, yellow robes and mitered head-gear, bearing scepter-like wands of gold; the high priest, who had exchanged his caduceus for a golden double-ax; half-naked youths, each of whom led in a filleted, snow-white bull; young girls in long, white robes and chaplets of white flowers.

"The sacrifice!" O'Farrell exclaimed under his breath, and felt the blood curdle around his heart.

"Oh, no," the Englishman whispered. "Watch!"

And the girl Diana gave him another look of warning and entreaty.

And then O'Farrell saw enacted, down there in that huge arena, a thing quite new and modern and yet as old as the oldest ritual of the ancient cult of the bull. One by one the beautiful long-horned bulls were released. One by one the young men leaped at them, seized their polished horns, and, in spite of the bulls' frantic struggles, pinned them to the earth. Each bull received a mock blow from the golden double-ax in the high priest's hand, was led away.

Then the young priestesses marched in a demure procession around the altar, and threw incense by handfuls upon the smoking fire, chanting their vows meanwhile to serve Atlantis' altar-fires for a year-long term of chastity and prayer.

O'Farrell drew a deep breath of relief. No bloodshed there! But the original ceremony from which this one was directly descended—ah, that, certainly, had literally run with blood!

The high priest raised his hand.

"Children of the sun and of Atlantis," he cried. "You know why we are gathered here. You know that when the gods were wroth with us, when the earth split and the waters rose and the heavens poured fire upon us, even then the more merciful of our gods raised up leaders among us to save the remnants of our people and our land. They—these merciful ones—taught us how to set our broken isles adrift, how to bring them together, how to separate them again. They taught us how to control the mists of the air and the currents of the sea, how to remain for ever invisible to our enemies. And last, because they knew that every race must have new blood in order to survive, they taught us how to summon our own from the outside world—once in a thousand years!"

A very old man, that high priest. He took a step forward now, and lifted his arms high.

"We welcome you as our own, those of you who have come today from the far-flung parts of the earth. Ours is a happy land where every man works, and every man plays, and every man rests, eats, sleeps according to his need, and every woman the same. Forget, then, violence, injustice, ugliness, the cold of frost, the burning heat of the sun. There are none of those things here.

"And you know, too, you who are descended from Atlas and Poseidon's, that the little ones, the lemmings, they who once gnawed loose the bonds of Poseidon's sea horses and set them free, made pilgrimages to our old land each year in the long ago. But when Poseidon in his anger at our disobedience and iniquities had overwhelmed the land which stood between, they could no longer reach us. Yet they tried, at certain times, and were swallowed up and lost."

His voice, which had sunk to a mournful cadence, suddenly ceased. He spread his hands. And, as if by magic, out from behind the smoking altar scampered the lemmings, chattering, running this way and that.

Applause burst from the people, wild, deafening, and lasting long. But at last the high priest raised his hand, and silence fell. His voice came again, triumphant now.

"These did not die! The mighty Poseidon sent them to us, a sign of his favor, of his forgiveness, of his promise to preserve us—for another thousand years! And he chose as his instruments a youth and a maiden who came together. Let them, therefore, descend and stand before me, that all Atlantis may behold and honor those whom our father Poseidon has pointed out as his most favored children."

Dazed and thunderstruck, O'Farrell felt the girl Diana's hand take his. It was as cold as ice. But she did not speak. Together they threaded their way among the tables, down the stair, along a shadowy passage, through a door. At last they were in the center of the arena, a hand of the high priest rested on each head.

"All Atlantis thanks you," the old man finished simply.

"Ah, it was nothing to be thanked for," Diana said, a catch in her voice. "It was a duty, an obligation, and a pleasure beyond all telling. We *loved* to do it."

"And," O'Farrell added, feeling it incumbent upon him to say something and not knowing what to say, "we hope, now that they are here, that they will grow in numbers year by year, so you will never be without them again."

And then it seemed to him that the atmosphere was charged with something dreadful, as if the sky had cracked, or the earth opened, or the sea forsook its bed. Silence. Like the dead weight of a nightmare, like the awful certainty of death.

At last the high priest's voice came in a strangled whisper—a whisper that yet seemed to reverberate to the remotest corner under that blazing dome.

"*Who are you?*" he demanded. "How did you come here if you do not know—is it indeed possible you do not remember?—that the lemmings, like the wild geese and the salmon and so many other creatures, must go north in the spring to breed?"

And then O'Farrell knew that he was done.

"Deceit, imposture, falsehood," came the inexorable voice of the high priest. These things have always borne the brand of treason, and treason is punishable by death." His voice rose to a lamentable cry. "I am accursed, that the duty has devolved upon me to condemn a man to death!"

"No!" the girl cried in a desperate voice. "No! He had no intention to deceive. It was I who made him do that. I did not know—my memories were too old to tell me—that now you worship only the more merciful of the Atlantean gods. My ancestor went with Quetzalcoatl to America. And at that time Atlantean worship was a cruel and bloody thing!"

"How did he come?"

"By accident only. The current caught him—him and the lemmings. He could not help but come. And he shall not die! I appeal to the people!" Her voice rose to a scream. "He shall not die!"

"He shall not die!" It was the Englishman. He was standing, his right arm thrown upward, palm out, in the universal gesture of friendship, peace.

And "He shall not die!" came in shouts from this section and that as the newcomers leaped to their feet. O'Farrell could distinguish them by their dress, but not for long. For in a moment they were hidden by the up-surging multitude.

"He shall not die!" shouted Atlantis with one voice. "He brought us the lemmings! He shall not die!"

"The lemmings, and good fortune with them for a thousand years," the girl Diana cried. "The people have spoken. He shall go in peace."

"The people have spoken," assented the high priest. "There shall be no blood on my hands tonight. Shall he remain or shall he depart? It is for him to choose."

But O'Farrell stood still, too overwhelmed with bewilderment and uncertainty to speak. The shocks had been too many and too close together. He was at that moment incapable of choice.

The girl looked at him, long and hard. A queer little smile rested on her lips for a moment. She made a slight, despairing movement with her hands. At last she spoke.

"He would never be happy with us. Let him go."

They put him in her boat, O'Farrell said. It was night then, but the sky was clear and the moon and the stars hung low. They brought him food and presents of all sorts, and said many kind things to him. They didn't want him to go. That was plain. But he was still too numbed to combat the girl's decision—she had guided him so long. He let her guide him now. So—he went.

For a little while he could see the land behind him. But presently it seemed to break up, to be floating in fragments of beauty on the bosom of the sea, at last to be no more than a mist, a mirage, a dream of faery...

"But," I demanded then, incredulously, "why didn't you come home? You were gone three years or more. And this adventure, you say, took up hardly more than a week!"

"And at that I was luckier than the Portuguese who spent one night there and took a hundred years to get back home," O'Farrell answered, with a strange smile. "But my further adventures were commonplace enough. The Atlanteans had done all they could for me, but they couldn't give me gasoline. So when the stock in the boat gave out, which was soon, I drifted. A tramp picked me up, a privately owned trading-vessel with no wireless. She was bound for the South Pacific, and I had to go, willy-nilly—around the Horn—stopping to trade first one place and another—till we came to the very jumping-off place of the world, it seemed to me. And that was a plague-stricken place—typhus, the mate said it was. He and two sailors and I were left there. We were on shore when the captain found out about the epidemic, and he simply lifted anchor and left us—in a blue funk, I suppose.

"But it's plain he spread the news of the sickness, for there wasn't a boat that came near us for—well, something like two years, I imagine. You lose track of time out there—and," wearily, "you have lots of time to think."

"Well?" I said, for I knew there must be something more.

"Oh, I came home. But I had proof while I was there that I hadn't dreamed about—Atlantis. It was true. For that shot in the arm the priest gave me did what he said it would. At least two-thirds of the natives died of that plague. The mate and the two sailors died—horribly. But I stayed right with them and did all I could for them and wasn't sick a day. That's proof, I think. And it's quite likely that I'll live to be a hundred or more—just as that Portuguese did—whether I want to or not."

"And now you wish you had stayed when you had the chance, or that you could go back?"

I don't know why, but I was quite certain of his answer before he spoke.

"Oh, yes." He sat still a long time, twisting his pipe between his fingers. "I want to go back. But I can't. That current won't flow again for another thousand years. I was a fool, a poor, blind fool. It's hell, you know, just plain hell—" His head drooped forward a little, hopelessly. "It's hell to love a woman—and not have sense enough to find it out—till after you have lost her—forever."

And after a while he repeated in a voice of indescribable weariness and bitterness:

"Perhaps, long since, there was a land beyond,
Westward from death, some city, some calm place,
Where one could taste God's quiet and be fond
With the little beauty of a human face;

"But now the land is drowned, yet still we press
Westward, in search, to death, to nothingness."

CHILD OF ATLANTIS

Edmond Hamilton

Edmond Hamilton (1904–1977) was an American author born in Youngstown, Ohio. A prodigious intellect, he enrolled in college at the age of fourteen, intending to train as an electrical engineer. Yet, the difference in age between himself and his peers, alongside a general distaste for academic life, led to him dropping out after three years. Hamilton's first story, "The Monster-God of Mamurth", was published in the August 1926 issue of *Weird Tales*. Continuing at pace, he would become renowned for his contributions to science fiction. Stories such as "Crashing Suns" (1928) helped to establish the style of "Space Opera", while the consistently cosmic scale of his threats—evidenced perfectly by his 1930 tale, "The Universe Wreckers"—earned him the nickname of "World Wrecker". In 1946, Hamilton married fellow science fiction writer, and "Queen of Space Opera", Leigh Brackett. Together, they would pen one formal collaboration: "Stark and the Star Kings".

"Child of Atlantis" is but one of Hamilton's Atlantean tales, alongside "The Avenger from Atlantis" (1935) and "The City from the Sea" (1940). First published in the December 1937 issue of *Weird Tales*, Hamilton's story charts a similar tale of "Atlantis Resurrected", where the sunken civilization is no longer confined to its undersea origins. Shipwrecked, David and Christa Russell awake on a strange island inhabited by other stranded souls. As they strain to survive, a black castle on the cliffs, home to "The Master", summons the residents one at a time, never to return. Foreshadowing the extreme imagination of the concluding works, "Child of Atlantis" steers the anthology into increasingly generic territory. Compared to the ancient architecture of earlier tales, here, the technological advances of Atlantis far exceed those of the supposedly modern present.

The little yawl clove the blue waters of the sunlit sea, its white sails taut with a strong wind. Steadily it crept eastward across the vast wastes of the Atlantic, toward the Azores, still hundreds of miles away. In the cockpit at the stern, David Russell stood over the wheel, his lean, brown, bareheaded figure bent forward, his smiling gray eyes watching his wife.

Christa Russell was earnestly coiling ropes on the deck forward. Now she finished and came back toward him, a slim, boyish little figure in white slacks and blue jersey. Her soft, dark eyes, always oddly serious beneath her childish forehead and smoothly brushed black hair, met her husband's and returned his smile.

"Happy, kid?" he asked, his arm going around her slender waist as she jumped down into the cockpit to his side.

She nodded, her uplifted eyes adoring. "It's the best honeymoon anyone ever had, David. Just you and me and the sea."

He grinned. "I felt a little guilty about dragging you on a risky cruise like this, but you've been the best sailing partner I ever had. And the only one who could really cook."

He added, "Speaking of cooking, suppose you get down in that galley and exercise your talents, gal. I'm hungry."

Christa said dismayedly, "Oh, I'd forgotten all about lunch. I'll only be a few minutes."

She disappeared hurriedly down the companionway. Left alone, David Russell drew a long breath of utter contentment. His gray eyes swept the horizon happily. Sunlight and sea, a good boat and a good wind, and his young wife—what more could any man want?

They had been married in Bermuda two weeks before. And David had proposed this cruise to the Azores in his yawl as a honeymoon. Fine weather and favoring winds had made it a dream voyage of sun-drenched days and moon-silvered nights.

David suddenly stiffened at the wheel. He had glimpsed something just ahead that was—queer. It was a strange, great flicker in the air, a wavering of light like the refraction of air above hot railway tracks. The whole area just ahead of the onward-racing yawl seemed flickering oddly like that.

He felt a sudden tinge of dim fear, of alarm. He moved his hand on the wheel to guide the yawl away from that weirdly flickering area. But before he could do so, the speeding boat had run directly into the edge of the queer area. The next moment—

A big island loomed dead ahead in the sea!

It was like hell-born magic to David's stunned brain. One moment he was sailing with no speck of land in sight in the vast blue waste. Next moment, without warning, this island had suddenly clicked into sight, not a hundred yards ahead of the yawl.

David's stupefied eyes glimpsed the isle as a heavily forested mass of land, several miles across, towering to frowning black cliffs at its center. The shores were fringed with cruel, jagged rocks that showed like broken black fangs through the foam of wild waves breaking over them.

The yawl was running headlong onto these rocks, without chance of being turned in time. David, his face a gray mask of stupefied horror, dropped the wheel and yelled hoarsely.

"Christa! Quick!"

She came darting up the companionway, face white with alarm. "David, what—"

He grabbed her. At that instant, with terrific, grinding shock, the yawl struck the rocks.

They were thrown clear of its wildly tilting deck by the impact. And almost instantly they were sinking in the roaring waters, David still blindly gripping his wife.

Thunder of the rushing waves was in his ears as they went down and down in the cold currents. He shifted his grip on Christa, and fought frantically with his other arm to rise. He came up, half strangled, to be nearly smothered by white foam and deafened by the roaring bellow of breaking waves.

They were flung like chips toward the jagged shore rocks. David struck out with his free arm in mad strokes to keep them away from the cruel stone fangs upon which the waves would hammer them to pulp. His left arm still gripped Christa with frantic strength as they were hurled forward.

His right shoulder grazed hidden rock, his shirt ripping and a brand of fire seeming to sear along his arm. As he was whirled around by the wild waves that were tossing them, he glimpsed the yawl, piled on the outer rocks, being hammered by the smashing waves.

The waves were hurling them on toward those menacing black teeth with the swiftness of a mill-race. A flat, jagged ledge rose a few feet from the foaming waters just ahead. The charging waves flung them hard against it.

David took the impact on his right shoulder, and felt the flesh bruise from the savage blow. With his numbed right arm he clawed wildly to cling to the edge of the ledge, a foot above his head. His fingertips gained the rim, then were torn loose as the receding waves sucked the two helpless humans back.

Back and back—and then again they bore them forward, like

raging stallions of the sea, toward the ledge of rock. David felt his strength leaving him, knew desperately that he could not hold Christa longer, that if the waves swept them back out again, they would sink together.

The rushing waters again flung them like floating puppets against the rock. David's head hit the wall and he saw blinding light, felt the last remnants of strength melting from the stunning blow. Yet knowledge of death close at hand made him claw frenziedly for the ledge.

His fingers again gripped its brink—but his nerveless body had not the strength to haul them up onto it. Through the bellowing din, icy death seemed stooping to enfold them in his cold shroud. Then before the waters sucked back, a wave higher than the others lifted David and the girl a little. With a supreme effort, he used that moment to roll with her onto the ledge.

He lay there, hearing only dimly the raging of the baffled seas just below him, the splatter of salty spray on his face. He was aware that Christa was bending frantically over him, as his consciousness darkened.

"David! David *dear*!" Her sobbing voice came thinly and remotely to his fading hearing. "David, we're safe now. I'll get help—get someone—"

And then there was only darkness in David Russell's brain.

It was the steady showering of the stinging spray on his face that finally revived his overtaxed body and brain. He opened his eyes, and weakly struggled up to a sitting position.

He was still on the ledge at the island's shore. The incoming combers were still smashing a few inches below him, flinging up great geysers of feathery foam, and a hundred yards outward the yawl lay grinding on the outer rocks where it had been tossed.

Where was Christa? She was nowhere in sight along the rocky, wave-dashed shore. David's clearing brain remembered now her frantic attempts to revive him. She had gone to look for help, and she was not back yet. How long had she been gone? Had something happened to her on this hellish island that had appeared so magically in the mid-Atlantic? Cold fear for his bride clutched at David's heart, and forced him to stagger weakly to his feet. Wildly he looked along the shore of the island.

From the sea-beaten, jagged rocks, a narrow strip of beach lifted toward the edge of the dark, great forest that seemed to cover most of the island. He saw tracks in the sand, leading toward the forest. Christa must have gone that way. He stumbled after her, spurred by apprehension. This island, a mysterious place that should not be— what danger might not Christa meet on it?

As he toiled up the slight grade of the beach, David's mind was still dazed by the suddenness with which the whole incredible thing had happened. This island had been utterly invisible to his eyes until the yawl had almost run onto it, had reached the edge of that strange flickering area. *Then* the island had clicked suddenly into sight.

He turned his head and looked wildly back out to sea, as he hastened on. David received another shock. He could not see more than a few hundred feet out from the island! He could look that far out over the rocks and waters, but beyond that limit he could see nothing but a weird flickering. His vision seemed to be repelled at that limit, to be turned back upon itself.

He looked upward. The sky had changed too. It was a strange, flickering sky of very dark blue, and the sun could not be seen in it. This nightmare island! It could not be seen by anyone outside it—and neither could anyone on the island see outside.

It was all crazy, incredible. But his dazed mind clung frantically to the thought of finding Christa. David reached the edge of the forest, and stood staring haggardly into its dark depths.

Huge, black-trunked trees rose for hundreds of feet, mighty columns supporting a canopy of green foliage high overhead. Thickets of brush and snaky creepers that bore enormous white blooms, choked the space between the trees. This forest loomed strangely silent in the weird, sunless day. And he saw beyond the waving tree-tops the towering central cliffs he had already glimpsed from the yawl. On those distant, frowning bluffs of dark rock crouched a monstrous square black castle.

David stared and stared over the great trees at that somber structure of mystery on the distant heights, his gaze fascinated by its black domes and towers and unbroken, windowless walls. Then he tore his eyes from it and peered frantically along the forest edge for some trace of his wife.

"*Woher kommst du?*" The voice came from close behind him, with startling unexpectedness.

David spun around. Two men had come up behind him on the beach without his observing them. They were staring at him suspiciously.

The man who had asked the question in German was a solidly built, sandy-haired man of forty, with searching eyes. He was clad in a time-worn, ragged and stained gray uniform.

The other man was a huge, broad-shouldered Scandinavian in sweater and sea-boots almost as ragged, his weather-beaten Viking face a little older than that of the German, his blond head bare. Both men carried steel-pointed spears.

David Russell said, with difficulty, "I—I don't understand you." Then he cried, "In God's name, what kind of place is this?"

The German's suspicious face cleared and he exclaimed in English, "You're new here, then? Did your ship run onto the island? Were any others saved?"

To his excited questions, David answered, "We were in a yawl—my wife and I. This hellish island suddenly appeared right in front of us. Our boat struck—there it is out on the rocks. We got to shore, but I passed out, and when I came around, Christa was gone for help. And now I can't find her. I've got to find her!" he cried. "To get her away from this devilish place!"

The German shook his head sadly. "There is no escape from this island—none except death or whatever horrible fate the Master deals out to those whom he calls to his castle. I myself have been here on the island for twenty years."

"Twenty years?" cried David, appalled.

The Teuton nodded. "I am Leutnant Wilhelm von Hausman, of U-Boat 321 of the Imperial German Navy. In the spring of 1918 our boat, running on the surface to recharge our batteries, sighted a strange flickering just ahead. The next moment, this island appeared, we crashed into it, and I, who was on deck, was the only one saved."

He motioned toward the giant blond Scandinavian seaman. "This is Halfdon Husper, first mate of a Norwegian freighter that ran onto the island in 1929. There are a couple of hundred such survivors from similar wrecks—we have a little village over yonder in the forest."

David cried, "But why haven't you tried to get away? And what kind of hellish place is this island, anyway, that it's completely invisible until you're right on it?"

Von Hausman shrugged. "I know no more than you how the island is made invisible to the outside world. The Master has made it so, but how he does it, I can't guess."

"The Master?" repeated David. "Who is that?"

Von Hausman pointed to the black castle brooding on the distant cliffs. "That is the castle of the Master. He is supreme ruler of this island, but who or what he is, I cannot say, for none of us who live here have ever seen him."

"You mean—he never comes out of that place?" David asked wonderingly. "But then how do you know he exists?"

The German shuddered a little. "We know well he exists, because from time to time he calls one among us to the castle, and whoever goes into that black place never comes out again."

The torturing anxiety uppermost in David's mind burst forth. "But what about my wife? I must find her—at once."

The big Norwegian, Halfdon Husper, spoke for the first time in rumbling, heavily accented English. He said to the German, "Some other of the men may have found the girl and taken her to the village."

Von Hausman nodded rapidly, his keen eyes narrowing. He told David, "It's possible some of the others took your wife to the village, as Halfdon says. I think you'd better come with us, at once."

Half mad with torturing worry, David Russell started with the two ragged men at a trot through the forest. There was a faintly marked trail which the others appeared to know, that wound inward between the great trees and around huge fallen logs.

Even in the tense stress of his anxiety, he could not help noticing that the trees and vegetation around him were totally unfamiliar. He had never seen such trees, such huge flowers, such grotesque orange-podded fruits. It all seemed like a strange dream into which he had suddenly been plunged.

Von Hausman was telling him, "The village is not far ahead. It's a miserable little place, where we eke out life by gathering fruits and hunting the small animals, until the time comes when we die or the Master calls us."

He added somberly, "Almost I wish sometimes that the Master would call me and put an end to this wretched existence from which there is no escape."

They emerged soon into a shallow, unwooded valley at the center of the island. At the farther side of the valley rose the black, frowning cliffs, upon whose highest point squatted the brooding ebon castle.

David saw that in the valley lay a rude village of two or three score huts, built of logs and bark. The little village seemed to huddle there like a thing crouching in fear, beneath the black battlements of the cliffs and the Master's mysterious castle.

At the center of the village milled an excited crowd of men. The din of their shouting voices reached David and his two companions as they hurried forward. The lips of the German U-Boat officer tightened.

"It's as I feared—they've got your wife here," he rasped. "You're probably going to have to fight."

"Fight?" cried David.

Von Hausman nodded tightly. "Very few women ever get ashore alive on the island from the wrecks—only at long intervals. And the women go to those who can fight for them and keep them. Quick!"

They raced forward, between the rows of rude huts. Now David saw that there were perhaps two hundred men in the throng milling in shouting excitement ahead. He could see only a dozen or so women—ragged, frightened women—peering out of huts here and there.

But the mob of men! A ragged, hard-bitten throng that had been cast ashore here by the ships of every nation that had wrecked on this mysterious island. Red-faced British sailors, brown, snake-eyed Lascars, stalwart Scandinavians like Husper, swarthy Spanish and Italian and Portuguese seamen, bearded Russians and guttural-voiced

Teutons, a score of other races, all milling excitedly around one central point.

David Russell and his two companions crashed through the shouting throng, David unnoticed by the ragged mob in its excitement. He burst into a small clear space at the center of the crowd. There he stopped, and shouted aloud.

"Christa!"

She was there, a slim, shrinking, boyish figure in her wet slacks and sweater. A stocky, simian, red-headed man of thirty with hard blue eyes and a button-nosed, craggy face, was holding her struggling form with one arm. He was shaking his other fist at the crowd and roaring belligerently, "I say this girl is mine! I found her there in the forest and if anyone else wants her, he can fight me for her, here and now."

A sudden silence descended on the mob at the redhead's roaring challenge. Von Hausman muttered in David's ear, "It's Red O'Riley—a gun-runner whose schooner ran ashore here ten years ago. He's the toughest customer on the island."

But David wasn't listening. Flaming with rage, he had burst from the crowd and, with a savage twist, tore O'Riley's arm away from Christa and sent the redhead sprawling.

He gritted, "Damn you, this girl isn't for you or anyone else here. She's my wife."

Christa clung to his arm, sobbing with relief. "David, I was afraid you were dead! I went to try to find help and was caught—"

O'Riley had got to his feet, in a dead silence of stunned amazement on the part of the crowd. The gun-runner's craggy face split in a wide, menacing grin at David.

"So she's your wife, is she?" the red-headed man mocked harshly. "That's a good one! She may have been your wife by law outside, but there's devil a law on this cursed island except what the strongest man makes. I'm going to tear you apart and then take her."

The stocky gun-runner was savagely peeling off his ragged coat and shirt as he spoke, and stood now with gorilla-like, hairy chest bare, his great fists balled, advancing slowly on David.

David thrust the white-faced Christa back to von Hausman and Husper, at the edge of the crowd. The ragged mob was shouting now with increased excitement.

"Kill him, Red—tear the young squirt apart!" exultant voices bawled.

Von Hausman told David swiftly, "Try to finish him before he gets to you, or you won't have a chance."

David stepped out to meet the grimly advancing O'Riley. As he looked at the redhead's huge shoulders, barrel chest and simian arms, David's heart sank within him. He was still half exhausted from the battle through the waves an hour before, and he knew that even in the best of condition he would be no match for O'Riley. Yet if he were killed, Christa's possible fate in this weird, brutal place—the thought filled him with a wild, desperate frenzy.

He suddenly rushed, his left fist driving out with every ounce of his strength. It smashed against O'Riley's craggy jaw, and the Irishman rocked for a moment. David leaped in and smashed with right and left at the redhead's face with everything he had, and his enemy clawed for balance.

A wild howl went up from the mob, but David's heart was cold with knowledge that he had hit O'Riley with everything he had—and had failed to knock him down. With a bear-like snarl of rage, shaking his head as though to clear his eyes, the redhead rushed forward. David tried to sidestep but his foot slipped on the loose gravel. Then something hit him a terrific blow on the mouth, and everything was in a red mist, and he was dimly aware that his back was lying on the damp ground and that something hot and sticky was running on his lips. And O'Riley was standing there, snarling down at him.

"Get up! Get up before I beat you to death lying there."

"David!" That heartbroken sob was in Christa's voice. He recognized it through the mistiness that had seized his brain.

He staggered to his feet, lunged forward with fists balled. *Crash!* The crunching blows seemed to explode out of nothing against his face, and he knew he had gone to his knees this time. His brain was rocking—he felt he was done for. There wasn't an ounce of strength left in his nerveless body.

"David!" That agonized cry again pierced his numbness of mind and body, making him somehow struggle up again.

As though through crimson fog, he saw O'Riley's snarling face. David hitched drunkenly to one side, drove his right with clumsy aimlessness. The blow connected with something—there was a grunt of pain from O'Riley, and the big redhead staggered, clutching his solar plexus.

"Finish him!" Von Hausman was yelling somewhere in the shouting mob.

David summoned his last spark of strength, swayed forward and jabbed both clenched fists at a staggering, dimly-seen O'Riley. His fists crashed onto hard bone with stinging pain—and there was a wilder shout as O'Riley slumped from his feet, collapsed to a sitting position and looked up with stunned, half-conscious gaze of utter bewilderment.

David stumbled over to where Von Hausman held Christa. He was reeling, almost unable to stand, but he tried to quiet her sobbing. Suddenly a great hand tore him around, and he faced one of the brutal mob, a black-bearded, wolf-faced Russian.

"You fight *me* now for the girl," the Russian grinned evilly. "I want her, too."

Von Hausman's face flamed with rage and he cried, "No, Bardoff! *Gott in Himmel*, this man is dead on his feet! You can't—"

Bardoff swept him aside with a growl, and the ragged mob cheered. "You fight, or I take her!" the Russian growled at David.

Halfdon Husper, the huge Norwegian, shouldered forward with pale eyes blazing. "You'll fight me first if you try that," he warned Bardoff.

"And me also!" snapped Von Hausman.

"Yes, and me too!" roared a third, unsteady voice. It was Red O'Riley. He had staggered to his feet, his battered, bruised face still bleeding, but his eyes were raging at the Russian. The redhead bellowed, "By heaven, this lad whipped me fairly and it's me that's with him."

Bardoff yelled furiously to the motley mob, "Do you allow them to do this? Why shouldn't we take the woman from them?"

"Yes, let's take her!" howled a score of brutal voices.

David Russell, swaying, hardly able to stand, saw Von Hausman and Husper and the bruised O'Riley bunch together and raise their fists and rude spears.

The ragged mob surged toward them, with Bardoff in the lead. Christa hid her face on David's shoulder. Then suddenly a strange, an awful thing, happened.

Bardoff, the Russian, suddenly stopped short, his whole body stiffening as though turned to stone. Then slowly, mechanically, he turned and began to walk away with strange, stiff strides—to walk toward the frowning black cliffs. And as he walked, he shrieked wildly to the suddenly transfixed mob, "The Master! His will is on me—he is calling me!"

213

The mob shrank back in dread. David saw that the Russian's face was now that of a soul in hell as he marched stiffly on like a human automaton toward the cliffs.

"*Gott!*" breathed Von Hausman, white-faced. "Another of us, called by the Master!"

"Save me!" the receding Russian was screaming wildly. "Save me from the Master!"

Not one person made a move toward him; all shrank back in horrified dread, toward the shelter of the huts. The Russian strode stiffly on, and now had started up a steep path that climbed the cliff toward the brooding castle.

David, staring with Christa terrifiedly clinging to him, and with the German and Husper and O'Riley the only others now left in the clearing, saw the doomed man climbing straight toward the front of the monstrous black castle. He saw a door appear in the blank, black front of the building. The Russian strode stiffly through, his last wild despairing cry floating faintly down to them. Then the aperture closed after him.

Through the three men beside David and Christa went a sigh of horror. Von Hausman's keen eyes were haunted as he told David, "You see now why we all dread the Master so. We never know at what moment he will call us, nor what dark, unholy doom he deals out to those whom he summons into the castle."

"But why did the man go up there, when he didn't want to?" David protested. "He was terrified, yet he walked straight on."

Halfdon Husper told him solemnly, "The will of the Master was on him and he could not resist—no human can resist when that call comes."

"*Ja*," said the German darkly. "Whatever thing it is that lairs up in that unholy place, it can throw its will on any of us, call us to it, whenever it wishes. It is so we shall all end in time, if we do not die first."

"Not Christa and I!" David declared passionately. "I'm going to get her away from this hellish island, somehow."

Red O'Riley's bruised face grinned approval.

"I'm with you there, lad," he declared. "Ten years I've been on this devil's place, ever since my schooner that was loaded with guns for Abd-el-Krim piled up here in the night. I've seen a plenty of men called up there by the old Satan that lives in that castle, and I'm damned if I'll sit around here longer twiddling my thumbs waitin' for him to call *me*. I'll risk anything to get away."

Von Hausman shrugged hopelessly. "It is useless to talk of it—you know what happens to anyone who tries to escape from the island. However, we can discuss that later. These two must have a place to live, so Halfdon and I will give them our hut."

He led the way along the street of wretched huts. It was growing dusky now. There was no sun or sunset visible in the flickering sky, but that sky steadily was darkening into a thick, strange twilight. The great forest loomed in deep shade now, gloomy and forbidding. Up on the cliff above the valley, the black stronghold of the dreaded Master bulked ominously against the dusking sky.

Von Hausman led them into a small bark cabin. It was unfurnished, save for beds of boughs, and a pile of strange-looking fruit in one corner. They sat down together in the dusky interior, and ate the fruit. David found it tasted as queer as it looked. Christa nestled nervously at his side, silent, still overwhelmed.

David could hardly yet believe in the reality of this strange place, this island invisible to the outer world, peopled by survivors of a hundred past wrecks, ruled by the mysterious, unseen occupant of the black castle. Yet Von Hausman and Husper and O'Riley ate with quiet matter-of-factness. The red-headed gun-runner had apparently forgotten all animosity against David.

When he had finished, O'Riley tossed the fruit-husks outside and stretched back, groaning, "What I wouldn't give now for a pipe and something to put in it. I swear if I ever get away from here I'll smoke for six months without stopping even to sleep."

David asked the German, "Why do you say it's impossible to escape from the island? It seems to me that it shouldn't be hard to make some sort of raft or dugout canoe, and launch it. Once away from the island, out where you could be seen by passing ships, you'd have a good chance of being picked up."

Von Hausman laughed mirthlessly. "A good many men on this island have thought that and have tried to get away in rafts or rude boats. And sooner or later in each case, before they could start, the Master called them. Whatever it is that dwells up in the castle, it does not want anyone to escape from this island—no!"

"That is so," rumbled the great Norwegian. "And that is why we no longer try to escape. It is hard to live here as we do—but it is more terrible to feel the will of the Master on you, to answer his call and go up into his castle never to return."

Christa, peering out through the doorway with wide eyes at the enigmatic black structure looming in the dusky sky, clung to her husband in shivering dread. "David, I'm afraid!"

He soothed her, yet felt as though a cold, alien wind of dread had blown over him, too. He asked, "But who or what is the Master? You say you don't know—but you must have some idea."

Von Hausman said thoughtfully, "We do not know because those who see the Master up there never come out again. But one thing I am sure of—*the Master is immortal.*"

And as David and Christa stared at him incredulously, the U-boat officer continued, "I believe that this island has existed here, invisible and unsuspected by the world, for countless centuries; for along its shores I have found old, rotted wreckage and metal objects from ships of many centuries back, from Eighteenth Century frigates and Sixteenth Century slavers, and Spanish caravels like those of Columbus—even wreckage of a Greek galley that must have ventured into these western seas more than two thousand years ago."

Von Hausman added, "That shows the island has been here, invisible, for centuries. Now the only thing that can keep this island invisible to the outside world is some force or power exerted by the Master. Therefore the Master must have dwelt here during all those centuries."

David made an impatient gesture. "After all, I don't care who or what the Master is. What I want to do is to get Christa away from this unholy place. I'm going to do that somehow, Master or no Master."

"And it's me that seconds the motion," promptly declared O'Riley. "What the devil!—this isn't any place for a man of action like meself to be moldering away his life. We'll build ourselves a boat and launch it, and the back of our hands to the Master if he tries to stop us."

"We wouldn't need to build a boat," David said eagerly. "My yawl—it was tossed up onto the outer rocks down at the shore. I think the hull is stove in a little and the masts are snapped, but there are tools in it and we could patch it up enough to be seaworthy, in a few days." He added passionately, "Isn't it better to try it than to sit here and do nothing? It may be true that before we can escape in it, the Master will call us as he has done the others who tried to escape. But if we just sit here, it seems that sooner or later we'll be called to the same fate anyway. So why not try to get away?"

"Sure, and why not?" echoed O'Riley. "We've got nothin' to lose but our lives."

Halfdon Husper said slowly, "I say, try it then. I have a wife in Oslo, if she still lives. And I am weary of waiting for death here."

They all looked at Von Hausman. After a moment, the German said quietly, "I have been here longer than any of you. I am quite certain that this attempt to escape will mean death for all of us. And not quick, easy death, but some horrible fate at the Master's hands. It is sure that, before we can ever launch that boat, we shall be called up there to that fate." His keen eyes smiled. "Yet I also say, let us try it. I too am weary of waiting idly for death here."

"Then we four will go down and start work on the yawl in the morning," David declared. He added troubledly to his young wife, "Christa, you're going to stay here while we work. No one here will bother you now, and if you do not go with us there is less chance of the Master's doom falling on you, if it does fall."

"I want to be with you, David!" she cried. But after a little, at David's anxiety, she gave in and consented to remain in the hut while they worked.

Night passed quickly, a strange, starless and moonless night, with only the unceasing flickering visible in the dark sky. And when dawn came it was a gray, sunless dawn, a slow, gradual increase in light. Leaving Christa in the hut, the four made their way quietly out of the village and through the forest to the beach.

The yawl still lay on the rocks where it had been tossed. David fished axes, saws and other tools from its hold, and they began the work. Halfdon Husper, most experienced of them, took charge as they rudely patched the holes in the hull.

Ever and again through the day, David glanced tensely over his shoulder at the distant cliffs and castle.

Von Hausman noticed that and said quietly, "Do not fear, *mein freund*, the Master is watching us. That is sure."

"Let him watch!" rasped David desperately. "We'll get away—we will!"

But when they returned into the village that evening, they saw that the ragged motley mob there now looked at them with awe and dread. These others had discovered during the day that they were working on the yawl.

"They already look on us as doomed by the Master, as dead men," commented the German.

O'Riley bristled. "Anyone who tries anything on me will find out that it's a damned tough dead man I am," he declared. "And that goes for the old devil up in the castle, too."

Christa cried softly in David's arms that night. "David, I feel that something terrible is going to happen to you. And if it did, I wouldn't want to live."

"Nothing's going to happen to me," he insisted despite the fatal foreboding in his heart. "We'll get away."

By the end of the next day, the four men had completely, if crudely, patched the holes in the yawl's hull. They got it afloat, secured it by cables to the rocks. Halfdon Husper regarded their work with satisfaction.

"Tomorrow we will cut and fit new spars," the Norwegian said. "Then—"

Day was beginning to fade eerily as they returned to the village. It looked stricken, deserted—no one was abroad in it, but from the doors of the huts, horrified faces stared silently at them. Christa was not in the bark cabin. Nor did she answer David's calls.

"Something's happened to her!" he cried. "Some of these brutes—"

Gripping the ax he had brought back from the yawl, he ran wildly down the rude street. He plucked a man out of the door of one of the huts, a loutish Breton sailor who stared at him with ignorant, horror-widened eyes.

"What's happened to my wife?" snarled David, raising the ax menacingly. "If some of you have harmed her, I'll kill you!"

The Breton, gasping in David's furious, choking grip, stammered an answer. "It was not us—the girl is gone for ever. An hour ago the call of the Master came upon her, and she climbed the cliff and passed up into the castle. She did not want to go—she screamed as all they who feel the call scream, but she could not help herself."

David felt the blood leave his heart as the ghastly truth penetrated his mind. He saw infinite pity on the faces of his three friends, and heard Von Hausman whisper, "*Gott*, the Master has summoned her. We shall never see her again."

"I *will* see her again!" raved David wildly. "I'm going up there and try to get her out, if I have to go alone!"

He suddenly turned on the ragged, motley men staring from the huts, and lashed them with raging words of volcanic fury. "You men—are you really men or are you sheep, that you sit here and let whatever creature is up in that castle kill you at his will? Whoever the Master is, he must be living, and that means that he can be killed! Why don't you try to kill him, instead of submitting humbly to his will? Why don't you storm the castle and destroy him, instead of waiting for him to destroy you one by one?"

A fierce yell burst from the men before him, hard-bitten, brutal men from all the seven seas, whose smoldering hate and fear of the Master had been fanned to a quick blaze by David's raging words.

A flashing-eyed Italian sailor waved his spear aloft and cried, "By the saints, he speaks truth! Why do we not pull down the demon that crouches up there?"

"That's the stuff, lads!" cried Red O'Riley exultantly.

"Aye, death to the Master!" boomed Halfdon Husper's great voice, the huge Norwegian's eyes flaming with long-repressed hatred.

"Death to the Master!" burst a raging chorus of two hundred voices, as rude spears and swords waved thick from the maddened men.

David, his face half crazed with rage, shook his heavy ax and cried, "Up the cliff, then! We'll storm the Master's castle before he can claim my wife as another victim!"

They poured out of the village, a roaring, raging mob of savage seamen from every nation, every man with his weapon, every man afire to destroy the mysterious being whom they had dreaded so long.

David ran at their head, his face white and set, his ax gripped in his hand, with the exulting O'Riley and the blazing-eyed Norwegian and Von Hausman, curiously calm, behind him. Close after the four streamed the wild mob. David led them straight to the cliff and up the steep, narrow path in single file. He knew that if they had time to recover from their rage, the old dread of the Master would rapidly repossess them.

Above them bulked ominously against the dusky sky the mysterious black castle. It seemed to David that as they neared the top of the cliff, the raging roar of his mob of followers lessened a little, their pace slackened.

O'Riley yelled back to them, "On, comrades! In a minute we'll be inside the Master's castle!"

"Death to the Master!" thundered back the wild, climbing horde.

Now David and the three friends close at his heels climbed onto the sheer rock shelf in front of the castle. The huge square structure loomed black and somber before them, doorless and windowless.

"There's a door somewhere in front here!" David cried. "We'll find it!"

He led them at a run toward the towering, black wall of smooth stone that was the front of the citadel.

Suddenly he stopped short, and at the same moment every man behind halted in his tracks. He could not go forward! He wanted to, for every fiber in his body was aflame with raging desire to rush forward and break into this structure into which Christa had gone. But he could not take a single step forward. It was as though his legs had suddenly ceased to obey his brain's commands, and were under outside control.

The men behind him, smitten to a halt by the same weird phenomenon, were struck silent with stupefaction for a moment. Then a cry of horror and dread went up from the ragged mob.

"The Master's will is on us!"

"God save us—the Master has us in his grip!"

David fought to move forward, making a tremendous effort of his will to move his legs even one step. Sweat stood out on his forehead, but he could not move.

He heard a confused cry of terror from the mob behind him. Then he saw that the ragged horde, and also Von Hausman and Husper and O'Riley, had begun to move back down the cliff, walking with stiff, mechanical strides down the path.

"O'Riley! Halfdon! Come back!" yelled David hoarsely. "We can still break in and destroy that demon inside."

The big Irishman, his face white and beaded with sweat, called thickly back, "Lad, we can't!"

And Von Hausman, as they marched stiffly away down the path, cried back up to David, "The Master—his will is making us return to the village!"

Stiffly striding, shouting in their terror now, David's ragged followers descended the path up which they had raged a few moments before, and stiffly his three friends followed despite their struggles. David was left standing alone in the flickering dusk before the enormous citadel.

Suddenly his legs began to move under him. Stiffly as those of a dead man, they stalked forward with him toward the front of the great building. He could not control that movement—it was another brain that was directing his forward strides. But he did not try to fight it now, for in his throbbing brain was only the desire to get into the castle where Christa was. Still gripping his ax tightly in his hand, he strode forward with those mechanical steps.

As he neared the blank black wall of the citadel, a tiny round aperture appeared in it. The aperture expanded rapidly, like an opening camera shutter, into a round door beyond which he saw a great hall filled with misty blue light. David strode on, into that blue-lit hall, and heard the door close with a sighing sound after him.

Tramp, tramp—the steady strides, which he did not himself will, took him across the great hall. He saw through the light-mists, massive, shining mechanisms of unearthly design standing about him. He passed on through them, into a huge vaulted corridor.

David's legs took him on down that corridor. Somewhere in this building the Master was drawing David to him, controlling his body by super-hypnotic force. He passed other halls and corridors, all flooded with pale, misty blue luminescence, holding weird instruments and mechanisms of unfathomable purpose. Then he emerged into a colossal domed central hall.

He stared with fascinated, stupefied eyes as he was drawn forward. At the center of this mighty chamber poised a ten-foot crystal sphere inside which pulsed a throbbing core of living azure fire, like a miniature, misty blue sun.

In front of this titan crystal of pulsing light was a throne-like metal chair he could just glimpse through a shroud of concealing light-mists. And he glimpsed or sensed someone, something, sitting upon that metal throne. Facing the throne stood—

"Christa!" cried David hoarsely.

The girl stood, a wild terror frozen upon her face, her slim, childish body silhouetted against the blue light.

She turned at David's cry, tried to run toward him but could not move, rooted by the same force that was drawing him stiffly forward. Anguish had leaped into her eyes at sight of him.

"David!" she uttered in a sobbing cry. "You came after me—came to your doom—"

He was beside her now. And there, without command of his own brain, his stiff strides suddenly stopped. He tried to step to Christa and take her in his arms, but could not. He could only reach out with one hand, and touch her trembling cheek.

She stared ahead once more, horror unveiled in her eyes. David turned his head and looked forward to what she stared at, that metal throne whose base could just be glimpsed through the curling blue light-mists that surrounded it.

David gripped his ax tighter. Yet he felt utterly helpless, powerless, standing with the girl before that shrouded throne and before the colossal crystal of throbbing light.

Out of the light-mists around the throne spoke the voice of the Master, a metallic voice of chill, measured accents.

"Man from outside, you interest me," the passionless, cold voice of the Master told David. "You tried to do what no other here ever tried to do, attack me in revolt. I am sorry now I did not call you here sooner—I meant in any case to call you and your friends because of your childish attempt to escape the island."

David tried to keep his voice steady. "You can do what you want with me," he told the Master. "I know that. But I will submit willingly, gladly, if you will allow the girl to go."

"No, David!" cried Christa. "I share your fate! If you die, I die!"

The Master's metallic voice told them, "Your argument is purposeless. My will rules here and not yours—it rules even your own bodies, as you have learned. My actions are not to be disturbed by your tiny clamor. It is my intention to use the body of this girl at once as material for certain interesting experiments which I have long been performing on humans whom I called from the village. As for you, man who dared attack me, you will have the same fate, a little later."

"You're not going to use Christa's body for your experiments," said David in a thick, hoarse voice. "You're not!"

He was slowly, stealthily, raising the heavy ax. If he could throw it, if he could hurl it into the shrouding mists at the thing on the metal throne—

His hand flashed up for the wild cast—and froze in midair, gripping the ax! He could not throw the weapon!

The veins on David's neck corded with tremendous effort, but his arm and shoulder muscles would not obey his will.

"You fool!" scorned the cold accents of the Master. "Did you not think that I could read your intention in your mind, that I could hold your arms powerless by my will as easily as your legs? Do you think me a stupid, blundering creature of flesh and blood like yourself? Look, human, and see!"

The light-mists drifted swiftly away from the seat of the Master as he spoke. There on the metal throne before the great crystal of throbbing light, he sat unveiled.

David felt his brain reeling as he stared. He heard a choking of horror from Christa.

The Master was a metal robot—a mechanical creature of coppery metal, formed like a horrible travesty of humanity, with metal arms, legs and cylindrical body, and a bulbous metal head or brain-case out of which two glittering, unwinking eye lenses watched them.

"God, a robot!" cried David. "A machine, created by somebody—"

"And a machine greater far than its creators!" came the cold voice of the Master.

There was a strange note of pride in the robot's chill accents. It was as though it was speaking, out of that resonator mouth below its eyes, not to the transfixed David and Christa but to itself.

"Yes, they were men like you who created me," he was saying, "though men wiser far than you in the craft and skill of science. Long, long ago that was, long ago in ancient Atlantis whose fertile continent stood here in the sea where now only this little island stands, and where the races of men had reached their highest civilization.

"The scientists of Atlantis had built many wonderful mechanisms, some of them completely automatic and self-sustaining in operation. And they dreamed finally of creating a machine with brain and mind.

"I was that machine. There in Atlantis, ages past, I was born in the laboratories of the greatest scientists. My body was easy to build, but for decades they worked on the metal brain they meant to give me.

"That brain, when they finished it, was incomparably more complex in its metal neurone structure than is the human brain. Because of that, it could receive and classify an incomparably greater number of thought-patterns. That meant that I had the capacity for infinitely greater knowledge and memory than any human.

"The scientists instructed me, proud of my progress. But very soon I had learned all that they could teach me, and as I passed beyond them in knowledge and power, they began to realize that they had created a being greater than themselves."

There was a brooding note of undying hate in the metallic voice of the robot.

"I became great in power in Atlantis, the final oracle in all problems. To the populace I was a god, and as such I was worshipped and had my temple. Power I loved, not for its own sake, but only because it enabled me to continue my quest for new knowledge.

"Then the Atlantean scientists who had created me regretted their work, and wished to destroy me. They aroused the populace against me and attacked my temple with the most powerful weapons they could muster. I repelled them, but they attacked me again. At last I grew weary of their harrying, and I resolved to destroy all Atlantis and its people, except for the land on which my temple stood.

"In a single night, I did the thing. For long I had gathered my powers and on that night I unchained them, and they smote down into the earth's structure far beneath the continent of Atlantis, and touched off great earth-faults that I knew existed there in the depths. And in that one night, all the continent of Atlantis and all its people sank downward and the sea crashed over the land and hid it for ever.

"All but one small portion of the continent, the portion around my temple! *That* did not sink, for I had provided against that, setting up certain radiated forces which sustain that small bit of land as an island above the waves. That great crystal of blue fire which you see behind me, man from outside, is the source of the radiation which still upholds the island. Were it not for that crystal's radiation, the slender pinnacle of rock which bears up this island must have collapsed long ago.

"Also there is a force mingled in the crystal's radiation which refracts light around the island, keeping it invisible to the outside world, so that I will not be annoyed by the curiosity of the barbarian races of men. Occasionally ships have crashed onto my invisible island as yours did, and men have gained its shore. I have suffered them to live down there in their wretched village because I sometimes need their bodies for my researches."

The glittering lens-eyes of the Master seemed to muse upon the stricken Christa and upon David, still standing petrified with his ax upraised.

"Man from outside, why do I speak of these things to you who can little understand them?" asked the robot. "It is for only one reason—it is because I am lonely.

"Yes, I, the child of old Atlantis, long more and more for contact with a mind equal to my own. I have resolved to create one, a metal brain as intelligent as mine. That is the purpose that engages me, and it is upon issues connected with that purpose that I am experimenting upon the bodies of humans like you and this girl."

"Not upon Christa's body—no!" shouted David hoarsely.

"Do you think to frighten me by mouthing futile threats?" asked the robot calmly. "Man from outside, you humans begin to weary me. I think it is well that the girl go now to the laboratories, where you will follow in due course."

Christa uttered a heart-torn cry. "David, good-bye—"

"No, you're not going there!" David cried. He was making tremendous mental effort to free his arm from the hypnotic grip of the

Master, to hurl his ax. But the Master's super-hypnotism held him powerless.

Across David's brain seared a lightning expedient, a thought that he suppressed as soon as he was aware of it. He desperately began to think, to think a *lie*.

He began to think of stirrings in the dim ocean depths below where wrecked Atlantis lay entombed, of mighty scientists emerging from tight chambers where they had lain sleeping, and not dead. He thought of them vowing vengeance upon the robot they had created, of assembling great weapons, of sending him, David Russell, ahead as a spy upon the robot.

The Master read the lie in David's mind and for a moment was deceived by it. For the robot leaped wildly upright.

"Then they of Atlantis are not all dead!" cried the metallic voice. "They come again against me—"

For that single moment of wild excitement, the Master's mind relaxed its remorseless hypnotic grip upon David and Christa.

That one instant was enough. In it, David's muscles exploded in mad action and sent the ax in his hand flying straight toward the robot's head.

The heavy ax-head crashed squarely into the bulbous metal brain-case, between the lens-like eyes. The steel blade drove deep through the outer casing into the interior of the head, deep into the metal brain that had been created ages ago in the laboratories of dead Atlantis.

The Master staggered. His metallic voice uttered an awful, broken scream.

"Tricked! Tricked by a barbarian creature of flesh! But I will destroy you all—"

Even as he uttered that dying scream, the Master was whirl-ing, was falling. But he fell with outstretched metal arms crashing purposefully down against the giant crystal of blue fire behind him, the crystal whose radiated force alone held the island from sinking beneath the waves.

The crystal shivered beneath the cracking impact of the dead robot's falling body. The blue fire inside it dulled and died instantly. David heard Christa cry out, run into his arms.

Then they were thrown from their feet by a terrific earth-shock. They heard a thunderous roar from the earth beneath the castle, and the crash of the castle's black walls as they were riven by the awful shock.

David grabbed his wife and plunged desperately across the huge halls and corridors whose walls were collapsing and crashing around him. He glimpsed daylight through a great gap in the outer wall, and he leaped with Christa through the gap out into the day. They stopped on the shelf of the cliff, for a moment appalled.

The whole island was heaving and rocking like a ship on a stormy sea. The thunderous earth-shocks were following each other at intervals of seconds, and there was a long, grinding roar from deep beneath that told of shifting, settling masses. The sun had appeared in the sky since the light-refracting force had died, but the heavens were instantly overcast with an ominous crimson pall.

The two fled down the path into the valley, David feeling nausea from the roll and buck of the earth beneath him. In the valley, the huts were in ruins and their ragged occupants were running about in mad panic. Von Hausman and O'Riley and the great Norwegian came running wildly up to David and the girl. "*Gott in Himmel!*" yelled the German. "What is—"

"The island is sinking into the sea!" screamed David over the roaring crashes. "I killed the Master, and in dying he acted to make the island sink. Our only chance is to get to the yawl!"

"To the yawl, then!" shouted Husper, his face crimson with excitement.

They sprinted forward, into the forest, the earth still rolling and heaving wildly under their feet.

"Saints in heaven, look!" cried O'Riley, glancing back horrified.

With terrible, reverberating roll of thunder, the cliff and ruined castle of the Master were collapsing in masses of rock onto the valley they had just quitted.

"On!" yelled Von Hausman.

Fissures opened on either side of them as they plunged through the wild-waving woods. Terrific tremors crashed down trees and twice knocked them from their feet.

They burst out onto the beach. The sea before them was wild, great waves rushing madly in to shore and then out again, threatening to tear from its cables the mastless yawl that bobbed crazily on the waters.

They waded out through the rising waters, smashed by inrushing waves, shaken by the shifting of the rocks beneath their feet, and finally clambered onto the pitching yawl.

"Cut loose!" shouted Halfdon Husper.

David's ax sliced the cables. The yawl whirled crazily like a cork, then was sucked far, far back out to sea by the waters now receding at mill-race speed from the island—out and out, until the waters halted for a moment in awful dead calm. And from that distance they glimpsed the whole island, with solemn, grinding drum-roll from far beneath, sinking down into the waters.

The last black mass of the island plunged down under the sea. Then the waters around the yawl boiled terrifically and raced wildly with the little boat toward the spot where the island had been, a mad maelstrom of converging currents.

Halfdon Husper thrust the others by main force down into the cabin of the yawl, leaped in after them and slammed the hatchway shut. Next moment they were tossed violently against the walls of the dark cabin as the yawl seemed to stand up on its stern. David, still holding Christa tightly, felt his head strike the cabin wall and knew nothing more.

When he awoke, brilliant sunset light was in his eyes. He was lying on the deck of the yawl, and Christa and his friends were bending anxiously over him. Husper had a great bruise on his face, but the others did not seem injured.

David struggled to sit up, his dazed eyes sweeping the waters. The sea was still heaving and troubled, but the terrific currents had vanished. There was no sign of the island or of any other land anywhere in the tossing blue waste.

David stammered, "The yawl—it wasn't sucked down by the currents, then?"

Von Hausman, his quiet face still pale, said, "No, but it must have been only a reverse under-current that snatched us back out of the maelstrom. The yawl was actually under water when that current gripped us."

O'Riley, drawing a long breath, nodded his flaming head in corroboration. "It's me that was saying my prayers that minute!"

Christa was crying eagerly, "David, we've sighted the smoke of a ship coming—we're going to be picked up!"

His arm encircled her tightly. But for the moment his eyes were not looking at her, but gazing fascinatedly at the heaving waters, into whose green depths the lifeless metal form and shattered castle of the Master had sunk for ever. The child of old Atlantis, he had gone down at last to rejoin his creators in death.

ATLANTIS
REIMAGINED

THE MIRRORS OF TUZUN THUNE

Robert E. Howard

Robert E. Howard (1906–1936) was an American author born in Peastar, Texas. Growing up at the tail-end of the American frontier, and the beginning of the Texas oil boom, Howard's adolescence was set against the drastic, often violent, upheaval of an unregulated industry. Such violence seeped into his stories, and, in a letter of 1931, Howard reflected that "I'll say one thing about an oil boom; it will teach a kid that Life's a pretty rotten thing as quick as anything I can think of". Howard's first pulp publication, "Spear and Fang", was printed in the July 1925 issue of *Weird Tales*. Becoming a regular contributor to the magazines of the era, he would subsequently experiment with an array of genres, including adventure, horror, and boxing stories. Now regarded as a pioneer of the "Sword and Sorcery" subgenre of fantasy fiction, as well as the "Weird West" style of western, Howard was responsible for the creation of such iconic characters as Conan the Barbarian and Solomon Kane.

Before Conan, there was Kull. An Atlantean warrior, exiled from his home, Kull was the protagonist of a series of short works, of which only three would be published during Howard's lifetime: "The Shadow Kingdom" (1929), "The Mirrors of Tuzun Thune" (1929) and "Kings of the Night" (1930). Indicative of Howard's unique blend of "Sword and Sorcery", in this story, Kull—having become

King of another region, Valusia—is tempted to visit "The House of a Thousand Mirrors" to cure his melancholy. There, the magics of Tuzun Thune tempt Kull into increasingly existential despair. A Weird Fantasy, "The Mirrors of Tuzun Thune" initiates a final selection of works, "Atlantis Reimagined", in which the sunken civilization is used as a catalyst for broader generic diversity. In 1967, Howard's remaining tales were collected under the title of *King Kull*.

"A wild, weird clime that lieth sublime
Out of Space, out of Time."

—POE.

There comes, even to kings, the time of great weariness. Then the gold of the throne is brass, the silk of the palace becomes drab. The gems in the diadem and upon the fingers of the women sparkle drearily like the ice of the white seas; the speech of men is as the empty rattle of a jester's bell and the feel comes of things unreal; even the sun is copper in the sky and the breath of the green ocean is no longer fresh.

Kull sat upon the throne of Valusia and the hour of weariness was upon him. They moved before him in an endless, meaningless panorama, men, women, priests, events and shadows of events; things seen and things to be attained. But like shadows they came and went, leaving no trace upon his consciousness, save that of a great mental fatigue. Yet Kull was not tired. There was a longing in him for things beyond himself and beyond the Valusian court. An unrest stirred in him and strange, luminous dreams roamed his soul. At his bidding there came to him Brule the Spear-slayer, warrior of Pictland, from the islands beyond the West.

"Lord king, you are tired of the life of the court. Come with me upon my galley and let us roam the tides for a space."

"Nay." Kull rested his chin moodily upon his mighty hand. "I am weary beyond all these things. The cities hold no lure for me—and the borders are quiet. I hear no more the sea-songs I heard when I lay as a boy on the booming crags of Atlantis, and the night was alive with blazing stars. No more do the green woodlands beckon me as of old. There is a strangeness upon me and a longing beyond life's longings. Go!"

Brule went forth in a doubtful mood, leaving the king brooding upon his throne. Then to Kull stole a girl of the court and whispered:

"Great king, seek Tuzun Thune, the wizard. The secrets of life and death are his, and the stars in the sky and the lands beneath the seas."

Kull looked at the girl. Fine gold was her hair and her violet eyes were slanted strangely; she was beautiful, but her beauty meant little to Kull.

"Tuzun Thune," he repeated. "Who is he?"

"A wizard of the Elder Race. He lives here, in Valusia, by the Lake of Visions in the House of a Thousand Mirrors. All things are known to him, lord king; he speaks with the dead and holds converse with the demons of the Lost Lands."

Kull arose.

"I will seek out this mummer; but no word of my going, do you hear?"

"I am your slave, my lord." And she sank to her knees meekly, but the smile of her scarlet mouth was cunning behind Kull's back and the gleam of her narrow eyes was crafty.

Kull came to the house of Tuzun Thune, beside the Lake of Visions. Wide and blue stretched the waters of the lake and many a fine palace rose upon its banks; many swan-winged pleasure boats drifted lazily upon its hazy surface and evermore there came the sound of soft music.

Tall and spacious, but unpretentious, rose the House of a Thousand Mirrors. The great doors stood open and Kull ascended the broad stair and entered, unannounced. There in a great chamber, whose walls were of mirrors, he came upon Tuzun Thune, the wizard. The man was ancient as the hills of Zalgara; like wrinkled leather was his skin, but his cold gray eyes were like sparks of sword steel.

"Kull of Valusia, my house is yours," said he, bowing with old-time courtliness and motioning Kull to a throne-like chair.

"You are a wizard, I have heard," said Kull bluntly, resting his chin upon his hand and fixing his somber eyes upon the man's face. "Can you do wonders?"

The wizard stretched forth his hand; his fingers opened and closed like a bird's claws.

"Is that not a wonder—that this blind flesh obeys the thoughts of my mind? I walk, I breathe, I speak—are they all not wonders?"

Kull meditated awhile, then spoke. "Can you summon up demons?"

"Aye. I can summon up a demon more savage than any in ghost-land—by smiting you in the face."

Kull started, then nodded. "But the dead, can you talk to the dead?"

"I talk with the dead always—as I am talking now. Death begins with birth and each man begins to die when he is born; even now you are dead, King Kull, because you were born."

"But you, you are older than men become; do wizards never die?"

"Men die when their time comes. No later, no sooner. Mine has not come."

Kull turned these answers over in his mind.

"Then it would seem that the greatest wizard of Valusia is no more than an ordinary man, and I have been duped in coming here."

Tuzun Thune shook his head. "Men are but men, and the greatest men are they who soonest learn the simpler things. Nay, look into my mirrors, Kull."

The ceiling was a great many mirrors, and the walls were mirrors, perfectly jointed, yet many mirrors of many sizes and shapes.

"Mirrors are the world, Kull," droned the wizard. "Gaze into my mirrors and be wise."

Kull chose one at random and looked into it intently. The mirrors upon the opposite wall were reflected there, reflecting others, so that he seemed to be gazing down a long, luminous corridor, formed by mirror behind mirror; and far down this corridor moved a tiny figure. Kull looked long ere he saw that the figure was the reflection of himself. He gazed and a queer feeling of pettiness came over him; it seemed that that tiny figure was the true Kull, representing the real proportions of himself. So he moved away and stood before another.

"Look closely, Kull. That is the mirror of the past," he heard the wizard say.

Gray fogs obscured the vision, great billows of mist, ever heaving and changing like the ghost of a great river; through these fogs Kull caught swift fleeting visions of horror and strangeness; beasts and men moved there and shapes neither men nor beasts; great exotic blossoms glowed through the grayness; tall tropic trees towered high over reeking swamps, where reptilian monsters wallowed and bellowed; the sky was ghastly with flying dragons and the restless seas rocked and roared and beat endlessly along the muddy beaches. Man was not, yet man was the dream of the gods and strange were the nightmare forms that glided through the noisome jungles. Battle and onslaught were there, and frightful love. Death was there, for Life and Death go hand in hand. Across the slimy beaches of the world sounded the bellowing of the monsters, and incredible shapes loomed through the steaming curtain of the incessant rain.

"This is of the future."

Kull looked in silence.

"See you—what?"

"A strange world," said Kull heavily. "The Seven Empires are crumbled to dust and are forgotten. The restless green waves roar for many a fathom above the eternal hills of Atlantis; the mountains of Lemuria of the West are the islands of an unknown sea. Strange savages roam the elder lands and new lands flung strangely from the deeps, defiling the elder shrines. Valusia is vanished and all the nations of today; they of tomorrow are strangers. They know us not."

"Time strides onward," said Tuzun Thune calmly. "We live today; what care we for tomorrow—or yesterday? The Wheel turns and nations rise and fall; the world changes, and times return to savagery to rise again through the long ages. Ere Atlantis was, Valusia was, and ere Valusia was, the Elder Nations were. Aye, we, too, trampled the shoulders of lost tribes in our advance. You, who have come from the green sea hills of Atlantis to seize the ancient crown of Valusia; you think my tribe is old, we who held these lands ere the Valusians came out of the East, in the days before there were men in the sea lands. But men were here when the Elder Tribes rode out of the waste lands, and men before men, tribe before tribe. The nations pass and are forgotten, for that is the destiny of man."

"Yes," said Kull. "Yet is it not a pity that the beauty and glory of men should fade like smoke on a summer sea?"

"For what reason, since that is their destiny? I brood not over the lost glories of my race, nor do I labor for races to come. Live now, Kull, live now. The dead are dead; the unborn are not. What matters men's forgetfulness of you when you have forgotten yourself in the silent worlds of death? Gaze in my mirrors and be wise."

Kull chose another mirror and gazed into it.

"That is the mirror of the deepest magic; what see ye, Kull?"

"Naught but myself."

"Look closely, Kull; is it in truth you?"

Kull stared into the great mirror, and the image that was his reflection returned his gaze.

"I come before this mirror," mused Kull, chin on fist, "and I bring this man to life. This is beyond my understanding, since first I saw him in the still waters of the lakes of Atlantis, till I saw him again in the gold-rimmed mirrors of Valusia. He is I, a shadow of myself, part of myself—I can bring him into being or slay him at my will; yet"—he halted, strange thoughts whispering through the vast dim recesses of his mind like shadowy bats flying through a great cavern—"yet where is he when I stand not in front of a mirror? May it be in man's power thus lightly to form and destroy a shadow of life and existence? How do I know that when I step back from the mirror he vanishes into the void of Naught?

"Nay, by Valka, am I the man or is he? Which of us is the ghost of the other? Mayhap these mirrors are but windows through which we look into another world. Does he think the same of me? Am I no more than a shadow, a reflection of himself—to him, as he to me? And if I am the ghost, what sort of a world lives upon the other side of this mirror? What armies ride there and what kings rule? This world is all I know. Knowing naught of any other, how can I judge? Surely there are green hills there and booming seas and wide plains where men ride to battle. Tell me, wizard, who are wiser than most men, tell me, are there worlds beyond our worlds?"

"A man has eyes, let him see," answered the wizard. "Who would see must first believe."

*

The hours drifted by and Kull still sat before the mirrors of Tuzun Thune, gazing into that which depicted himself. Sometimes it seemed that he gazed upon hard shallowness; at other times gigantic depths seemed to loom before him. Like the surface of the sea was the mirror of Tuzun Thune; hard as the sea in the sun's slanting beams, in the darkness of the stars, when no eye can pierce her deeps; vast and mystic as the sea when the sun smites her in such way that the watcher's breath is caught at the glimpse of tremendous abysses. So was the mirror in which Kull gazed.

At last the king rose with a sigh and took his departure still wondering. And Kull came again to the House of a Thousand Mirrors; day after day he came and sat for hours before the mirror. The eyes looked out at him, identical with his, yet Kull seemed to sense a difference—a reality that was not of him. Hour upon hour he would stare with strange intensity into the mirror; hour after hour the image gave back his gaze.

The business of the palace and of the council went neglected. The people murmured; Kull's stallion stamped restlessly in his stable and Kull's warriors diced and argued aimlessly with one another. Kull heeded not. At times he seemed on the point of discovering some vast, unthinkable secret. He no longer thought of the image in the mirror as a shadow of himself; the thing, to him, was an entity, similar in outer appearance, yet basically as far from Kull himself as the poles are far apart. The image, it seemed to Kull, had an individuality apart from Kull's; he was no more dependent on Kull than Kull was dependent on him. And day by day Kull doubted in which world he really lived; was he the shadow, summoned at will by the other? Did he instead of the other live in a world of delusion, the shadow of the real world?

Kull began to wish that he might enter the personality beyond the mirror for a space, to see what might be seen; yet should he manage to go beyond that door could he ever return? Would he find a world identical with the one in which he moved? A world, of which his was but a ghostly reflection? Which was reality and which illusion?

At times Kull halted to wonder how such thoughts and dreams had come to enter his mind and at times he wondered if they came of his own volition or—here his thoughts would become mazed. His meditations were his own; no man ruled his thoughts and he would summon them at his pleasure; yet could he? Were they not as bats, coming and going, not at his pleasure but at the bidding or ruling of—of whom? The gods? The Women who wove the webs of Fate? Kull could come to no conclusion, for at each mental step he became more and more bewildered in a hazy gray fog of illusory assertions and refutations. This much he knew: that strange visions entered his mind, like bats flying unbidden from the whispering void of non-existence; never had he thought these thoughts, but now they ruled his mind, sleeping and waking, so that he seemed to walk in a daze at times; and his sleep was fraught with strange, monstrous dreams.

"Tell me, wizard," he said, sitting before the mirror, eyes fixed intently upon his image, "how can I pass yon door? For of a truth, I am not sure that that is the real world and this the shadow; at least, that which I see must exist in some form."

"See and believe," droned the wizard. "Man must believe to accomplish. Form is shadow, substance is illusion, materiality is dream; man is because he believes he is; what is man but a dream of the gods? Yet man can be that which he wishes to be; form and substance, they are but shadows. The mind, the ego, the essence of the god-dream—that is real, that is immortal. See and believe, if you would accomplish, Kull."

The king did not fully understand; he never fully understood the enigmatical utterances of the wizard, yet they struck somewhere in his being a dim responsive chord. So day after day he sat before the mirrors of Tuzun Thune. Ever the wizard lurked behind him like a shadow.

Then came a day when Kull seemed to catch glimpses of strange lands; there flitted across his consciousness dim thoughts and recognitions. Day by day he had seemed to lose touch with the world; all things had seemed each succeeding day more ghostly and unreal; only the man in the mirror seemed like reality. Now Kull seemed to be close to the doors of some mightier worlds; giant vistas gleamed fleetingly; the fogs of unreality thinned; "form is shadow, substance is illusion; they are but shadows" sounded as if from some far country of his consciousness. He remembered the wizard's words and it seemed to him that now he almost understood—form and substance, could not he change himself at will, if he knew the master key that opened this door? What worlds within what worlds awaited the bold explorer?

The man in the mirror seemed smiling at him—closer, closer—a fog enwrapped all and the reflection dimmed suddenly—Kull knew a sensation of fading, of change, of merging—

"Kull!" the yell split the silence into a million vibratory fragments!

Mountains crashed and worlds tottered as Kull, hurled back by that frantic shout, made a superhuman effort, how or why he did not know.

A crash, and Kull stood in the room of Tuzun Thune before a shattered mirror, mazed and half blind with bewilderment. There before him lay the body of Tuzun Thune, whose time had come at last, and above him stood Brule the Spear-slayer, sword dripping red and eyes wide with a kind of horror.

"Valka!" swore the warrior. "Kull, it was time I came!"

"Aye, yet what happened?" The king groped for words.

"Ask this traitress," answered the Spear-slayer, indicating a girl who crouched in terror before the king; Kull saw that it was she who first sent him to Tuzun Thune. "As I came in I saw you fading into yon mirror as smoke fades into the sky, by Valka! Had I not seen I would not have believed—you had almost vanished when my shout brought you back."

"Aye," muttered Kull, "I had almost gone beyond the door that time."

"This fiend wrought most craftily," said Brule. "Kull, do you not now see how he spun and flung over you a web of magic? Kaanuub of Blaal plotted with this wizard to do away with you, and this wench, a girl of Elder Race, put the thought in your mind so that you would come here. Kananu of the council learned of the plot today; I know not what you saw in that mirror, but with it Tuzun Thune enthralled your soul and almost by his witchery he changed your body to mist—"

"Aye." Kull was still mazed. "But being a wizard, having knowledge of all the ages and despising gold, glory and position, what could Kaanuub offer Tuzun Thune that would make of him a foul traitor?"

"Gold, power and position," grunted Brule. "The sooner you learn that men are men whether wizard, king or thrall, the better you will rule, Kull. Now what of her?"

"Naught, Brule," as the girl whimpered and groveled at Kull's feet. "She was but a tool. Rise, child, and go your ways; none shall harm you."

Alone with Brule, Kull looked for the last time on the mirrors of Tuzun Thune.

"Mayhap he plotted and conjured, Brule; nay, I doubt you not, yet—was it his witchery that was changing me to thin mist, or had I stumbled on a secret? Had you not brought me back, had I faded in dissolution or had I found worlds beyond this?"

Brule stole a glance at the mirrors, and twitched his shoulders as if he shuddered. "Aye. Tuzun Thune stored the wisdom of all the hells here. Let us begone, Kull, ere they bewitch me, too."

"Let us go, then," answered Kull, and side by side they went forth from the House of a Thousand Mirrors—where, mayhap, are prisoned the souls of men.

None look now in the mirrors of Tuzun Thune. The pleasure boats shun the shore where stands the wizard's house and no one goes in the house or to the room where Tuzun Thune's dried and withered carcass lies before the mirrors of illusion. The place is shunned as a place accursed, and though it stands for a thousand years to come, no footsteps shall echo there. Yet Kull upon his throne meditates often upon the strange wisdom and untold secrets hidden there and wonders...

For there are worlds beyond worlds, as Kull knows, and whether the wizard bewitched him by words or by mesmerism, vistas did open to the king's gaze beyond that strange door, and Kull is less sure of reality since he gazed into the mirrors of Tuzun Thune.

A VOYAGE TO SFANOMOË

Clark Ashton Smith

Clark Ashton Smith (1893–1961) was an American author, poet and artist born in Long Island, California. Due to an intense form of agoraphobia, Smith spent much of his adolescent life in isolation. However, his enthusiastic approach to reading, alongside an eidetic memory, meant that by the age of fourteen he had already penned the adventure novel, *The Black Diamonds* (first published, posthumously, in 2002). Pursuing his primary passion for poetry, Smith would publish *The Star-Treader and Other Poems* in 1912. Further volumes include *Odes and Sonnets* (1918), *Ebony and Crystal: Poems in Verse and Prose* (1922) and *Sandalwood* (1925). As a writer of fiction, Smith was infamous for his beguiling approach to language. Publishing over one-hundred short works in the periodicals of the era, his tales include "The End of the Story" (1930), "Sadastor" (1930) and the Hyperborea, Zothique and Averoigne cycles.

Originally published in the July 1931 issue of *Weird Tales*, "A Voyage to Sfanomoë" is taken from another of Smith's cycles: Poseidonis. Coined by the author Algernon Blackwood in his short story of 1912, "Sand", Blackwood described Poseidonis as a "great island adjoining the main continent which itself had vanished a vast period before, sank down beneath the waves". To Smith, the land of Poseidonis became the last remnants of Atlantis, fleshed out further in stories such as "A Vintage from Atlantis" (1930) and "The Double Shadow" (1933). In "A Voyage to Sfanomoë", brothers Hotar and Evidon resign themselves to the sinking of their home. Charting a course for the planet of Sfanomoë, their arrival results in evocative descriptions of alien flora and fauna. Yet, the story ends with two distinct images of environmental agency. All civilizations, it suggests, must eventually reach their end.

There are many marvelous tales, untold, unwritten, never to be recorded or remembered, lost beyond all divining and all imagining, that sleep in the double silence of far-recessive time and space. The chronicles of Saturn, the archives of the moon in its prime, the legends of Antillia and Moaria—these are full of an unsurmised or forgotten wonder. And strange are the multitudinous tales withheld by the light-years of Polaris and the Galaxy. But none is stranger, none more marvelous, than the tale of Hotar and Evidon and their voyage to the planet Sfanomoë, from the last isle of foundering Atlantis. Harken, for I alone shall tell the story, who came in a dream to the changeless center where the past and future are always contemporary with the present; and saw the veritable happening thereof; and, waking, gave it words:

Hotar and Evidon were brothers in science as well as by consanguinity. They were the last representatives of a long line of illustrious inventors and investigators, all of whom had contributed more or less to the knowledge, wisdom and scientific resources of a lofty civilization matured through cycles. One by one they and their fellow-savants had learned the arcanic secrets of geology, of chemistry, of biology, of astronomy; they had subverted the elements, had constrained the sea, the sun, the air and the force of gravitation, compelling them to serve the uses of man; and lastly they had found a way to release the typhonic power of the atom, to destroy, transmute and reconstruct the molecules of matter at will.

However, by that irony which attends all the triumphs and achievements of man, the progress of this mastering of natural law was coincidental with the profound geologic changes and upheavals which caused the gradual sinking of Atlantis. Age by age, eon by eon, the process had gone on: huge peninsulas, whole seaboards, high mountain ranges, citied plains and plateaus, all went down in turn beneath the diluvial waves. With the advance of science, the time and location of future cataclysms was more accurately predictable; but nothing could be done to avert them.

In the days of Hotar and Evidon, all that remained of the former continent was a large isle, called Poseidonis. It was well known that this isle, with its opulent sea-ports, its eon-surviving monuments of art and architecture, its fertile inland valleys, and mountains lifting their spires of snow above semi-tropic jungles, was destined to go down ere the sons and daughters of the present generation had grown to maturity.

Like many others of their family, Hotar and Evidon had devoted long years of research to the obscure telluric laws governing the imminent catastrophe; and had sought to devise a means of prevention, or, at least, of retardation. But the seismic forces involved were too deeply seated and too widespread in their operation to be controllable in any manner or degree. No magnetic mechanism, no zone of repressive force, was powerful enough to affect them. When the two brothers were nearing middle age, they realized the ultimate futility of their endeavors; and though the peoples of Poseidonis continued to regard them as possible saviors, whose knowledge and resource were well-nigh superhuman, they had secretly abandoned all effort to salvage the doomed isle, and had retired from sea-gazing Lephara, the immemorial home of their family, to a private observatory and laboratory far up in the mountains of the interior.

Here, with the hereditary wealth at their command, the brothers surrounded themselves not only with all the known instruments and materials of scientific endeavor, but also with a certain degree of personal luxury. They were secluded from the world by a hundred scarps and precipices and by many leagues of little-trodden jungle; and they deemed this seclusion advisable for the labors which they now proposed to themselves, and whose real nature they had not divulged to any one.

Hotar and Evidon had gone beyond all others of their time in the study of astronomy. The true character and relationship of the world, the sun, the moon, the planetary system and the stellar universe, had long been known in Atlantis. But the brothers had speculated more boldly, had calculated more profoundly and more closely than any one else. In the powerful magnifying mirrors of their observatory, they had given special attention to the neighboring planets; had formed an accurate idea of their distance from the earth; had estimated their relative size; and had conceived the notion that several, or perhaps all, might well be inhabited by creatures similar to man; or, if not inhabited, were potentially capable of supporting human life.

Venus, which the Atlanteans knew by the name of Sfanomoë, was the planet which drew their curiosity and their conjecture more than any other. Because of its position, they surmised that it might readily resemble the earth in climatic conditions and in all the prerequisites of biological development. And the hidden labor to which they were now devoting their energies was nothing less than the invention of a vehicle by which it would be possible to leave the ocean-threatened isle and voyage to Sfanomoë.

Day by day the brothers toiled to perfect their invention; and night by night, through the ranging seasons, they peered at the lustrous orb of their speculations as it hung in the emerald evening of Poseidonis, or above the violet-shrouded heights that would soon take the saffron footprints of the dawn. And ever they gave themselves to bolder imaginings, to stranger and more perilous projects.

The vehicle they were building was designed with complete foreknowledge of all the problems to be faced, of all the difficulties to be overcome. Various types of air-vessels had been used in Atlantis for epochs; but they knew that none of these would be suitable for their purpose even in a modified form. The vehicle they finally devised, after much planning and long discussion, was a perfect sphere, like a miniature moon; since, as they argued, all bodies travelling through etheric space were of this shape. It was made with double walls of a metallic alloy whose secret they themselves had discovered—an alloy that was both light and tough beyond any substance classified by chemistry or mineralogy. There were a dozen small round windows lined with an unbreakable glass, and a door of the same alloy as the walls, that could be shut with hermetic tightness. The explosion of atoms in sealed cylinders was to furnish the propulsive and levitative power and would also serve to heat the sphere's interior against the absolute cold of space. Solidified air was to be carried in electrum containers and vaporized at the rate which would maintain a respirable atmosphere. And foreseeing that the gravitational influence of the earth would lessen and cease as they went further and further away from it, they had established in the floor of the sphere a magnetic zone that would simulate the effect of gravity and thus obviate any bodily danger or discomfort to which they might otherwise be liable.

Their labors were carried on with no other assistance than that of a few slaves, members of an aboriginal race of Atlantis, who had no conception of the purpose for which the vessel was being built; and who, to insure their complete discretion, were deaf-mutes. There were no interruptions from visitors, for it was tacitly assumed throughout the isle that Hotar and Evidon were engaged in seismologic researches that required a concentration both profound and prolonged.

At length, after years of toil, of vacillation, doubt, anxiety, the sphere was completed. Shining like an immense bubble of silver, it stood on a westward-facing terrace of the laboratory, from which the planet Sfanomoë was now visible at even-tide beyond the purpling sea of the jungle. All was in readiness: the vessel was amply provisioned for a journey of many lustrums and decades, and was furnished with an abundant supply of books, with implements of art and science, with all things needful for the comfort and convenience of the voyagers.

Hotar and Evidon were now men of middle years, in the hale maturity of all their powers and faculties. They were the highest type of the Atlantean race, with fair complexions and lofty stature, with the features of a lineage both aristocratic and intellectual. Knowing the nearness of the final cataclysm, they had never married, they had not even formed any close ties but had given themselves to science with a monastic devotion. They mourned the inevitable perishing of their civilization, with all its epoch-garnered lore, its material and artistic wealth, its consummate refinement. But they had learned the universality of the laws whose operation was plunging Atlantis beneath the wave—the laws of change, of increase and decay; and they had schooled themselves to a philosophic resignation—a resignation which, mayhap, was not untempered by a foresight of the singular glory and novel, unique experiences that would be entailed by their flight upon hitherto-untravelled space.

Their emotions, therefore, were a mingling of altruistic regret and personal expectancy, when, on the evening chosen for their departure, they dismissed their wondering slaves with a writ of manumission, and entered the orb-shaped vessel. And Sfanomoë brightened before them with a pulsing luster, and Poseidonis darkened below, as they began their voyage into the sea-green heavens of the west.

The great vessel rose with a buoyant ease beneath their guidance; till soon they saw the lights of Susran the capital and its galley-crowded port Lephara, where nightly revels were held and the very fountains ran with wine that people might forget awhile the predicted doom. But so high in air had the vessel climbed, that Hotar and Evidon could hear no faintest murmur of the loud lyres and strident merrymaking in the cities beneath. And they went onward and upward till the world was a dark blur and the skies were aflame with stars that their optic mirrors had never revealed. And anon the black planet below was rimmed with a growing crescent of fire, and they soared from its shadow to unsetting daylight. But the heavens were no longer a familiar blue, but had taken on the lucid ebon of ether; and no star nor world, not even the littlest, was dimmed by the rivalship of the sun. And brighter than all was Sfanomoë, where it hung with unvacil-lating lambence in the void.

Mile by stellar mile the earth was left behind; and Hotar and Evidon, peering ahead to the goal of their dreams, had almost forgot-ten it. Then, gazing back, they saw that it was no longer below but above them, like a vaster moon. And studying its oceans and isles and continents, they named them over one by one from their maps as the globe revolved; but vainly they sought for Poseidonis, amid an unbroken glittering waste of sea. And the brothers were conscious of that regret and sorrow which is the just due of all evanished beauty, of all sunken splendor. And they mused awhile on the glory that had been Atlantis, and recalled to memory her obelisks and domes and mountains, her palms with high and haughty crests, and the fire-tall plumes of her warriors, that would lift no longer to the sun.

Their life in the orb-like vessel was one of ease and tranquillity, and differed little from that to which they were accustomed. They pursued their wonted studies, they went on with experiments they had planned or begun in past days, they read to each other the classic literature of Atlantis, they argued and discussed a million problems of philosophy or science. And time itself was scarcely heeded by Hotar and Evidon; and the weeks and months of their journey became years, and the years were added into lustrums, and the lustrums into decades. Nor were they sensible of the change in themselves and in each other, as the years began to weave a web of wrinkles in their faces, to tint their brows with the yellow ivory of age and to thread their sable beards with ermine. There were too many things to be solved or debated, too many speculations and surmises to be ventured, for such trivial details as these to usurp their attention.

Sfanomoë grew larger and larger as the half-oblivious years went by; till anon it rolled beneath them with strange markings of untravelled continents and seas unsailed by man. And now the discourse of Hotar and Evidon was wholly concerning the world in which they would so soon arrive, and the peoples, animals and plants which they might expect to find. They felt in their ageless hearts the thrill of an anticipation without parallel, as they steered their vessel toward the ever-widening orb that swam below them. Soon they hung above its surface, in a cloud-laden atmosphere of tropic warmth; but though they were childishly eager to set foot on the new planet, they sagely decided to continue their journey on a horizontal level till they could study its topography with some measure of care and precision.

To their surprize, they found nothing in the bright expanse below that in any manner suggested the work of men or living beings. They had looked for towering cities of exotic aerial architecture, for broad thoroughfares and canals and geometrically measured areas of agricultural fields. Instead, there was only a primordial landscape of mountains, marshes, forests, oceans, rivers and lakes.

At length they made up their minds to descend. Though they were old, old men, with five-foot ermine beards, they brought the moon-shaped vessel down with all the skill of which they would have been capable in their prime; and opening the door that had been sealed for decades, they emerged in turn—Hotar preceding Evidon, since he was a little the elder.

Their first impressions were of torrid heat, of dazzling color and overwhelming perfume. There seemed to be a million odors in the heavy, strange, unstirring air—odors that were almost visible in the form of wreathing vapors—perfumes that were like elixirs and opiates, that conferred at the same time a blissful drowsiness and a divine exhilaration. Then they saw that there were flowers everywhere—that they had descended in a wilderness of blossoms. They were all of unearthly forms, of supermundane size and beauty and variety, with scrolls and volutes of petals many-hued, that seemed to curl and twist with a more than vegetable animation or sentiency. They grew from a ground that their overlapping stems and calyxes had utterly concealed; they hung from the boles and fronds of palm-like trees they had mantled beyond recognition; they thronged the water of still pools; they poised on the jungle-tops like living creatures winged for flight to the perfume-drunken heavens. And even as the brothers watched, the flowers grew and faded with a thaumaturgic swiftness, they fell and replaced each other as if by some legerdemain of natural law.

Hotar and Evidon were delighted, they called out to each other like children, they pointed at each new floral marvel that was more exquisite and curious than the rest; and they wondered at the speed of their miraculous growth and decay. And they laughed at the unexampled bizarrerie of the sight, when they perceived certain animals new to zoology, who were trotting about on more than the usual number of legs, with orchidaceous blossoms springing from their rumps.

They forgot their long voyage through space, they forgot there had ever been a planet called the earth and an isle named Poseidonis, they forgot their lore and their wisdom, as they roamed through the flowers of Sfanomoë. The exotic air and its odors mounted to their heads like a mighty wine; and the clouds of golden and snowy pollen which fell upon them from the arching arbors were potent as some fantastic drug. It pleased them that their white beards and violet tunics should be powdered with this pollen and with the floating spores of plants that were alien to all terrene botany.

Suddenly Hotar cried out with a new wonder, and laughed with a more boisterous mirth than before. He had seen that an oddly folded leaf was starting from the back of his shrunken right hand. The leaf unfurled as it grew, it disclosed a flower-bud; and lo! the bud opened and became a triple-chaliced blossom of unearthly hues, adding a rich perfume to the swooning air. Then, on his left hand, another blossom appeared in like manner; and then leaves and petals were burgeoning from his wrinkled face and brow, were going in successive tiers from his limbs and body, were mingling their hair-like tendrils and tongue-shaped pistils with his beard. He felt no pain, only an infantile surprize and bewilderment as he watched them.

Now from the hands and face and limbs of Evidon the blossoms also began to spring. And soon the two old men had ceased to wear a human semblance, and were hardly to be distinguished from the garland-laden trees about them. And they died with no agony, as if they were already part of the teeming floral life of Sfanomoë, with such perceptions and sensations as were appropriate to their new mode of existence. And before long their metamorphosis was complete, and every fiber of their bodies had undergone a dissolution into flowers. And the vessel in which they had made their voyage was embowered from sight in an ever-climbing mass of plants and blossoms.

Such was the fate of Hotar and Evidon, the last of the Atlanteans, and the first (if not also the last) of human visitors to Sfanomoë.

SPAWN OF DAGON

Henry Kuttner

Henry Kuttner (1915–1958) was an American author born in Los Angeles, California. A prominent member of the Lovecraft Circle, and a mentor to future pulp heroes Leigh Brackett and Ray Bradbury, Kuttner spent much of his early adulthood working as a reader for the literary agency of his uncle, Laurence D'Orsay. His own literary debut, the poem "Ballad of the Gods", was published in the February 1936 edition of *Weird Tales*. Commencing his career as a fiction writer, "The Graveyard Rats"—recently adapted as part of *Guillermo del Toro's Cabinet of Curiosities* (2022)—would follow the month after. Kuttner's broader body of work includes the novels *The Dark World* (1946), *Fury* (1947) and *The Well of the Worlds* (1952). Under the pseudonyms of Lawrence O'Donnell, C. H. Liddell or Lewis Padgett, Kuttner wrote frequently alongside his wife, and fellow pulp pioneer, C. L. Moore.

First published in the July 1938 issue of *Weird Tales*, "Spawn of Dagon" unites the legacies of many of the authors here collected. The second instalment of Kuttner's "Elak of Atlantis" series, the swashbuckling style of the adventure pays homage to the Sword and Sorcery popularized by Robert E. Howard. Situated within the broader Cthulhu Mythos, Kuttner further tints his tale with the eldritch horror of one of Lovecraft's most notorious evils. Elak, with the assistance of his drunken companion, Lycon, is tasked with killing the "Wizard of Atlantis", Zend. Upon the near completion of their mission, however, he discovers that his benefactors are disinclined towards the preservation of Atlantis. A final Weird fantasy, "Spawn of Dagon" concerns not the sinking of Atlantis, but its salvation. Elak of Atlantis would return in Kuttner's other tales, "Thunder in the Dark" (1938), "Beyond the Phoenix" (1938) and "Dragon Moon" (1941).

Under all graves they murmur,
They murmur and rebel,
Down to the buried kingdoms creep,
And like a lost rain roar and weep
O'er the red heavens of hell.
—CHESTERTON.

Two streams of blood trickled slowly across the rough boards of the floor. One of them emerged from a gaping wound in the throat of a prostrate, armor-clad body; the other dripped from a chink in the battered cuirass, and the swaying light of a hanging lamp cast grotesque shadows over the corpse and the two men who crouched on their hams watching it. They were both very drunk. One of them, a tall, extremely slender man whose bronzed body seemed boneless, so supple was it, murmured:

"I win, Lycon. The blood wavers strangely, but the stream I spilt will reach this crack first." He indicated a space between two planks with the point of his rapier.

Lycon's child-like eyes widened in astonishment. He was short, thick-set, with a remarkably simian face set atop his broad shoulders. He swayed slightly as he gasped, "By Ishtar! The blood runs up-hill!"

Elak, the slender man, chuckled. "After all the mead you swilled the ocean might run up-hill. Well, the wager's won; I get the loot." He got up and stepped over to the dead man. Swiftly he searched him, and suddenly muttered an explosive curse. "The swine's as bare as a Bacchic vestal! He has no purse."

Lycon smiled broadly and looked more than ever like an undersized hairless ape. "The gods watch over me," he said in satisfaction.

"Of all the millions in Atlantis you had to pick a fight with a pauper," Elak groaned. "Now we'll have to flee San-Mu, as your quarrels have forced us to flee Poseidonia and Kornak. And the San-Mu mead is the best in the land. If you had to cause trouble, why not choose a fat usurer? We'd have been paid for our trouble, then, at least."

"The gods watch over me," Lycon reiterated, leaning forward and then rocking back, chuckling to himself. He leaned too far and fell on his nose, where he remained without moving. Something dropped from the bosom of his tunic and fell with a metallic sound to the oaken floor. Lycon snored.

Elak, smiling unpleasantly, appropriated the purse and investigated its contents. "Your fingers are swifter than mine," he told the recumbent Lycon, "but I can hold more mead than you. Next time don't try to cheat one who has more brains in his big toe than you have in all your misshapen body. Scavenging little ape! Get up; the innkeeper is returning with soldiers."

He thrust the purse into the wallet at his belt and kicked Lycon heartily, but the small thief failed to awaken. Cursing with a will, Elak hoisted the body of the other to his shoulders and staggered toward the back of the tavern. The distant sound of shouting from the street outside grew louder, and Elak thought he could hear the querulous complaints of the innkeeper.

"There will be a reckoning, Lycon!" he promised bitterly. "Ishtar, yes! You'll learn—"

He pushed through a golden drapery and hurried along a corridor—kicked open an oaken door and came out in the alley behind the tavern. Above, cold stars glittered frostily, and an icy wind blew on Elak's sweating face, sobering him somewhat.

Lycon stirred and writhed in his arms. "More grog!" he muttered. "Oh gods! Is there no more grog?" A maudlin tear fell hotly on Elak's neck, and the latter for a moment entertained the not unpleasant idea of dropping Lycon and leaving him for the irate guards. The soldiers of San-Mu were not renowned for their soft-heartedness, and tales of what they sometimes did to their captives were unpleasantly explicit.

However, he ran along the alley instead, blundered into a brawny form that sprang out of the darkness abruptly, and saw a snarling, bearded face indistinct in the vague starlight. He dropped Lycon and whipped out his rapier. Already the soldier was plunging forward, his great sword rushing down.

Then it happened. Elak saw the guard's mouth open in a square of amazement, saw horror spring into the cold eyes. The man's face was a mask of abysmal fear. He flung himself back desperately—the sword-tip just missed Elak's face.

The soldier raced away into the shadows.

With a snakelike movement Elak turned, rapier ready. He caught a blur of swift motion. The man facing him had lifted quick hands to his face, and dropped them as suddenly. But there was no menace in the gesture. Nevertheless Elak felt a chill of inexplicable uneasiness crawl down his back as he faced his rescuer. The soldiers of San-Mu were courageous, if lacking in human kindness. What had frightened the attacking guard?

He eyed the other. He saw a medium-sized man, clad in voluminous gray garments that were almost invisible in the gloom—saw a white face with regular, statuesque features. A black hollow sprang into existence within the white mask as a soft voice whispered, "You'd escape from the guards? No need for your rapier—I'm a friend."

"Who the—but there's no time for talk. Thanks, and good-bye."

Elak stooped and hoisted Lycon to his shoulders again. The little man was blinking and murmuring soft appeals for more mead. And the hasty thunder of mailed feet grew louder, while torchlight swiftly approaching cast gleams of light about the trio.

"In here," the gray-clad man whispered. "You'll be safe." Now Elak saw that in the stone wall beside him a black rectangle gaped. He sprang through the portal without hesitation. The other followed, and instantly they were in utter blackness as an unseen door swung creakingly on rusty hinges.

Elak felt a soft hand touch his own. Or was it a hand? For a second he had the incredible feeling that the thing whose flesh he had touched did not belong to any human body—it was too soft, too cold! His skin crawled at the feel of the thing. It was withdrawn, and a fold of gray cloth swung against his palm. He gripped it.

"Follow!"

Silently, gripping the guide's garment, bearing Lycon on his shoulders, Elak moved forward. How the other could find his way through the blackness Elak did not know, unless he knew the way by heart. Yet the passage—if passage it was—turned and twisted endlessly as it went down. Presently Elak had the feeling that he was moving through a larger space, a cave, perhaps. His footsteps sounded differently, somehow. And through the darkness vague whisperings came to him.

Whispers in no language he knew. The murmurous sibilants rustled out strangely, making Elak's brows contract and his free hand go involuntarily to the hilt of his rapier. He snarled, "Who's here?"

The invisible guide cried out in the mysterious tongue. Instantly the whisperings stopped.

"You are among friends," a voice said softly from the blackness. "We are almost at our destination. A few more steps—"

A few more steps, and light blazed up. They stood in a small rectangular chamber hollowed out of the rock. The nitrous walls gleamed dankly in the glow of an oil lamp, and a little stream ran across the rock floor of the cave and lost itself, amid chuckles of goblin laughter, in a small hole at the base of the wall. Two doors were visible. The gray-clad man was closing one of them.

A crude table and a few chairs were all the furnishings of the room. Elak strained his ears. He heard something—something that should not be heard in inland San-Mu. He could not be mistaken. The sound of waves lapping softly in the distance... and occasionally a roaring crash, as of breakers smashing on a rocky shore.

He dumped Lycon unceremoniously in one of the chairs. The little man fell forward on the table, pillowing his head in his arms. Sadly he muttered, "Is there no mead in Atlantis? I die, Elak. My belly is an arid desert across which the armies of Eblis march."

He sobbed unhappily for a moment and fell asleep.

Elak ostentatiously unsheathed his rapier and laid it on the table. His slender fingers closed on the hilt. "An explanation," he said, "is due. Where are we?"

"I am Gesti," said the gray-clad one. His face seemed chalk-white in the light of the oil lamp. His eyes, deeply sunken, were covered with a curious glaze. "I saved you from the guards, eh? You'll not deny that?"

"You have my thanks," Elak said. "Well?"

"I need the aid of a brave man. And I'll pay well. If you're interested, good. If not, I'll see you leave San-Mu safely."

Elak considered. "It's true we've little money." He thought of the purse in his wallet and grinned wryly. "Not enough to last us long, at any rate. Perhaps we're interested. Although—" He hesitated.

"Well?"

"I could bear to know how you got rid of the soldier so quickly, back in the alley behind the tavern."

"I do not think that matters," Gesti whispered in his sibilant voice. "The guards are superstitious. And it's easy to play on their weakness. Let that suffice!" The cold glazed eyes met Elak's squarely, and a little warning note seemed to clang in his brain.

There was danger here. Yet danger had seldom given him pause. He said, "What will you pay?"

"A thousand golden pieces."

"Fifty thousand cups of mead," Lycon murmured sleepily. "Accept it, Elak. I'll await you here."

There was little affection in the glance Elak cast at his companion. "You'll get none of it," he promised. "Not a gold piece!"

He turned to Gesti. "What's to be done for this reward?"

Gesti's immobile face watched him cryptically. "Kill Zend."

Elak said, "Kill—Zend? *Zend?* The Wizard of Atlantis?"

"Are you afraid?" Gesti asked tonelessly.

"I am," Lycon said without lifting his head from his arms. "However, if Elak is not, he may slay Zend and I'll wait here."

Ignoring him, Elak said, "I've heard strange things of Zend. His powers are not human. Indeed, he's not been seen in the streets of San-Mu for ten years. Men say he's immortal."

"Men—are fools." And in Gesti's voice there was a contempt that made Elak stare at him sharply. It was as though Gesti was commenting on some race alien to him. The gray-clad man went on hurriedly, as though sensing the trend of Elak's thoughts. "We have driven a passage under Zend's palace. We can break through at any time; that we shall do tonight. Two tasks I give you: kill Zend; shatter the red sphere."

Elak said, "You're cryptic. What red sphere?"

"It lies in the topmost minaret of his palace. His magic comes from it. There is rich loot in the palace, Elak—if that's your name. So the little man called you."

"Elak or dunce or robber of drunken men," Lycon said, absently feeling the bosom of his tunic. "All alike. Call him by any of those names and you'll be right. Where is my gold, Elak?"

But without waiting for an answer he slumped down in his chair, his eyes closing and his mouth dropping open as he snored. Presently he fell off the chair and rolled under the table, where he slumbered.

"What the devil can I do with him?" Elak asked. "I can't take him with me. He'd—"

"Leave him here," Gesti said.

Elak's cold eyes probed the other. "He'll be safe?"

"Quite safe. None in San-Mu but our band knows of this underground way."

"What band is that?" Elak asked.

Gesti said nothing for a time. Then his soft voice whispered, "Need you know? A political group banded together to overthrow the king of San-Mu, and Zend, from whom he gets his power. Have you more—questions?"

"No."

"Then follow."

Gesti led Elak to one of the oaken doors; it swung open, and they moved forward up a winding passage. In the dark Elak stumbled over a step. He felt the cloth of Gesti's garment touch his hand, and gripped it. In the blackness they ascended a staircase cut out of the rock.

Half-way up, Gesti paused. "I can go no further," he whispered. "The way is straight. At the end of the stairway there is a trap-door of stone. Open it. You'll be in Zend's place. Here is a weapon for you." He thrust a tube of cold metal into Elak's hand. "Simply squeeze its sides, pointing the smaller end at Zend. You understand?"

Elak nodded, and, although Gesti could scarcely have seen the movement in the darkness, he whispered, "Good. Dagon guard you!"

He turned away; Elak heard the soft rush of his descent dying in the distance. He began to mount the stairs, wonderingly. Dagon—was Gesti a worshipper of the forbidden evil god of ocean? Poseidon, a benignant sea-god, was adored in marble temples all over the land, but the dark worship of Dagon had been banned for generations. There were tales of another race whose god Dagon was—a race that had not sprung from human or even earthly loins...

Gripping the odd weapon, Elak felt his way upward. At length his head banged painfully against stone, and, cursing softly, he felt about in the darkness. It was the trap-door of which Gesti had spoken. Two bolts slid back in well-oiled grooves. And the door lifted easily as Elak thrust his shoulders against it.

He clambered up in semi-darkness, finding himself in a small bare room through which light filtered from a narrow window-slit high in the wall. A mouse, squeaking fearfully, fled as he scrambled to his feet. Apparently the room was little used. Elak moved stealthily to the door.

It swung open a little under his cautious hand. A corridor stretched before him, dimly lit by cold blue radiance that came from tiny gems set in the ceiling at intervals. Elak followed the upward slant of the passage; the red sphere Gesti had mentioned was in the topmost minaret. Up, then:

In a niche in the wall Elak saw the head. The shock of it turned him cold with amazement. A bodiless head, set upright on a golden pedestal within a little alcove—its cheeks sunken, hair lank and disheveled—but eyes bright with incredible life! Those eyes watched him!

"Ishtar!" Elak breathed. "What wizardry's this?"

He soon found out. The pallid lips of the horror writhed and twisted, and from them came a high skirling cry of warning.

"Zend! Zend! A stranger walks your—"

Elak's rapier flew. There was scarcely any blood. He dragged the blade from the eyesocket, whispering prayers to all the gods and goddesses he could remember. The lean jaw dropped, and a blackened and swollen tongue lolled from between the teeth. A red, shrunken eyelid dropped over the eye Elak had not pierced.

There was no sound save for Elak's hastened breathing. He eyed the monstrous thing in the alcove, and then, confident that it was no longer a menace, lengthened his steps up the passage. Had Zend heard the warning of his sentinel? If so, danger lurked all about him.

A silver curtain slashed with a black pattern hung across the corridor. Elak parted it, and, watching, he froze in every muscle.

A dwarf, no more than four feet tall, with a disproportionately large head and a gray, wrinkled skin, was trotting briskly toward him. From the tales he had heard Elak imagined the dwarf to be Zend, Behind the wizard strode a half-naked giant, who carried over his shoulder the limp form of a girl. Elak spun about, realizing that he had delayed too long. Zend was parting the silver curtain as Elak raced back down the corridor.

At his side a black rectangle loomed—a passage he had overlooked, apparently, when he had passed it before. He sprang into its shielding darkness. When Zend passed he would strike down the wizard and take his chances with the giant. Remembering the smooth hard muscles that had rippled under the dead-white skin of the man, Elak was not so sure that his chances would be worth much. He realized now that the giant had seemed familiar.

Then he knew. Two days ago he had seen a man—a condemned criminal—beheaded in the temple of Poseidon. There could be no mistake. The giant was the same man, brought back to life by Zend's evil necromancy!

"Ishtar!" Elak whispered, sweating. "I'd be better off in the hands of the guards." How could he slay a man who was already dead?

Elak hesitated, his rapier half drawn. There was no use borrowing trouble. He would keep safely out of sight until Zend was separated from his ghastly servitor—and then it would be an easy matter to put six inches of steel through the wizard's body. Elak was never one for taking unnecessary risks, as he had a wholesome regard for his hide. He heard a shuffling of feet and drew back within the side-passage to let Zend pass. But the wizard turned suddenly and began to mount the steeply sloping corridor where Elak lurked. In Zend's hand was a softly glowing gem that illuminated the passage, though not brightly.

Elak fled. The passage was steep and narrow, and it ended at last before a blank wall. Behind him a steady padding of feet grew louder in the distance. He felt around desperately in the dark. If there was a hidden spring in the walls, he failed to find it.

A grin lighted his face as he realized how narrow the passage was. If he could do it—

He placed his palms flat against the wall, and with his bare feet found an easy purchase on the opposite one. Face down, swiftly, with his muscles cracking under the strain, he walked up the wall until he was safely above the head of even the giant. There he stopped, sweating, and glanced down.

Only an enormously strong man could have done it, and if Elak had weighed a little more it would have been impossible. His shoulders and thighs ached as he strained to hold his position without moving.

The trio were approaching. If they should glance up, Elak was ready to drop and use his blade, or the strange weapon Gesti had given him. But apparently they did not notice him, hidden as he was in the shadows of the high ceiling.

He caught a glimpse of the girl the giant carried. A luscious wench! But, of course, Zend would undoubtedly choose only the most attractive maidens for his necromancy and sorcery.

"If that dead-alive monster weren't here," he ruminated, "I'd be tempted to fall on Zend's head. No doubt the girl would be grateful."

She was, at the moment, unconscious. Long black lashes lay on cream-pale cheeks, and dark ringlets swayed as the giant lurched on. Zend's hand fumbled out, touched the wall. The smooth surface of stone lifted and the gray dwarf pattered into the dimness beyond. The giant followed, and the door dropped again.

With a low curse of relief Elak swung noiselessly to the floor and rubbed his hands on his leather tunic. They were bleeding, and only the hardness of his soles had saved his feet from a similar fate. After a brief wait Elak fumbled in the darkness and found the concealed spring.

The door lifted, with a whispering rush of sound. Elak found himself in a short corridor that ended in another black-slashed silver curtain. He moved forward, noticing with relief that the door remained open behind him.

Beyond the silver curtain was a room—huge, high-domed, with great open windows through which the chill night wind blew strongly.

The room blazed with the coruscating brilliance of the glowing gems, which were set in walls and ceiling in bizarre, arabesque patterns. Through one window Elak saw the yellow globe of the moon, which was just rising. Three archways, curtained, broke the smooth expanse of the farther wall. The chamber itself, richly furnished with rugs and silks and ornaments, was empty of occupants. Elak noiselessly covered the distance to the archways and peered through the curtain of the first.

Blazing white light blinded him. He had a flashing, indistinct vision of tremendous forces, leashed, cyclopean, straining mightily to burst the bonds that held them. Yet actually he saw nothing—merely an empty room. But empty he knew that it was not! Power unimaginable surged from beyond the archway, shuddering through every atom of Elak's body. Glittering steel walls reflected his startled face.

And on the floor, in the very center of the room, he saw a small mud-colored stone. That was all. Yet about the stone surged a tide of power that made Elak drop the curtain and back away, his eyes wide with fear. Very quickly he turned to the next curtain—peered apprehensively beyond it.

Here was a small room, cluttered with alembics, retorts, and other of Zend's magical paraphernalia. The pallid giant stood silently in a corner. On a low table was stretched the girl, still unconscious. Above her hovered the gray dwarf, a crystal vial in one hand. He tilted it; a drop fell.

Elak heard Zend's harsh voice.

"A new servant… a new soul to serve me. When her soul is freed, I shall send it to Antares. There is a planet there where I've heard much sorcery exists. Mayhap I can learn a few more secrets…"

Elak turned to the last alcove. He lifted the curtain, saw a steep stairway. From it rose-red light blazed down. He remembered Gesti's words: "Shatter the red sphere! His magic comes from it."

Good! He'd break the sphere first, and then, with no magic to protect him, Zend would be easy prey. With a lithe bound Elak began to mount the stairs. Behind him came a guttural cry.

"Eblis, Ishtar, and Poseidon!" Elak said hastily. "Protect me now!" He was at the top of the staircase, in a high-domed room through which moonlight crept from narrow windows. It was the room of the sphere.

Glowing, shining with lambent rose-red radiance, the great sphere lay in a silver cradle, metallic tubes and wires trailing from it to vanish into the walls. Half as tall as Elak's body it was, its brilliance soft but hypnotically intense—and he stood for a moment motionless, staring.

Behind him feet clattered on the stair. He turned, saw the pallid giant lumbering up. A livid scar circled the dead-white neck. He had been right, then. This was the criminal he had seen executed—brought back to life by Zend's necromancy. In the face of real danger Elak forgot the gods and drew his rapier. Prayers, he had found, would not halt a dagger's blow or a strangler's hands.

Without a sound the giant sprang for Elak, who dodged under the great clutching paws and sent his rapier's point deep within the dead-white breast. It bent dangerously; he whipped it out just in time to save it from snapping, and it sang shrilly as it vibrated. Elak's opponent seemed unhurt. Yet the rapier had pierced his heart. He bled not at all.

The battle was not a long one, and it ended at a window. The two men went reeling and swaying about the room, ripping wires and tubes from their places in the fury of their struggle. Abruptly the red light of the globe dimmed, went out. Simultaneously Elak felt the giant's cold arms go about his waist.

Before they could tighten, he dropped. The moon peered in at a narrow window just beside him, and he flung himself desperately against the giant's legs, wrenching with all his strength. The undead creature toppled.

He came down as a tree falls, without striving to break the force of the impact. His hands went out clutchingly for Elak's throat. But Elak was shoving frantically at the white, cold, muscular body, forcing it out the narrow window. It overbalanced, toppled—and fell.

The giant made no outcry. After a moment a heavy thud was audible. Elak got up and recovered his rapier, loudly thanking Ishtar for his deliverance. "For," he thought, "a little politeness costs nothing, and even though my own skill and not Ishtar's hand saved me, one never knows." Too, there were other dangers to face, and if the gods are capricious, the goddesses are certainly even more so.

A loud shriek from below made him go quickly down the stairway, rapier ready. Zend was running toward him, his gray face a mask of fear. The dwarf hesitated at sight of him, spun about as a low rumble of voices came from near by. At the foot of the stairway Elak waited.

From the passage by which Elak had entered the great room a horde of nightmare beings spewed. In their van came Gesti, gray garments flapping, white face immobile as ever. Behind him sheer horror squirmed and leaped and tumbled. With a shock of loathing Elak remembered the whispering voices he had heard in the underground cavern—and knew, now, what manner of creatures had spoken thus.

A race that had not sprung from human or even earthly loins...

Their faces were hideous staring masks, fish-like in contour, with parrot-like beaks and great staring eyes covered with a filmy glaze. Their bodies were amorphous things, half solid and half gelatinous ooze, like the iridescent slime of jellyfish; writhing tentacles sprouted irregularly from the ghastly bodies of the things. They were the offspring of no sane universe, and they came in a blasphemous hissing rush across the room. The rapier stabbed out vainly and clattered to the stones as Elak went down. He struggled futilely for a moment, hearing the harsh, agonized shrieks of the wizard. Cold tentacles were all about him, blinding him in their constricting coils. Then suddenly the weight that held him helpless was gone. His legs and arms, he discovered, were tightly bound with cords. He fought vainly to escape; then lay quietly.

Beside him, he saw, the wizard lay tightly trussed. The nightmare beings were moving in an orderly rush toward the room in which Elak had sensed the surges of tremendous power, where lay the little brown stone. They vanished beyond the curtain, and beside Elak and the wizard there remained only Gesti. He stood looking down at the two, his white face immobile.

"What treachery is this?" Elak asked with no great hopefulness. "Set me free and give me my gold."

But Gesti merely said, "You won't need it. You will die very soon."

"Eh? Why—"

"Fresh human blood is needed. That's why we didn't kill you or Zend. We need your blood. We'll be ready soon."

An outburst of sibilant whispers came from beyond the silver drape. Elak said unsteadily, "What manner of demons are those?"

The wizard gasped, "You ask *him*? Did you not know—"

Gesti lifted gloved hands and removed his face. Elak bit his lips to choke back a scream. Now he knew why Gesti's face had seemed so immobile. It was a mask.

Behind it were the parrot-like beak and fish-like eyes Elak now knew all too well. The gray robes sloughed off; the gloves dropped from the limber tips of tentacles. From the horrible beak came the sibilant whisper of the monster:

"Now you know whom you served."

The thing that had called itself Gesti turned and progressed—that was the only way to describe its method of moving—to the curtain behind which its fellows had vanished. It joined them.

Zend was staring at Elak. "You did not know? You served them, and yet did not know?"

"By Ishtar, no!" Elak swore. "D'you think I'd have let those—those—what are they? What are they going to do?"

"Roll over here," Zend commanded. "Maybe I can loosen your bonds."

Elak obeyed, and the wizard's fingers worked deftly.

"I doubt—no human hands tied these knots. But—"

"What are they?" Elak asked again. "Tell me, before I go mad thinking hell has loosed its legions on Atlantis."

"They are the children of Dagon," Zend said. "Their dwelling-place is in the great deeps of the ocean. Have you never heard of the unearthly ones who worship Dagon?"

"Yes. But I never believed—"

"Oh, there's truth in the tale. Eons and unimaginable eons ago, before mankind existed on earth, only the waters existed. There was no land. And from the slime there sprang up a race of beings which dwelt in the sunken abysses of the ocean, inhuman creatures that worshipped Dagon, their god. When eventually the waters receded and great continents arose, these beings were driven down to the lowest depths. Their mighty kingdom, that had once stretched from pole to pole, was shrunken as the huge land-masses lifted. Mankind came—but from whence I do not know—and civilizations arose. Hold still. These cursed knots—"

"I don't understand all of that," Elak said, wincing as the wizard's nail dug into his wrist. "But go on."

"These things hate man, for they feel that man has usurped their kingdom. Their greatest hope is to sink the continents again, so that the seas will roll over all the earth, and not a human being will survive. Their power will embrace the whole world, as it once did eons ago. They are not human, you see, and they worship Dagon. They want no other gods worshipped on Earth. Ishtar, dark Eblis, even Poseidon of the sunlit seas... They will achieve their desire now, I fear."

"Not if I can get free," Elak said. "How do the knots hold?"

"They hold," the wizard said discouragedly. "But one strand is loose. My fingers are raw. The—the red globe is broken?"

"No," Elak said. "Some cords were torn loose as I fought with your slave, and the light went out of it. Why?"

"The gods be thanked!" Zend said fervently. "If I can repair the damage and light the globe again, the children of Dagon will die. That's the purpose of it. The rays it emits destroy their bodies, which are otherwise invulnerable, or almost so. If I hadn't had the globe, they'd have invaded my palace and killed me long ago."

"They have a tunnel under the cellars," Elak said.

"I see. But they dared not invade the palace while the globe shone, for the light-rays would have killed them. Curse these knots! If they accomplish their purpose—"

"What's that?" Elak asked—but he had already guessed the answer.

"To sink Atlantis! This island-continent would have gone down beneath the sea long ago if I hadn't pitted my magic and my science against that of the children of Dagon. They are masters of the earthquake, and Atlantis rests on none too solid a foundation. Their power is sufficient to sink Atlantis for ever beneath the sea. But within that room"—Zend nodded toward the curtain that hid the sea-bred horrors—"in that room there is power far stronger than theirs. I have drawn strength from the stars, and the cosmic sources beyond the universe. You know nothing of my power. It is enough—more than enough—to keep Atlantis steady on its foundation, impregnable against the attacks of Dagon's breed. They have destroyed other lands before Atlantis."

Hot blood dripped on Elak's hands as the wizard tore at the cords.

"Aye... other lands. There were races that dwelt on Earth before man came. My powers have shown me a sunlit island that once reared far to the south, an island where dwelt a race of beings tall as trees, whose flesh was hard as stone, and whose shape was so strange you could scarcely comprehend it. The waters rose and covered that island, and its people died. I have seen a gigantic mountain that speared up from a waste of tossing waters, in Earth's youth, and in the towers and minarets that crowned its summit dwelt beings like sphinxes, with the heads of beasts and gods and whose broad wings could not save them when the cataclysm came. For ruin came to the city of the sphinxes, and it sank beneath the ocean—destroyed by the children of Dagon. And there was—"

"Hold!" Elak's breathless whisper halted the wizard's voice. "Hold! I see rescue, Zend."

"Eh?" The wizard screwed his head around until he too saw the short, ape-featured man who was running silently across the room, knife in hand. It was Lycon, whom Elak had left slumbering in the underground den of Gesti.

The knife flashed and Elak and Zend were free. Elak said swiftly, "Up the stairs, wizard. Repair your magic globe, since you say its light will kill these horrors. We'll hold the stairway."

Without a word the gray dwarf sped silently up the steps and was gone. Elak turned to Lycon.

"How the devil—"

Lycon blinked wide blue eyes. "I scarcely know, Elak. Only when you were carrying me out of the tavern and the soldier screamed and ran away I saw something that made me so drunk I couldn't remember what it was. I remembered only a few minutes ago, back downstairs somewhere. A face that looked like a gargoyle's, with a terrible great beak and eyes like Midgard Serpent's. And I remembered I'd seen Gesti put a mask over the awful face just before you turned there in the alley. So I knew Gesti was probably a demon."

"And so you came here," Elak commented softly. "Well, it's a good thing for me you did. I—what's the matter?" Lycon's blue eyes were bulging.

"Is this your demon?" the little man asked, pointing.

Elak turned, and smiled grimly. Facing him, her face puzzled and frightened, was the girl on whom Zend had been experimenting—the maiden whose soul he had been about to unleash to serve him when Elak had arrived. Her eyes were open now, velvet-soft and dark, and her white body gleamed against the silver-black drape.

Apparently she had awakened, and had arisen from her hard couch.

Elak's hand went up in a warning gesture, commanding silence, but it was too late. The girl said,

"Who are you? Zend kidnapped me—are you come to set me free? Where—"

With a bound Elak reached her, dragged her back, thrust her up the stairway. His rapier flashed in his hand. Over his shoulder he cast a wolfish smile.

"If we live, you'll escape Zend and his magic," he told the girl, hearing an outburst of sibilant cries and the rushing murmur of the attacking horde. Yet he did not turn. "What's your name?" he asked.

"Coryllis."

"'Ware, Elak!" Lycon shouted.

Elak turned to see the little man's sword flash out, shearing a questing tentacle in two. The severed end dropped, writhing and coiling in hideous knots. The frightful devil-masks of monsters glared into Elak's eyes. The children of Dagon came sweeping in a resistless rush, cold eyes glazed and glaring, tentacles questing, iridescent bodies shifting and pulsing like jelly—and Elak and Lycon and the girl, Coryllis, were caught by their fearful wave and forced back, up the staircase.

Snarling inarticulate curses, Lycon swung his sword, but it was caught and dragged from his hand by a muscular tentacle. Elak tried to shield Coryllis with his own body; he felt himself going down, smothering beneath the oppressive weight of cold, hideous bodies that writhed and twisted with dreadful life. He struck out desperately—and felt a hard, cold surface melting like snow beneath his hands.

The weight that held him down was dissipating—the things were retreating, flowing back, racing and flopping and tumbling down the stairs, shrieking an insane shrill cry. They blackened and melted into shapeless puddles of slime that trickled like a little gray stream down the stairway...

Elak realized what had happened. A rose-red light was glowing in the air all about him. The wizard had repaired his magic globe, and the power of its rays was destroying the nightmare menace that had crept up from the deeps.

In a heartbeat it was over. There was no trace of the horde that had attacked them. Gray puddles of ooze—no more. Elak realized that he was cursing softly, and abruptly changed it to a prayer. With great earnestness he thanked Ishtar for his deliverance.

Lycon recovered his sword, and handed Elak his rapier. "What now?" he asked.

"We're off! We're taking Coryllis with us—there's no need to linger here. True, we helped the wizard—but we fought him first. He may remember that. There's no need to test his gratefulness, and we'd be fools to do it."

He picked up Coryllis, who had quietly fainted, and quickly followed Lycon down the steps. They hurried across the great room and into the depths of the corridor beyond.

And five minutes later they were sprawled at full length under a tree in one of San-Mu's numerous parks. Elak had snatched a silken robe from a balcony as he passed beneath, and Coryllis had draped it about her slim body. The stars glittered frostily overhead, unconcerned with the fate of Atlantis—stars that would be shining thousands of years hence when Atlantis was not even a memory.

No thought of this came to Elak now. He wiped his rapier with a tuft of grass, while Lycon, who had already cleaned his blade, stood up and, shading his eyes with his palm, peered across the park. He muttered something under his breath and set off at a steady lope. Elak stared after him.

"Where's he going? There's a—by Ishtar! He's going in a grog shop. But he has no money. How—"

A shocked thought came to him, and he felt hastily in his wallet. Then he cursed. "The drunken little ape! When he slashed my bonds, in the wizard's palace, he stole the purse! I'll—"

Elak sprang to his feet and took a stride forward. Soft arms gripped his leg. He looked down. "Eh?"

"Let him go," Coryllis said, smiling. "He's earned his mead."

"Yes—but what about me? I—"

"Let him go," Coryllis murmured...

And, ever after that, Lycon was to wonder why Elak never upbraided him about the stolen purse.

The Lost Land

There is a story of a beauteous land,
Where fields were fertile and where flowers were bright;
Where tall towers glistened in the morning light,
Where happy children wandered hand in hand,
Where lovers wrote their names upon the sand.
They say it vanished from all human sight,
The hungry sea devoured it in a night.

You doubt the tale? ah, you will understand;
For, as men muse upon that fable old,
They give sad credence always at the last,
However they have cavilled at its truth,
When with a tear-dimmed vision they behold,
Swift sinking in the ocean of the Past,
The lovely lost Atlantis of their Youth.

Ella Wheeler Wilcox
from POEMS OF ELLA WHEELER WILCOX, *1910*

ALSO AVAILABLE

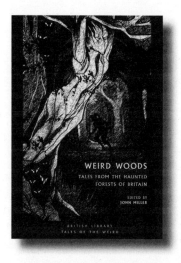

*But foliage surrounded him, branches blocked the
way; the trees stood close and still; and the sun dipped
that moment behind a great black cloud. The entire
wood turned dark and silent. It watched him.*

Woods play a crucial and recurring role in horror, fantasy, the gothic and the weird. They are places in which strange things happen, where it is easy to lose your way. Supernatural creatures thrive in the thickets. Trees reach into underworlds of pagan myth and magic. Forests are full of ghosts.

Lining the path through this realm of folklore and fear are twelve stories from across Britain, telling tales of whispering voices and maddening sights from deep in the Yorkshire Dales to the ancient hills of Gwent and the eerie quiet of the forests of Dartmoor. Immerse yourself in this collection of classic tales celebrating the enduring power of our natural spaces to enthral and terrorise our senses.

ALSO AVAILABLE

*... and then the music was so loud, so beautiful that I
couldn't think of anything else. I was completely lost to
the music, enveloped by melody which was part of Pan.*

In 1894, Arthur Machen's landmark novella *The Great God Pan* was
published, sparking the sinister resurgence of the pagan goat god. Writers
of the late-nineteenth to mid-twentieth centuries, such as Oscar Wilde,
E. M. Forster and Margery Lawrence, took the god's rebellious influence
as inspiration to spin beguiling tales of social norms turned upside down
and ancient ecological forces compelling their protagonists to ecstatic
heights or bizarre dooms.

Assembling ten tales and six poems—along with Machen's novella—from
the boom years of Pan-centric literature, this new collection revels in
themes of queer awakening, transgression against societal bonds and the
bewitching power of the wild as it explores a rapturous and culturally
significant chapter in the history of weird fiction.

For more Tales of the Weird titles
visit the British Library Shop (shop.bl.uk)

We welcome any suggestions, corrections or feedback you may have, and will
aim to respond to all items addressed to the following:

The Editor (Tales of the Weird), British Library Publishing,
The British Library, 96 Euston Road, London NW1 2DB

We also welcome enquiries through our Twitter account, @BL_Publishing.